THE DISAPPEARANCE OF

EMBER CROW

THE DISAPPEARANCE OF
EMBER CROW

AMBELIN
KWAYMULLINA

CANDLEWICK PRESS

Copyright © 2013 by Ambelin Kwaymullina

First U.S. edition 2016

Library of Congress Catalog Card Number 2015931428
ISBN 978-0-7636-7843-2

16 17 18 19 20 21 BVG 10 9 8 7 6 5 4 3 2 1

Printed in Berryville, VA, U.S.A.

This book was typeset in Garamond.

Candlewick Press
99 Dover Street
Somerville, Massachusetts 02144

visit us at www.candlewick.com

For Chris — beloved guardian,
faithful companion, and great soul;
and for Mum, Blaze, Zeke, and Paulina:
we are here.

THE PACK

I was wolf.

I was among the Pack. And everything was as it should be. Mostly. I had no shaggy coat of reddy-brown fur and couldn't run as fast on all fours as the others. I tried to make up for it by moving as quickly as possible on my inadequate two legs and by growing out my hair, which was almost the same as fur. It was the right color, too. Brown, like my skin. Except my skin was covered, hidden beneath the blue jacket, shirt, and pants I needed as protection against the cold. The differences between myself and the rest of the Pack made me want to pace and shake out the fur I didn't have. But doing that would reveal my worry to the others, and worrying—when our territory was free of other predators and when the Pack was healthy and prey plentiful—wasn't wolf. And I was wolf.

There was a stirring in the warm darkness of the den. Pack Leader raised his head, sniffed once, and rolled to his feet. Ears pricked and noses lifted as everyone waited for instructions. Pack Leader's golden eyes focused on me. The others flopped back into sleep, while I leaped into a half-crouch. I couldn't stand completely, because I would've hit my head on the dirt ceiling of our underground burrow. Besides, standing upright made me tall in an unwolf-like way. Pack Leader loped out, and I followed, darting under the tree root that arched over the mouth of the den.

Outside, the world was cold and gray with the light that came right after sun-wakes. As I wriggled out, the wind tore through the forest, rushing into my ears, making strange whispering noises that almost seemed to be words. I barked, loud and fierce. The odd breeze went away. I cast a hopeful glance at Pack Leader to see if he'd noticed my victory. All he did was sit down, lift his nose, and sniff again. There was obviously *something* out here, and it wasn't the wind.

I sniffed as deep as I could. Scents raced up my

nose and exploded into my head. I took a single, giddy bound into the forest, then skidded to an undignified halt. How embarrassing. Not daring to look at Pack Leader, I held myself still, doing my very best to make it seem as though I'd been trying to find a better position to smell from. This time I separated out the scents, searching for whatever had made Pack Leader bring me out of the den. Rain, coming later today. The sharp tang of eucalyptus from the leaves of the huge tuart trees, and the lighter, minty smell of the peppermints that grew beneath them. The muskiness of tree cats slumbering in branches high above us, the sweet headiness of waratah flowers, and . . . oh, rabbit! I yipped, bouncing in place. Pack Leader didn't move. He wasn't taking me on a hunt, and my head drooped. He didn't seem to think I was worthy to kill with the other wolves, or even to share in the meat.

He'd see, though. I was a good wolf.

I went back to sniffing, finally catching the scent of something that was not forest, or prey, or wolf. It belonged to the ones that the wolves thought of as the *other* Pack. The human pack. Two were headed this way. They drew closer, near enough for me to make out their individual scents. Pictures flashed into my head, first of a thin, olive-skinned girl with long black curls. Then of a male, tall and brown, with eyes that were the color of tuart leaves. I knew these humans. I couldn't remember how, but it was well enough to give them wolf names. *Looks Ahead* and *Fleet Foot*. And . . . wait, there was a third, walking behind the others. I knew him, too. Pale skin, blue eyes, black hair. *Flies High.* Limbs quivering with joy, I put my nose to the air, breathing in his smell. I wanted to run through the forest and scamper around Flies High as if I were a silly pup.

Until my joy was swamped by a crashing wave of dread.

I lifted my lip and growled. Pack Leader snapped at me, and I cowered, bewildered. *Flies High isn't a threat?*

Then why did I want to chase him away?

The humans came into view, walking through the trees. They were wearing the same coverings I was, except in different colors. Blue on Looks Ahead and Fleet Foot, greeny-brown on Flies High.

With a wary glance at Pack Leader, I opened my jaws, releasing a low breath that had a tiny rumble at the edges. Pack Leader's ears flicked in my direction, but he let it pass.

The humans stopped. Fleet Foot spoke. "I think we're scaring her."

"You mean *I'm* scaring her," Flies High said.

Somewhere, a wolf howled, a single, lonely note of distress. I twisted, searching for the hurt wolf. The sound seemed to be everywhere and nowhere, and I realized it was coming from *inside* my head. Bewildered, I whined at Pack Leader, who fixed a golden gaze on me. He didn't speak, but I understood him. *Be calm. I am your Pack Leader, and I am here.*

Looks Ahead took a step toward me and paused, waiting to see what I would do. I didn't do anything, because I wasn't afraid, at least not of her. Pack Leader was here, and besides, Looks Ahead was—a pup? No, that wasn't quite right. She was full grown and yet somehow pup-like, in need of protection and not a threat. She reached me in five hesitant paces and crouched down. "Ash? We all miss you. Don't you want to come back to us?"

More pictures flooded into my mind. A fire. Endless caves. And a lot of human faces—brown eyed, blue eyed, dark skinned, light skinned . . . I didn't like it. It reminded me of a time when I was not wolf, which was impossible. I had always been wolf. I gave my head a furious shake, trying to get rid of the images.

Looks Ahead straightened and spoke to the others. "I think we should tell her."

"She's here because she couldn't cope," Flies High replied. "Telling her might push her right over the edge."

"She always comes when we need her!"

"Ordinarily, yes. But I think we can all agree this behavior isn't normal. She's running away, Georgie. And I'm not sure she even knows what she's running from."

I didn't understand what the two of them were talking about, and the third one, Fleet Foot, kept staring at me. "Connor, do her eyes seem a little yellow to you?"

For some reason, that made them all stare. I bared my teeth, ready to spring if they attacked. Then Flies High turned away, running a hand through his hair. "They *are* gold. I should have seen it."

The howling wolf that only I seemed to hear returned, keening in pain. I pawed at my skull as Fleet Foot spoke. "My animal is a hawk, remember? I have better eyesight than anyone else in the Tribe."

Looks Ahead glanced from them to me and back again. "You think she's changing into a wolf?"

"I don't know," Fleet Foot replied. "We've really got no idea what could happen to her. No one in the Tribe has ever lived with their animals the way she's been living with the wolves."

"I live with my spiders!" Looks Ahead protested.

"It isn't the same," Flies High said. "You aren't trying to *be* a spider. We have to tell her. And if it doesn't work — I'm using my ability to drag her out of here."

I didn't know what an ability was, and the wailing of the wolf in my head seemed to mean it wasn't anything good. I lunged, snapping at Flies High.

Looks Ahead shouted, "That's enough!"

There was a powerful note of command in her voice, and I froze, astonished. She wasn't a pack leader, but she sounded like one. "You have to listen to me now, Ash. This is important."

She crouched down again. Then she tilted her head to one side, blinked pale-green eyes, and spoke three words that shattered the world into pieces.

"Ember is missing."

THE DISAPPEARANCE

Ember is missing.

The words reverberated through my body. Everything split into two as different realities competed for dominance: the world of wolves—fur and den and Pack—and that of humans—clothes and cave and Tribe. I longed to abandon myself to the wolf world. I couldn't.

Because Ember was missing and she was important.

A face appeared in my mind. Round cheeks, red hair, and fair skin. Strange eyes, one blue and one brown. *Ember.*

Grabbing hold of the image, I followed it back to the other Pack, the other world. A kaleidoscope of pictures came together, the same ones I'd seen before, only now I understood them. The fire we cooked our meals on, the caves where Ember had her lab and Georgie made her maps of the future, and where we all slept when the weather was cold. The many faces of the Tribe.

My Tribe.

What was I doing here? I was filthy, covered in dirt, and crouching on the ground. I straightened, and reeled. Too tall, too high! But I forced myself to stay upright, staggering to the nearest tree and waving the others away when they moved closer. I leaned against the trunk and the dizziness eased, the tuart giving me the balance I couldn't find on my own. *My Firstwood.* I dug my fingers into the rough gray bark and pressed my feet into the earth, needing to connect to the forest that had been my home ever since I'd run away from my parents.

When the dizziness was gone, I glanced over at Looks Ahead. No, at *Georgie.* *"Wharrrr..."* I stopped. My words were coming out as growls. Human sounds, I had to make human sounds. At least I couldn't hear the howling anymore, although I didn't like the silence in my mind, either. There was an emptiness where something should have been.

Being a human was already complicated. "What . . . do . . . you . . . mean, missing?"

"She didn't come back from Gull City. Do you remember, she went to see the Serpent? We don't know what happened after she got there, of course—"

"Stop!" Images were popping into my head. Buildings and winding streets. Waves pounding on sand. And an enormous glowing snake. "I can't underrrr . . . understand you."

I gave up on speaking, directing a forlorn glance at Pack Leader where he lay in the dirt. He turned his head away. I had to deal with this on my own.

Flies High—Connor—broke the silence. "Ashala."

Hearing him say my name was as shattering as hearing "Ember is missing," although for a different reason. Connor was the only one who ever said it that way, drawing the word out over three beats. *A-shay-la.* I love you.

Memories of him sparked like lights, a lightning storm of shared laughter and adventure and passion. It became at once easier and harder to find my center as a human instead of a wolf. Easier, because I remembered being a leader, a fighter, a girl. Harder, because I knew what I'd done to Connor, the thing that had sent me fleeing to the wolves to begin with.

My skin heated in shame and I stared miserably into his blue eyes.

His flawless features showed no emotion, which meant nothing. He was good at hiding what he felt. He'd had to be, because he'd spent years living among Citizens, concealing the air-controlling ability that would've got him thrown into detention.

"Five weeks ago," he said, measuring out each word to be sure I'd understand, "Ember went to Gull City. Do you remember that?"

I did. It was almost the last thing that had happened before everything had gone wrong between us, and I'd run to the wolves. "She went to meet someone?" No, that wasn't quite right. She'd gone to *find* someone. "The Serpent?"

Georgie clapped her hands together. "That's right, Ash!"

There were two pictures in my head. A clear one of a huge snake, and a much hazier one of a tall man. My brain was insisting that they were *both* the Serpent. Only how could they be? Then I realized. There really was a giant snake, an ancient spirit who lived in a lake in the forest. But the man . . . the man, Ember had invented. *She made up a rebel, and we called him the Serpent.*

I dredged up the knowledge I needed. Our imaginary rebel was trying to overthrow the Citizenship Accords, the law that made anyone born with an ability an "Illegal." Our abilities were supposed to make us a threat to the Balance, the harmony of the world. Most Illegals were locked up in detention centers, except for those few whose abilities were considered "benign" enough to be given an Exemption from the accords. Or the ones who ran away, like us. We'd started rumors about the "Serpent" to give the government someone else to chase besides the Tribe.

Recently, though, we'd heard stories that some guy claiming to be the Serpent had started appearing at rallies against the Citizenship Accords. So Ember had gone to Gull City to check it out.

"She was supposed to be back ages ago! Why didn't anyone go after her?"

"I *did* go after her," Daniel answered patiently. "When she didn't come back after a couple of weeks, I Ran to the storage unit." He paused, eyeing me, and added, "Ah — that is, I used my ability, which lets me run very fast —"

"I know what your ability is," I informed him with wolfish dignity. Although it did take a moment for the words "storage unit" to mean anything to me. *The one that belongs to Daniel's Grandma Bessie, which we use as a place to hide in Gull City.* "Ember wasn't there?"

"No. She left a note saying she was fine and not to go searching for her."

I muddled my way through that. It was dangerous for Ember to go off alone. Only not as dangerous as it used to be. Because . . . because . . . oh, yes! Things were better for Illegals now. Belle Willis, a reformer, had recently been elected Prime of Gull City, and she'd cut back on all the enforcer patrols and the spot Citizenship checks. Besides which, Ember had an entirely genuine Citizenship tattoo, so even if she got checked, she'd pass. Like Connor, she'd managed to fool an Assessor into thinking she didn't have an ability.

"She might not really be missing," I said. "She might be doing, I don't know, Ember stuff!" I liked that idea. Cheered up, I expanded upon it. "Didn't she say before she left that she might try to contact some old friends of her dad? People who are involved in the reform movement?"

"We thought that, too," Georgie chimed in. "Until the dog came."

"The *what*?"

"The dog. I think he's a Labrador."

I was confused again, only this time it wasn't in an

13

I-was-a-wolf-and-now-I'm-not kind of way. It was more of a comfortable, familiar kind of way, as if it was usual for Georgie to not make any sense.

She continued, totally unaware that she was confusing me, and that was normal, too. "The dog brought the stone." She nudged Daniel. "Show her!"

Daniel reached into his pocket and held out a small gray rock. "This was in a canister attached to the dog's collar."

I darted over to snatch up the stone before retreating to the tree.

"Do you understand what it is?" Connor asked.

"Yeah. A rock."

"No, it's —"

"I'm kidding. I know what it is."

He gave me a look that was somewhere between exasperation and hurt. *Stupid, Ashala.* Only I didn't know how to act around him, what to say. It had been easier being a wolf.

I focused on the stone, which was at least something I could deal with. Ember's ability meant that she could manipulate memories, including sharing them between people by putting a memory into — well, anything. The last time she'd done it, she'd used river stones. Exactly the same as the one I was holding.

I rolled the rock between my fingers. It wasn't giving me one of her memories or anyone else's—not yet. She had locked away whatever fragment of a life the stone held with a password, as she had before.

"Has anyone activated it?"

Georgie shook her head. "We didn't understand the note."

"What note?"

Daniel reached into his pocket again, pulling out a folded piece of paper. "We figured it was meant for you, Ash."

I unfolded it eagerly, only to find it was covered in strange scratchings that I couldn't understand. Words. They were words. I'd forgotten how to read. I glared at the note until the scratchings finally made sense. *Do you remember the story of the girl who wanted to die?*

"Do you know what she means?" Georgie asked.

"I think so. Give me a minute, okay?"

I edged back, leaning against the tree and staring at the note. Ember loved her stories. She'd told me, once, about a girl who wanted to die, until someone spoke six words to her that made her want to live instead. I was such an idiot; it had taken me an embarrassingly long time to realize Ember was talking about herself.

15

When Georgie and I had arrived in the Firstwood four and a half years ago, Ember was already here. A runaway, the same as the rest of us. Only she'd run with her dad, and he'd died on the way to the forest. I thought back to that first conversation, trying to remember exactly what I'd said that had made such a difference to Ember. She'd been heartbroken over losing her dad. And I'd known what it was like to be knocked out by grief, because my little sister had died right before I left Gull City. The difference was that I'd had someone who needed me to get back up again. I'd had Georgie.

And suddenly, I knew the six words that had made Ember want to live.

I needed space to breathe for this. I glanced at the others, my gaze skittering past Connor to rest somewhere between Georgie and Daniel. "Can you all move away a bit?"

Everyone stepped back and then, when I kept staring, stepped back farther still. I slid to the ground, the rock in my hands. The earth was damp, but there was no point in trying to stay on my feet. The memory would be overwhelming; they always were.

Pack Leader padded over and lay down beside me. *I am here.* I wanted to reach out and ruffle his fur. I didn't. He wasn't a pet. Instead I nodded at him, and he gave me a toothy grin in return.

I held the rock up to my mouth, cupping it between my hands.

"You're not alone," I whispered. "You've got us."

Energy emanated from the stone, buzzing into my hands, up my arms, and spreading through my head.

And I was yanked into a moment in Ember's life.

THE MESSAGE

I placed the mirror on the ground and sat cross-legged in front of it. The solar lamp to the right of the glass cast enough light through the gloomy interior of the storage unit for me to see my reflection—short red curls, mismatched eyes, and a worried expression. This was how Ash would see me when she accessed this memory. I attempted a smile, only rather than making me look less anxious, it made me seem slightly crazed.

Giving up on the smile, I spoke instead. "Hi, Ash. This memory is a message. From me to you. I'm going to give it to Nicky—that's the dog—to take to you, and it's to show you . . . I mean, to tell you . . ."

My words were tangled, like my emotions and thoughts. I took a moment to unravel some of the knottiness that was twisting my stomach and tried again. "I know you've experienced someone else's memories before, but that was different. The last time you saw small snapshots of Connor's life. This is . . . more. You'll understand every second of what I'm thinking and feeling."

There, that was better. An explanation. I was good at explanations. I went on in a more confident tone, "It's like this, Ash. You and I both know that there is no rebel Illegal who calls himself the Serpent, except someone claiming to be that person is appearing at rallies against the Citizenship Accords. And from the descriptions we've heard of him, I might know who he is."

Had I said too much? I didn't think so, but I was walking a very fine line. If I ran into—I jerked my thoughts away from names. If I ran into certain people, I wanted to be able to say that I hadn't told Ashala anything about them. Because it was difficult to lie to them. Not impossible, but not easy, and I didn't want to take any chances.

"Ash, if the Serpent is who I think he is, then there could be these other people around him, and some of them are . . . they're bad people. If he's alone, I'll, um, sort some things out with him, and be back before you know it. If he's not . . ." I stopped speaking, because I

19

had to. My voice had begun to waver in anticipation of how the sentence ended. I completed it silently instead. *If he's not, I don't know when I'm coming home.* That was why I was saying good-bye.

Reaching out, I pressed my fingers to the cold glass and called up memories, letting them play out in my head. One memory after another, of things I'd experienced since the day I first met Ashala Wolf. Discovering my connection to the huge black crows that stared beadily down from the trees of the Firstwood. The good times Ash and Georgie and I shared, first with the three of us, and then with others when more Illegals came to the Firstwood. Our triumph over Neville Rose, Chief Administrator of Detention Center 3. We'd snatched sixteen detainees out from under his nose and exposed his plan to take over the government of Gull City. That had been six months ago now. After that, it seemed as though the Tribe could do anything. I hoped they could. I hoped they'd be all right, if I was really gone forever.

I smiled, a genuine smile this time, for all that happiness. A smile for the forest. For my crows. For my friends. For Ash.

"Look after Nicky, won't you? And please don't try to find me. If I stay away, it's because I've chosen to." She would try, I knew that, but she wouldn't succeed. At least, not in locating me, although it was inevitable that she'd discover some of the knowledge I'd hoped never to have to share.

The glass in front of me was growing misty. I blinked back the tears. "However this ends, you're probably going to find out some things about me, and they're not nice things. But, Ash, even after you know, do you think you could remember the good? And whatever you end up discovering—try to think of me kindly. If you can."

THE PLAN

Blackness. Then light. Dirt. Trees.

I am Ashala, and I am in the Firstwood.

That much was clear. Nothing else was.

What did she mean, "not nice things"? And how could she have hidden her suspicions about the man claiming to be the Serpent?

"Ash?"

Georgie's voice. I stared past Pack Leader to where Connor and Daniel and Georgie stood. Their faces were better than a mirror for showing me a reflection; I could measure exactly how bad I looked by the flare of concern in their eyes, the way Connor took a single step before stumbling to a halt, uncharacteristically graceless. I'd pushed him away, and now he wasn't sure how I'd react if he came any closer. I was sorry he'd stopped. I stomped on that feeling.

He deserved better than me.

"Ash!" Georgie again. "Has something happened to Ember?"

She was afraid. I couldn't let Georgie be afraid. "She's okay. Or she was when the memory happened. Only . . ." I let one hand fall to the ground, crept my fingers across the earth until I was touching Pack Leader's fur. "I don't think she's coming back. Not anytime soon."

"Why not?" Georgie sounded as bewildered as I'd felt a moment ago.

"I don't know!"

Even I could hear the edge of desperation in my voice. Pack Leader turned his head in my direction and huffed reprovingly. *Get ahold of yourself.* I drew back, a little hurt—and realized that expecting him to coddle me at this moment was a human reaction. Wolves didn't fall to pieces when one of their own was gone. If a Pack member died, that was to be mourned and accepted. But if one was missing . . .

I reached back, gripping the tree, and hauled myself

up. My legs were trembling, made shaky by too many shocks, but I made it all the way upright. Then I stepped away from the tuart and staggered.

Daniel started forward to help.

Connor caught his arm, spoke in a sharp voice. "No. Leave her."

To anyone else that might have sounded cruel. Not to me. I regained my balance and met Connor's eyes in a bittersweet moment of understanding.

In my head, a wolf yipped, flinging out a challenge to the world. I understood what I was hearing now. The wolf-voice was Connor's emotions. He and I were linked, and had been ever since Ember helped us share memories. Sometimes I felt what he was feeling and sometimes he felt what I was. *Maybe that means Em and I are linked now, too?* Except she'd said once that her ability worked differently when it was one of her own memories, and if I could feel what she was feeling, I wasn't conscious of it. All I was aware of right now was Connor's emotions and mine.

We both knew that it was time for me to lead my Pack.

"Ember . . ." My voice was hoarse, weak. I frowned and began again. "Ember said in the memory that if she didn't come back, it would be because she'd chosen to stay away. I think she's trying to protect us."

"Protect us from what?" Georgie asked.

"I'm not exactly sure." I gathered pieces of information together. "People connected with the fake Serpent. And she also said . . ." It was hard to tell them the rest. I fought the ridiculous urge to protect Em from criticism and shoved words out of my mouth. "She said she thought she might know who the guy pretending to be the Serpent is."

Daniel and Connor spoke as one. "Who?"

"She didn't say. She didn't say anything else really."

My chest tightened in a familiar sensation, as if a rock were sitting on my heart. If it got much heavier, I wouldn't be able to breathe.

"Do you know if she met up with the Serpent?" Connor asked.

I shook my head.

"If she's still searching for him, we could try to find her at the next rally," he pointed out. "And even if Ember—or the Serpent—aren't there, there'll be people at that rally who were at the last one. Someone might have seen who she was with, where she went."

An idea. The weight on my chest grew lighter.

"Does anyone know when the next rally is?"

"Just over a month," Daniel answered. "We haven't gone through the things in her lab yet, either."

Two ideas. I scrabbled for another and found one. "Have you tried talking to the crows?"

"Not yet."

I swiveled, scanning the trees. *There!* A big glossy one perched in the distance. A male, I could tell by the red eyes. I focused my attention on the bird and yelled, "Hey, crow!"

The crow didn't move. He didn't seem to know I was there at all. Or maybe he couldn't understand what I was saying. It wasn't always possible to communicate with someone else's animal.

I tried again. "Ember's gone. You must know that she's left the Firstwood, and wherever she is, I think she might be in trouble. Can you help us find her?"

The crow just sat there, silent and — smug? I got the distinct feeling he was ignoring me on purpose, and he didn't seem to be a bit concerned about Ember. I shouldn't have been surprised. Crows weren't Pack animals the way wolves were. They were independent, contrary creatures, and Ember was part-crow to them, like I was part-wolf to the wolves. They'd assume she was clever enough to take care of herself. Crows thought they were clever enough to outwit anyone or anything.

"We could get Keiko to talk to them," Georgie suggested. "Or Coral."

Those two were Chirpers, bird-speakers. I wasn't sure they'd have any luck, either. It was still worth a try. "I guess we'll have to."

"We could check the storage unit as well," Daniel said. "I did search it after I found the note, in case there was something else there. But I could go back."

I considered that. Ember had been inside the unit in the memory, although that had probably been before Daniel had gone through it. She certainly wouldn't be there now, though, and I doubted she'd have been careless enough to leave something behind.

"We'll start with the lab," I said. Where Ember probably hadn't left any clues, either. "And then the rally." Which was just over a month away. None of this was a very good plan. But it was all I had. I tried to think if there was anything I'd missed, and remembered something else. "What happened to the dog who brought the message? Is someone looking after him?"

"About ten someones," Connor replied. "All of the younger kids."

That was all right, then. Tribe children knew how to take care of an animal.

"Ash?" Georgie touched my arm. "I could try to *See*."

I glanced at her, and she added brightly, "Because if we knew where she was *going* to be, we could be there before she is."

It was a nice offer, except I knew the limitations of Georgie's ability. At any given moment there were thousands of possible futures, and it was hard for her to control which future she Saw into, or for how long. Nor was it easy to interpret her visions.

On the other hand, I wasn't overwhelmed with options.

"That's a good idea, Georgie. Any clue might be—"

I sputtered to a halt as a sudden gust of wind blew a leaf into my mouth. The wind grew stronger, and branches waved above me. This time I understood the words made by the rustling leaves.

Granddaughter, Granddaughter . . .

The Serpent. *My* Serpent. The giant snake who lived in the lake and was my many-times grandfather. In the old world, the one that had been destroyed by the Reckoning, the Serpent had created my people, my "race." It was hard to believe that humans used to care about things like different-shaped eyes, or different-colored skin. Now all that mattered were the lines between Citizen, Exempt, and Illegal.

Grandpa had been trying to contact me for days, only I hadn't understood. Or maybe I hadn't wanted to understand. He was part of the human life that I'd been trying to leave behind. I was never going to forgive myself if he wanted to tell me something about Ember.

I shouted into the air, "I'm coming."

Daniel eyed me warily, and Georgie with curiosity. They thought I was talking at nothing.

"It's her grandfather," Connor explained. "He wants to see her."

How had he known that? Usually no one else could hear Grandpa. I stared at him, puzzled. He stared back, revealing nothing.

"Georgie and I can go to the caves while you're at the lake," Daniel said. "I'll search the lab."

"And I'll try to find Em. In the future," Georgie put in.

"Go ahead and try," I told her. "But, Daniel, leave the lab to me. I was the one who was in there most, besides Ember. If there's something out of place, I'm more likely to spot it." It was a good reason, only it wasn't quite the truth. If there were not-nice things about Ember to be discovered, I should be the one to find them. Whatever they were, I'd understand, and I'd explain to everyone else so they understood as well. "Do the rest of the Tribe know she's gone?"

"They know she's away," Daniel replied. "Not that she's missing."

"Then don't ask the Chirpers to talk to the crows yet. It'll panic everybody, and I doubt those birds are going to be much help anyway. I'll go through the lab first."

Daniel nodded. He brushed his hand against Georgie's arm, and the two of them walked away, strolling into the forest together.

I shifted to face Connor. "Can you . . . um . . ."

He folded his arms. "I am coming with you."

I toyed with the idea of sending him back to the caves. *He won't go.* And Ember had once said I should never give an order that I thought might not be obeyed. *Yeah, right. Be honest, Ash. You don't want him to leave.*

My gaze shifted to Pack Leader, who was still lying beneath the tree. He rolled to his feet and came over to butt his head against my leg. Telling me I had to go back to being human. He'd always known that I would, I realized. It was why he'd stopped me from hunting.

The Tribe didn't eat the flesh of animals. We couldn't. It would break the pact I'd made with the trees when I'd first come here, to care for the forest and all the life in it.

I stared down into Pack Leader's yellow eyes. For over a month, I'd run with him. It had been glorious. But it wasn't my world. Reaching out, I brushed my hand lightly over his ears. "In another life."

His jaw dropped into a grin. For a second, I could almost see it, an existence where I'd been born into the clarity of thought and intensity of sensation that was wolf.

Then he turned away from me and loped back to the den.

I turned away from him and strode into the Firstwood.

THE LAKE

We walked through the crisp morning air, Connor matching his pace to mine. I stole a quick glance at him. There was something different about how he looked, something not quite right, only I wasn't sure what. I tried to puzzle it out. His hair was falling over his sculpted face as usual, and he was wearing what he always wore, the greeny-brown shirt and pants that he'd dyed himself. The color made it difficult to see him against the trees. Connor tended to think in terms of a defensive advantage, a habit he'd got into when he'd been an enforcer . . . and it dawned on me. It was the way he was *moving* that was wrong. Too tense, too contained. Exactly how he'd walked when he was an enforcer.

Connor had worked for the government for years, pretending to be a Citizen, all part of a plan to strike back at the man who killed his mother. Then that man died of a stroke and Connor had joined the Tribe. He normally moved easily here, weaving between the trees and loping across the ground with the rise and fall of the earth. The only other person who fit in so completely with the Firstwood was . . . well, me.

Now he was separate. Walking *in* the forest and not with it. Keeping too many emotions shut away.

Or maybe he was in pain.

Before I could stop myself, I blurted out, "Is your arm okay?"

"It's fine. Penelope Mended it. You know that."

Eight words, and every one bitten out. *I shouldn't have asked about his arm.* "You don't have to come with me, you know. I can do this alone."

"Yes, you've made it abundantly clear that you don't want me around."

"Because it's dangerous for you!" The memory of blood and splintered bone flashed through my mind. My stomach lurched. "I *broke* your arm."

"It wasn't your fault," he replied in a tone edged

33

with impatience. "Your ability was going haywire; you weren't in control."

"You think that makes it better? Being out of control of an ability like mine?"

Sleepwalking was a powerful but unpredictable talent. When I used it, I experienced everything as part of a vivid dream, and whatever changes I made in my dream really happened in the world around me. Except since I always thought I was only dreaming, and didn't know I was affecting reality, I could decide to do some strange things.

And now I wasn't having dreams at all. "The nightmares . . . Connor, I can't tell a friend from an enemy when I'm Sleepwalking anymore. I could have snapped you in half, and I don't want to hurt you."

He choked off an incredulous laugh. "So your solution was to leave me? Do you really think that didn't *hurt*?"

I swung to face him. "At least you were safe."

"I never asked you to keep me safe!"

"You never had to," I shouted. "I could have killed you!"

We glared at each other, caught in the same tangle of anger and pain we'd been in before I went to the wolves. I'd left because I was terrified I'd do something to him that a Mender couldn't heal. I was still terrified. He still wasn't. "Connor, I can't . . . Ember's missing, and I have to see my grandpa. There isn't time for this."

In my head those words had sounded reasonable. Out loud they sounded like an excuse.

He stepped back, jaw clenched, and gestured in the direction of the lake. "Go ahead, Ashala. Run away. Again."

I snarled at him, an instinctive wolf reaction to someone prodding at an unhealed wound. Then I stomped off into the forest, leaving him to follow. Hoping he wouldn't.

Not a bit surprised when he did.

We went on in angry silence. When we reached the water I strode right in, as much to get away from Connor as for any other reason. "Grandpa?" I called. "Are you there?"

Everything was quiet. The lake rippled where I'd disturbed the shallows, but the purple depths of the center were still. Was he angry because he'd been calling me for a while and I hadn't come? Either that or I was doing this wrong. My grandfather lived here and spoke on the wind, but I'd never actually seen him appear in this world. The first time I'd encountered Grandpa, I'd been close to death. I'd met him in the greater Balance, the place where everyone's souls go when we die. Or at least that's where I thought I'd been. The whole experience had been pretty weird.

I waded in farther. "Grandpa! Come out!"

Was that movement beneath the surface? I took another step.

Something seized hold of my leg and yanked me under.

Water rushed into my mouth and up my nose as I was dragged through the lake. I choked, flailed, and stupidly tried to yell. Then whatever was pulling me along let me go. I was deep under water, only I wasn't drowning.

It should have been impossible to breathe. To float, neither rising nor sinking. To see as clearly through water as I would through air.

Except nothing seemed to be impossible when it came to Grandpa.

Light shone and eventually resolved into a single sinuous shape. The shape coiled and curved until I was staring into the reproachful eyes of an enormous blue-scaled snake. **You did not come when I called.**

"I know. I'm sorry, I was—"

And you are throwing away my gift.

"You never gave me a . . . oh." He meant Connor.

Because Connor had died when we escaped Detention Center 3, and it had been Grandfather, working through me, who'd brought him back to life.

We have been speaking, he and I. You should not have left him.

"I was trying to protect him! And since when do you talk to Connor anyway?"

Grandpa tilted his massive head to one side. **He is of the forest. You are of the forest. You will both be needed in what is to come.**

I wasn't sure what that meant, and I didn't want to talk about Connor. "Listen, about my friend Ember—"

He interrupted. **I have been traveling.**

A picture of a giant snake slithering through the streets of Gull City flashed into my head. Except that was ridiculous. I wasn't sure how he moved through the world, but he had to do it in a way no one could see. "I hope you had a good trip, Grandpa. About Ember—"

I am concerned about this world. So are the others.

He was trying to tell me something in his usual cryptic way. I pushed my worry for Em aside for a moment. "Others?"

Ancient beings from the many lands of the world before. I am not the only old spirit to have come

through the great chaos. None of us wishes this world to become like the last one.

The great chaos was what Grandpa called the Reckoning, the environmental cataclysm that had destroyed the old world. "You do know everything's different from how it was before, right?" I wasn't sure how much he understood about the way things were now. After he'd sung the Firstwood into life, hundreds of years ago, he'd gone into a deep sleep, and he'd only been awake for about six months. I tried to explain. "The only reason the, um, great chaos happened at all was because people abused the environment and broke down the life-sustaining systems of the earth. No one does that anymore."

Harm to the earth was not all that ended what you call the old world. Everything connects, Granddaughter. But not everyone sees those connections. He twisted away, rolling through the water. **You must learn to understand your power.**

That was one piece of advice I didn't need. "I know. Don't you think I know? I could barely manage when I wasn't having nightmares!"

Sleepwalking is your ability. It is not your power.

"Then what's my power?"

38

He swirled upward, surrounding me in glowing coils until all I could see was shining blue light. His voice floated down from somewhere above. **Some truths cannot be told. They can only be discovered.**

"What does that mean?"

He didn't answer, which meant I was supposed to figure it out for myself. I was still puzzling over it when he spoke again. **Your friend is not lost.**

My heart leaped. "Ember? Grandpa, do you know where she is?"

She is where she has chosen to be.

"Can you help me find her?"

Silence again. "Grandpa," I called desperately, "if you know anything that would help, please tell me!"

He came swooping downward until his huge head was level with mine. **Beware the angels.**

And he vanished.

I was alone in the cold depths of the lake, and I couldn't breathe. Water surged, pushing me upward to the surface. Within seconds I broke through and sucked in a lungful of air. On my second breath, an invisible force seized hold of my body, propelling me out of the lake and onto the shore.

I collapsed onto my knees at Connor's feet.

"Are you all right?" he demanded.

"Yeah."

Air swirled, drying out my clothes until they were damp instead of plastered to my skin. I shifted into a more comfortable position on the sandy ground, watching as Connor sat at my side. "Thanks for pulling me out."

He stared at me for a moment longer, making sure I really was okay. Then he asked, "Did you find out anything about Ember?"

"Kind of. As usual, Grandpa wasn't making a lot of sense. He did say that Em's not lost, though. She's . . ." I paused, trying to remember the exact words. "He said, 'She is where she has chosen to be.'"

"That probably means she's all right at least."

"I hope so." *And he said that I should beware the angels. . . .* Only I couldn't tell him that. Because Grandpa might have been talking about Connor.

I'd thought of Connor as an angel ever since Georgie pointed out how his perfect features resembled the old-world statues that flanked the entrance to the Gull City Museum. Except why would Grandpa tell me to beware of Connor? The only reason I could think of was because I might hurt him. Again. And if I told Connor about Grandpa's warning, he'd know I was thinking that, and we'd end up in the same fight for the second time today.

"Did he tell you anything else?"

Had Connor sensed I was hiding something? "Grandpa wasn't really interested in Ember," I said quickly. "He's worried about, I don't know, the world. He was going on about connections. I didn't understand it." I rested my arms on my knees and added, "Maybe you could ask him. He said you'd been talking."

"I could hardly talk to you," Connor pointed out coolly.

I flushed and stared at the ground.

After a moment, he sighed and said, "Your grandfather and I have been speaking about when I was dead. And then not dead."

My head jerked up. "You're okay, aren't you?"

His lips curved into a smile. "I'm fine. Just different."

"Different how?" I grabbed hold of his arm. "Are you sick? Why didn't you tell me?"

"I'm not sick. And I didn't tell you because you won't talk about my death."

"Oh."

"I understand why, Ashala. It was worse for you than for me."

"How could it *possibly* have been worse for me?"

He covered my hand with his own. "You were the one left behind. I know what that's like. I watched you nearly die twice in Detention Center Three."

I should have pulled away from him. I couldn't. It was taking every scrap of willpower I had not to move closer. "Connor. How are you different?"

"I am both more of this world and less than I was before." He stared over the water. "Sometimes I am so . . . present in this place that I could tell you the individual shapes of every leaf on every tree. Other times it's as if I am closer to something else. A greater spirit that underlies what is. But," he added, his gaze shifting back to me, "you understand that. Don't you?"

"Yes." Because that was how it was for me as well. I'd felt it from the moment I arrived, long before I'd met Grandpa and realized I was descended from the ancient being who had brought life to the Firstwood. I'd always known that I was connected to this place. And now so was Connor. *He is of the forest. You are of the forest.* . . . Connor didn't have an animal, yet, and it occurred to me that maybe his link was with the forest itself. Or with Grandpa.

"Connor? I'm sorry you couldn't talk to me."

His hand tightened on mine, his blue eyes stormy and challenging. "Don't be sorry. Be here."

I will.

But I swallowed those reckless words before they could escape.

Connor read the answer in my silence. He let go and rose to his feet. "We should search the lab."

This was horrible. I hated it and I couldn't fix it. "Yeah. We should."

Then a voice roared into my mind, **GGGGRRRRRRRR!**

THE ADJUSTMENT

I jumped. Connor glanced at me questioningly, and I mouthed, "Jaz."

Closing my eyes, I called out in my head. *Jaz?*

No answer.

Jaz?

Oh. You can talk.

Of course I can talk!

I was trying to speak to you in wolf language because you'd gone wolfy. Did I get it right?

Jaz, that's . . . I mean, you can't just growl. Who told you I was with the wolves?

Silence. He must have been far away if it was taking

him a while to respond. Jaz still had trouble mind-speaking over long distances, although he was getting much better at it and had a far greater range than any of the other wild children who made up his Tribe. Of course, he'd had more practice. Jaz had been the first kid to be adopted by the saurs, which was how he'd acquired some of the big lizards' telepathic powers.

Finally, an answer came. **Daniel. Georgie. Connor. I have to keep up with the news now I'm the leader of my own Tribe, Ash.**

In other words he'd been gossiping. *Listen, Ember—*

Is missing. I know. He wasn't having trouble reaching me anymore; he must have moved into range. **I tried to contact you a little while ago and couldn't. Georgie said you were talking to your grandfather about Em.**

I was. He wasn't very helpful, though.

Maybe he doesn't know anything.

I think he likes being tricky.

You shouldn't talk about him that way!

I forgot, sometimes, that Jaz—who wasn't impressed by much on this earth—took my grandfather *very* seriously. Grandpa had created the saurs, the same way he'd created the trees and all the other life around here when the Reckoning ended over three hundred years ago. To the lizards, and to the children who made up the Saur Tribe, my grandfather was a creature of legend. *Sorry, Jaz. I'm a bit upset about Em.*

She's probably gone to have an adventure.

She's missing, Jaz. She's not on any adventure.

You worry too much, Ash.

And you don't worry enough! I sighed. *What are you calling for? Nothing's wrong, is it?*

Not wrong exactly . . .

Is someone hurt?

No, nothing like that. I need to talk to you in person, is all.

When Jaz wanted to talk to me face-to-face it was usually because one of his Tribe members had been experimenting with their ability and there'd been some kind of disaster. *What happened? Did Giovanni drain another lake?*

No! And it was totally unfair of you to blame him for taking that water when he was only trying to put out the fire.

The fire you started. Please tell me nothing is burning, Jaz.

I promised you we'd be more careful, didn't I? I need to see you about Leader business. I've been waiting to speak to you for a whole week, Ash.

He had? And "Leader business" meant something

big, something that concerned both my Tribe and his. *Where do you want to meet?*

On the grasslands. At the Five Sisters.

Five Sisters was the saur name for a set of small hills grouped in a loose circle. *I'm a few hours away.*

I'm almost there. I'll wait for you.

I opened my eyes. Connor was watching me. "I have to go see Jaz," I told him. "Leader business."

He nodded, and I hauled myself to my feet. It seemed to take a lot of energy. The day felt long already, and I was no closer to finding Ember.

"You should change into dry clothes," Connor said.

"I'm fine."

"You're shivering."

"I'll dry out on the way. It's a long walk."

"You don't have to walk. We'll fly. *After* you change. Aside from anything else, I don't think you want Jaz to see the way you look right now."

"What's wrong with the way I look?"

"Your clothes are filthy and torn, and your hair is matted. You seem . . . a little wild."

Really? I stared down at my grubby self. *He has a point.* And "Leader business" sometimes meant I had to talk Jaz out of a stupid idea. It was better that I seemed as if I was in control. "Fine. I'll change."

47

It didn't take long to reach the caves, or to put on a pair of Gull City–blue pants plus a matching shirt and jacket. When I tried to fix my hair, the brush kept getting stuck in snarls. I made a trip to the storeroom where the Tribe kept useful things that we'd picked up on runs into cities and towns, and grabbed a pair of scissors and a mirror. Then I returned to the cavern that Connor and I had chosen as our room. It opened onto the forest, so there was more than enough light for me to see by as I started cutting through the tangles.

When I was done, I examined myself critically. My hair was now a ragged mop, the ends barely touching my shoulders, and there were red highlights that hadn't been there before. I moved the mirror closer, checking out my eyes. There was definitely a hint of gold around my irises. I was still a little bit wolf, and I found that comforting. The Pack was with me, even though I wasn't with them.

I stopped on the way out to tell Georgie and Daniel I was going to see Jaz. Well, I told Daniel—Georgie was totally absorbed in tying together bits of vine and string and objects into one of her maps of future possibilities. She didn't say if she'd found out anything about Ember, and I couldn't tell, because her maps always looked like giant messes to me. Then I rejoined Connor at the entrance.

The two of us soared upward, slow until we cleared the trees and then fast over the top of the Firstwood. The wind rushing past made it impossible to talk, which was good because it meant I could focus on staying calm. If I panicked, he'd pick up on it, and I didn't want him knowing how much it bothered me to do this. I'd loved flying with him once. But the two of us had been hurtling through the sky when we'd been attacked as we left Detention Center 3. Now whenever we flew, I had occasional flashes of that sickening tumble to the earth, and the sound Connor's body made as it hit the ground and broke. *If not for my grandpa . . .*

Trying to distract myself, I stared down at the trees beneath me. We were moving too quickly to see anything except a blur of green, but the Tribe was down there somewhere. They'd be spread throughout the Firstwood at this time of the day, going about the tasks that were part of making a life in the forest. I imagined Micah and Nell and Charlie and Jin, our Leafers, tending to the food garden. And some of the cooking team would be making the long trek to get honey from the waratah flowers. They got a bit obsessed with storing honey at this time of year, before winter arrived and the flowers became dormant. *Stefan and Benny and Mai, maybe.* Keiko was probably with them, for no better reason than that she never passed up an opportunity to wander through the forest. I had no idea who was on washing duty. I imagined golden-haired Trix and dark-eyed Andreas cleaning the breakfast dishes in a stream. Unless one of the Waterbabies was doing it, in which case they'd bring water to the dishes rather than the other way around.

Thinking of them all was enough to steady me as we left the Firstwood behind to fly above a sea of yellow grasses. On we went, until we finally floated down to land amid the hills that made up the Five Sisters. Jaz wasn't here. I frowned and spun in a slow circle, searching for him. All I could see were rocky hills and long grass. And the grass wasn't flattened the way it would have been if a saur had trampled over it. *He said he'd meet us!*

What if something had gone wrong, something to do with the Leader business he wanted to talk about? What if he was missing as well?

I cast a worried glance at Connor — and gasped as a fireball appeared out of nowhere and hurtled toward his back.

"Connor, watch out!"

He was already moving, flinging himself to the side. The fireball blazed into the space where he'd been, stopped dead, and vanished.

A black-haired, black-eyed boy popped up from out of the grass. "No fair, Connor! Ash warned you."

Connor stood, brushing himself off. "I moved before she spoke, Jaz. I could hear something coming through the air. But," he added in an approving tone, "most enforcers would have turned in the direction of the sound. You would have hit them right in the face."

"It's no good getting the better of ordinary enforcers! I have to be able to beat the best. That's you."

"Have you two gone insane?" I choked. "What do you think you're doing?"

"Practicing fighting the government," Jaz answered. "I try to ambush Connor, and he has to escape without using his ability, as if he's an enforcer."

"Since when have you been doing that?"

"I dunno, a while. Connor's been teaching me lots of stuff. Tactics, and camouflage—see my clothes?"

I did. Jaz was wearing a shirt and pants of yellowy-brown that was hard to distinguish from the grass. He must have dyed them; none of the seven cities had that color clothing. "And," he continued enthusiastically, "check this out."

He pointed to one of the Five Sisters and intoned, "Hatches-with-Stars! Emerge!"

For a second, everything was still. Then the hill moved.

No, not the hill. A lizard the size of a pony who'd been coiled around the base.

Hatches-with-Stars skittered over to us, claws tearing at the ground and tail sweeping behind her. She'd been born late; it meant she was little, for a saur, and her scales were pale blue instead of black. Normally. Right now, she was covered in red dust. She stopped and reared up on her hind legs, displaying the rocks that had been — glued? — all over her body.

"What have you done to her?" I demanded.

Jaz rolled his eyes. "Don't worry, it all comes off."

Connor examined Hatches with interest. "It's very good, Jaz. Although in most situations you'd *want* people to see a saur coming. It tends to encourage fleeing in terror."

"Yeah. I only thought of that afterward. Plus to really make it work you have to puff up the grass to hide the saur footprints, which takes ages."

I looked from Connor to Jaz and back again. I'd known they were talking, but I hadn't realized they were . . . really talking. What else had I missed while I'd been wolf?

Hatches sank to her feet and lounged on the ground, licking the dirt off her scales. Jaz grabbed hold of my arm. "Come on, Ash. We need to speak."

He pulled me along, stopping at the very edge of the circle formed by the Five Sisters. "What do you think you're doing?" he hissed.

"What are you talking about?"

"Connor. You *know* I'm talking about Connor. I admit I wasn't sure about the guy at first, but he's pretty useful. And you're making him crazy."

"It's not that simple. I hurt him."

"A broken arm? That's nothing. If I lose control of my ability, I set people on fire."

"You're not asleep when you use your ability! It's not possible for you to lose control the way I can. And it could've been much worse than a broken arm."

Jaz suddenly seemed very tall for an eleven-year-old boy. "Connor is unhappy, Ash. Your whole Tribe has been unhappy 'cause you left them. You'd never let *me* get away with that."

Taken aback, I gazed into his dark, oddly grown-up eyes. This wasn't the first time Jaz had surprised me with what he'd become. He'd literally transformed when he'd joined the saurs, gaining hair and eyes as black as saur scales. Then, when he'd been captured by the government, he'd turned his fellow detainees into a fiercely loyal band of rebels. There was hardly any trace left now of the irresponsible thief he'd been when he first joined my Tribe.

Jaz was a leader. Right at this moment, he was a better leader than me.

I cast a guilty glance at where Connor was sitting next to Hatches. He said something to her. She raised her head to trill at him, and he laughed. It had been too long since I'd seen him do that.

Jaz must have decided that he'd made his point, because he added, "Anyway, Connor wasn't what I wanted to talk to you about. Well, not the only thing. I've got news. About the Adjustment."

My head jerked back to him. The Adjustment was the proceeding that was going to determine the fate of my old enemies, Neville Rose and Miriam Grey. "What about it?"

"They're holding it at Detention Center Three. In six weeks."

"What?" I shifted until I could see the center in the distance. It sat on stony earth, about twenty meters from the far-off edge of the grasslands. It still seemed to loom. "Are you sure? How do you even know?"

"The saurs."

"How do *they* know?"

"People hang around the front gate of the center and talk. If it's quiet and the wind's blowing the right way, the saurs can overhear what's being said from the grasslands. They have super-good ears, you know."

Saur spies. And I supposed that it did make a kind of sense for the Adjustment to be held in the center. It was supposed to restore order, to "adjust" the world back into harmony when the Balance had been seriously disturbed. The government must have figured there was no better place to restore harmony than the one where Neville and Grey had harmed the Balance to begin with. I'd been their prisoner in that place — and the fact that I'd put myself there on purpose to infiltrate the center hadn't made the experience any less terrifying.

Neville and Grey were evil people.

"Ashala?" Connor's voice. I twisted to find he was standing right beside me. When had he moved so close? "Are you all right?"

"I'm fine."

"Are you sure?" Jaz asked. "Because your breathing is a bit funny and you keep making a fist."

I looked down at my right hand, unclenched it, and spoke to Connor. "They're holding the Adjustment at the center."

"Ah." He studied my face. "They're coming back as prisoners, Ashala."

"I know."

He reached out and gently pried my fingers from my palm. I hadn't even realized I'd made another fist. Connor let me go and said, "They're coming back to die."

That might well be true. It was possible that the Adjuster would decide that the only way to make good the disharmony that Neville and Grey had caused was by sending them back to the greater Balance. It didn't quite seem right to Balance life with death to me, only I couldn't feel sorry at the thought of them being dead. Grey was an insane beast who found pleasure in causing pain, and Neville was even worse. A clever, calculating monster, taking a gleeful delight in tricking everyone into believing he was a kindly old man.

I was still afraid of them. I hadn't realized that until now.

Jaz nudged me. "You know, Ash, even if the government doesn't execute them, they'll force them to spend the rest of their lives making things up to the Balance. They broke, what, two accords? Three?" He ticked them off on his fingers. "Neville's hidden stash of those streaker weapons — *totally* against the Advanced Weaponry Accords. Building a secret rhondarite mine — not allowed, under the Three Mines Accords. And making a memory-reading computer thing . . ." His voice trailed off and he threw a hopeful glance in my direction.

I got into the spirit of it, finishing the sentence for him. "Completely and *utterly* against the Benign Technology Accords. No proof of that one, though, since we swiped their machine."

"Not to mention," Connor put in, "inspiring such terror in the detainee children in their care that they fled onto the grasslands and were tragically eaten by saurs."

That drew a smile from me. We'd engineered the *perfect* escape for Jaz and the rest of the detainees. No one came searching for Illegals they thought were dead.

I repeated Connor's words to myself. *They're coming back as prisoners. They're coming back to die.* And we'd gotten the better of them once before. With that I found I could focus, directing my thoughts to what it meant to have the Adjustment here. It was a rare event—there'd only been seventeen Adjustments ever. People didn't commit major crimes against the Balance very often. In fact, I didn't think anyone had ever managed to break so many sets of accords before.

I scowled. "Having that Adjustment here means everyone's going to be paying attention to this part of the world. I don't like it."

"Nor do I," Connor agreed. "But we've never been a big enough problem for the government to throw the kind of resources at the Firstwood that they'd need to in order to capture us. As long as we don't do anything to provoke them, I think we'll be all right."

"My Tribe is increasing patrols," Jaz announced. "We've got it all planned. If anyone comes onto the grasslands, we'll get the saurs to deal with them. No one's going to blame any of us for what the saurs do."

He was right about that. Everyone knew that being eaten was a basic hazard of walking onto saur territory, and the lizards themselves were in no danger from the government. Their armored scales made them virtually indestructible. Plus, saurs were generally held in awe and respect as one of the first new species to be born after the end of the Reckoning. It was part of the reason we'd used the lizards when we'd been engineering the escape. . . . *Uh-oh*.

"Jaz," I said urgently, "there will be people at the Adjustment who were at Detention Centre Three when you escaped." Everyone who'd been there was a witness to Neville and Grey's crimes, and the Adjuster would want to hear from them. "You *can't* let any of them spot you, not when you're supposed to be dead. If anybody ever finds out we faked the detainee deaths . . ."

"I'm not an idiot, Ash! I'll stay too far away for anyone to get a good look. Besides, no one cared enough to remember our faces."

"Dr. Wentworth cared," I pointed out. Rae Wentworth was a Mender who'd worked in the center. She had an Exemption from the Citizenship Accords, so she could openly use her ability, and she'd done her best to take care of everyone being held there. I was positive that she'd remember every last detainee, which made me grateful the others had changed so much that there was no danger of her recognizing any of them. They'd been adopted by the saurs after they'd escaped with Jaz, and they were all black haired and black eyed now. But Jaz had joined the saurs before he went to the center, so he looked exactly the same as when he'd been in there. "You have to be careful, Jaz."

"I will," he answered cheerfully. "You worry *way* too much, Ash."

He was probably right about that. Except the whole situation disturbed me, and not only because of Neville and Grey. Everything felt . . . unstable. Not just in the Tribe with Ember missing and my ability going wrong, but everywhere. Ember had warned me after Belle Willis won the Prime election not to get complacent simply because things had started improving for Illegals. She'd said that the most dangerous times to be a member of an oppressed group was when the oppression began and when it ended. Those were the moments when everyone who'd gained from the oppression had the most to lose. *And,* she'd said, her mismatched eyes brooding and sad, *threatened people are dangerous people, Ash.*

A trilling noise broke into my troubled thoughts. I blinked at Hatches, who'd risen to her feet and was prancing in place.

Jaz nodded at her. "I know, I know." To me, he said, "I've got to go. Hatches and I have things to do. I'll mindspeak you if the saurs hear anything else about the Adjustment."

I hugged him, and he hugged me back. Then he stepped away, frowning slightly. "You know what Georgie says about you, Ash? She says you're like a mother bird that's terrified of her chicks falling out of the nest."

"I am not!"

He continued as if I hadn't spoken. "Except she says the only real way to keep anyone from falling is to teach them how to fly." His gaze flicked to Connor. "And he already knows how to fly. So get over it."

"*Jaz!*"

He grinned at me, winked at Connor, and ran over to leap onto Hatches's back.

Another second, and the two of them were gone, skittering off into the grasslands.

THE NUMBERS

There was a moment of awkward silence.

"Jaz had no right. . . . He's not—he doesn't think things through!"

"Oh, I don't know. He made a lot of sense to me."

I glared at Connor. There was a gleam of laughter lurking in his eyes, and his lips were curved into the hint of a smile.

I felt my mouth twitch upward in response. Tried to make it turn back down again.

Failed.

I giggled, then laughed. Connor laughed, too, and the sound of our shared merriment rang out across the grasslands. Something seemed to fly out of me with that laughter, lifting from my chest and making it easier to breathe. I tipped my head to the sky and inhaled, savoring the sweet scent of the grass, the solidity of the ground beneath my feet, and Connor's steadying presence beside me. I felt . . . human. And glad to be so.

I threw Connor a smile that was partly left over from laughing, and partly from sheer joy at seeing him as he was right now: shoulders relaxed, hair falling over his face, eyes alight. I wanted to reach out to him, only doing that would remove all distance between us, and I wasn't sure I was ready for that. Instead I said, "Let's walk."

We wandered in the direction of the Firstwood. It was good to walk, to fall into the familiar rhythm of striding side by side with Connor. I didn't speak, and neither did he; I think we were both wary of saying something that would shatter the fragile peace between us. Besides, I needed some time to think about what had happened since I'd heard the words "Ember is missing."

I tried to be wolf-like about it, sifting through things one at a time. The news about the Adjustment had been a blow. But it didn't seem as if there was anything that could be done, other than the plans we'd already made. Then there was my malfunctioning ability. I'd handled the whole thing badly by running away, I could admit that. But I still didn't know how to get past the crippling fear of harming Connor worse than I already had. Which left Ember's disappearance, and I was no further along in finding her. I didn't even have anything to go on, other than Grandpa's cryptic message. *Beware the angels.*

My first instinct had been that he was warning me about hurting Connor. But what if he wasn't? After all, he'd said angels with an "s," and there was only one Connor. Except I couldn't see how angels were a clue to finding Ember. Angels were old-world beings that probably didn't exist anymore, if they ever did exist. Connor had never thought they were real. But Alexander Hoffman had written about them, in the *Histories of the Reckoning.* And there was a poem about them, too, although it was only a kids' counting rhyme.

"Do you remember exactly what Hoffman said about angels?" I asked. "In the *Histories?*"

Connor looked startled, and I realized it must seem like a really weird question. I cast around for a reason to have asked it. If I told him about Grandpa's warning, he'd want to know why I hadn't said anything before, and that conversation wasn't going to go well. "Ember said something about angels once," I lied. "Probably nothing important. I just don't want to ignore anything that might help her."

He gazed at me for a second longer. Then he shrugged and said, "It's a couple of lines about angels walking the earth during the Reckoning."

"That's it?"

"And that they would guide humanity in the new world that would emerge from the old. I've told you before—"

"You don't believe they exist. I know."

"They were supposed to be messengers of some sort of god, Ashala. So it's unlikely that Hoffman was talking about actual angels. Because he certainly didn't believe in gods."

No, he didn't. The first line of the "Instructions for a Better World" was *There are no gods. Only an inherent Balance between all life* . . .

"If he wasn't talking about actual angels, what was he talking about?"

"I don't know. Some scholars think he meant extraordinary people who would be leaders once the Reckoning ended. Or maybe he was a little confused."

"He couldn't have been confused! He was *Hoffman*."

"The reference to the angels is in the eighth volume of the *Histories*. He would have been pretty old by the time he was writing that one."

He had a point there. People were fairly certain the ninth volume was the last one Hoffman had actually written himself and the remaining six had been put together by his followers writing under Hoffman's name. The Reckoning had lasted over a hundred years; Hoffman couldn't possibly have lived through the whole thing. "Just because he was old doesn't mean he was crazy."

"I didn't say crazy, I said confused."

There was a note of amusement in his voice. I eyed him suspiciously.

"What's so funny?"

"The way you talk about Hoffman. The way everyone does. As if he was an all-seeing, all-knowing savior."

"He *was* a savior! He foresaw the Reckoning, and he tried to save people — and no one would've been able to rebuild a society when it ended without all the inventions and writings he left behind."

"I know that. Except . . . they ram Hoffman down our throats in enforcer training, because they use his work to justify the Citizenship Accords."

"Hoffman didn't think Illegals were a threat to the

Balance; Ember told me that. The government just tries to make out as if he did. Ever since the flood." That was what had started the Citizenship Accords in the first place — a Skychanger had caused a flood that drowned a city, back when the world's ecosystems had still been unstable in the aftermath of the Reckoning.

"I'm not saying he was against Illegals," Connor replied. "But most of what they told me during training was wrong, and I knew it. Hearing all about Hoffman in that context — I guess it made me question him, too." He sighed. "You know, our entire society is based on his vision of a perfect existence, and we all take every word he wrote as absolute truth. Which makes Alexander Hoffman kind of like the type of religious figure that our society doesn't have."

I frowned, digesting that. I felt distinctly uncomfortable at any criticism of Hoffman. He'd been the one to tell everyone about the Balance, and I knew how right he was about that. I'd *felt* the harmony of life when I'd come to the Firstwood. Although I guessed my grandpa was part of that Balance, and I didn't think Hoffman had ever written about ancient earth spirits. Maybe even he couldn't know everything.

"What exactly did Ember say about angels?" Connor asked.

"Um, nothing. I don't think it's important." Then, both to distract him and because I wanted him to know, I added, "Connor, in the memory, she said I was going to find out bad things about her."

"What kind of bad things?"

"I have no idea! Except it can't be to do with her life in the Firstwood, because there's nothing I don't know about that."

"What about her life before?"

"Well, I know her dad was heavily involved in the reform movement in Spinifex City, and he had contacts all over the world. He got sick, and they came here, using the tunnels beneath the forest, the ones that are collapsed now. He died on the way."

Three sentences, and it was a pretty good summary of all the information I had. I'd never noticed until now how little Ember had really told me. Then again, most of the Tribe didn't talk about their lives before, because their stories weren't happy ones. Too many of us had run from parents who would've handed us to the government in a heartbeat if they knew we had abilities. We all started over in the Firstwood.

"Do you think everything could be connected somehow?" I asked. "That the Adjustment could have something to do with Ember going missing?"

"Anything's possible, although I don't see an immediate link."

I didn't, either, but he was better at figuring out how things fit together than me. *Except there's pieces missing from this puzzle.* The things Ember hadn't said. The secrets she'd concealed. "I can't understand why she kept things from me!"

"She might have been afraid of disappointing you. Ember needs you to think well of her, Ashala, more than anyone else in the Tribe."

"I would never judge her."

"You don't know what she's hiding."

"It doesn't *matter.* She's my best friend!"

He smiled one of the heart-stopping smiles that always left me a little breathless. "You would say that. You don't love anyone halfway."

I smiled back, and the two of us walked on — in silence again, but not an uncomfortable one. Eventually, we reached the Firstwood and made our way through the trees, following the trail that led to the caves.

We hadn't gotten very far when a black dog came pounding out of the forest.

The Labrador took a huge leap and planted two paws on my waist. *Ember's dog?* It had to be. "Sit! Um, Nicky, sit!"

He sat, staring up at me adoringly. I petted his head. He slobbered all over my hand. "He's *really* friendly."

Connor was watching the dog in bemusement. "He didn't react quite so enthusiastically to anyone else. Are you sure you don't know him?"

"Never seen him before. And the kids were supposed to be taking care of him. What's he doing so far from camp?"

"You can't keep a dog penned up in a forest, and they would have been able to judge whether he could watch out for himself," Connor replied. "He did make it all the way to the Firstwood on his own, remember."

As if to prove his independence, Nicky bounded off. Then he stopped, waiting for me to follow.

"Woof! *Woof!*"

"We're going in that direction anyway, silly."

Nicky barked again, more urgently this time. Uneasiness threaded through me. "Connor, I think we should get back."

We followed the dog, jogging to keep up. He never ran too far ahead; he was clearly taking us somewhere. *Should we fly?* Only I wasn't sure where Nicky was going, and we'd outdistance him in the air. *You're jumpy because of everything that's happened. There's probably nothing to worry about.*

70

Only it didn't *feel* like there was nothing to worry about.

There was a sudden whoosh of air along the trail in front of us. Another second and Daniel materialized. He must have been pushing his Running ability hard; that was the only time he was impossible to see.

"What's wrong?" I demanded.

"It's Georgie. She's lost. In a future."

I didn't need to hear that twice, nor did Connor. Air pressed in around me, and the two of us began to float upward. "Bring the dog!" I called to Daniel as Connor and I neared the treetops. Then we cleared the forest and shot through the sky.

We hurtled along at incredible speed. It still wasn't fast enough for me. *I have to reach Georgie!* I'd always been the only one who could pull her back into reality when she got so caught up in a future that she couldn't tell a possibility from the real world. Connor and I plummeted down to land at the northeastern entrance to the cave system. I charged forward only to have him grab hold of my arm. "Look, Ashala!"

I looked, and saw them. *Spiders.* They were everywhere, crawling over the walls and spilling over the entrance in a boiling mass of furry gray bodies.

"I could try to blow them out of the way," Connor offered.

"We can't hurt them; they're Georgie's animal. Besides, there's hundreds . . . thousands . . . um, lots."

I stared at the spiders in frustration. I wanted to run right on through. I'd be risking my life if I did. A bite from one of the big ones would kill in seconds, and while they usually understood to leave us alone, they obviously weren't thinking straight right now. "I'm going to try to talk to them."

Connor cast a doubtful glance at me.

"It's not the same as Ember's crows," I told him. "You know how strong Georgie's link is with the spiders, and they're frantic. They understand something's wrong with her. I'm sure I can get through to them."

He let go of me, and I inched closer to the entrance. Not very much closer, but I hoped the spiders would appreciate the gesture.

"Hello, spiders. It's me, Ashala. Georgie's best friend—well, one of them. Ember isn't here." I tried to radiate calm. Animals could sense when someone was anxious. It was hard when it was making me *really* nervous to be standing in the vicinity of all those huge fuzzy bodies . . . twitching legs . . . miniature eyes . . . *Stop it, Ash!*

"I know we've never exactly been friends"—*because I'm terrified of you*—"but we both care about Georgie, and she's in trouble. You *know* she's in trouble. And I can help her."

Slowly, the spiders began to shift, retreating from the entrance in a creepy living carpet. They moved off the floor and walls, huddling onto the ceiling where they usually lived. There were still a lot more of them than normal, but they weren't going crazy any longer.

Connor held out his arm. "We go together. Do you know exactly where she is?"

I clasped hold of him. "She's in the cavern where she's been building her latest set of maps."

"You're certain of that?"

"Positive. I stopped by to see her before."

We barreled into the cave system, propelled by air down one corridor after another until we finally burst in on Georgie. She was sitting on the floor, writing on the ground with a piece of chalky stone. The spiders above were making little wailing noises; it sounded as if there were hundreds of them up there.

I crouched down in front of Georgie. Connor stood at my side, ready to fly us out if he needed to. Reaching out, I pushed back Georgie's hair so I could study her face in the soft glow of the solar lamps. Her pale eyes were staring at nothing, and her mouth was forming soundless words.

It was no wonder the spiders were crying; I wanted to howl, too. "Georgie, it's Ash. Can you hear me? You have to come back."

She didn't respond. I hauled her onto her feet. Her hand was twitching, moving through air like she was still writing. I pried the stone from her fingers and threw it away. The spiders went quiet. I didn't know if that was better or worse.

Grabbing hold of Georgie's shoulders, I flat-out yelled, "Come back. *I can't lose you, too!*"

For a horrible second there was no change. Then she gave a slow blink; once, then again. "Ash?"

"Yes! Yes, it's me."

She looked around the cave as if she'd never seen it before. "Is this the real world?"

I almost laughed in relief at the familiar question. "Yes, Georgie. This is the real world."

Her gaze wandered down to the markings. I turned her away from them. "This world is real and the other one, whatever you were Seeing, that was a future. It wasn't real."

To Connor I whispered, "Get food, water. *Now.*"

He left, and I steered Georgie across the floor and through an opening that led into a smaller cave. There were no solar lamps in this one, but the far wall was peppered with small holes that let in light from outside, enough for me to see by as I settled Georgie onto her bedroll. She liked to sleep here sometimes, near her maps. I sat next to her and gripped her hand. "See, these are the caves, your caves, Georgie. And the spiders are quiet now; I think they were really worried about you. They're pretty scary when they're upset— or at any other time. . . ."

On I went, anchoring Georgie in the present with the touch of my hand and the sound of my voice. There was a familiar whooshing noise and Daniel appeared, holding Nicky in his arms. He set the dog down and came to sit opposite us. I kept on talking as Nicky sniffed around the cave and Daniel watched Georgie with quiet, focused intensity.

Eventually, Connor returned, bringing with him a flask of water, a jar of honey, and some of the flat, nutty bread we baked in the ashes of a fire. He handed the flask to me and the food to Daniel before retreating back into the other cavern. He knew better than to crowd Georgie with too many people right now.

Daniel and I got Georgie to drink and eat. She started to seem better — more solid somehow, and definitely present in this world. I heaved a sigh of relief. Georgie hadn't gotten lost in a really long time. *It was my fault.* I'd asked her to find Ember, and she must have tried so hard that she'd become trapped in whatever future she'd Seen.

She finished off the piece of bread she was eating and yawned. "I'm tired, Ash."

"You should sleep." I shifted to the side so she could lie down. She pressed her head into the pillow, and I stroked her hair as her breathing grew heavy. Most people looked unguarded when they slept, more vulnerable. Georgie's face didn't change, because she didn't have any walls between herself and the world. I was glad she was here, cocooned in her caves with her spider-guardians, where no one would bother her. None of the Tribe could come into this side of the cave system unless they were accompanied by me, Daniel, Connor, or Ember. Georgie had asked me once if she should add more Tribe members to the list of people the spiders allowed into this part of the caves. I'd told her no, for the same reason that very few of the Tribe knew that Georgie could See the future. She needed to be protected from the pressure of other people's expectations, and to have a place where she could be completely herself.

After a while, Connor stuck his head around the opening. "Ashala. I think you should come and see this."

I hesitated.

"I'll stay with Georgie," Daniel said.

He was about the only other person I'd trust to watch over her; I didn't know what it was between the two of them, but he'd always understood Georgie in a way very few people did. I nodded and followed Connor out, Nicky trotting at my heels.

Connor had moved the solar lamps, setting them in a circle that enclosed the marks on the floor. I stood at his side, staring down at what Georgie had written. Brackets. Numbers. Letters. Weird symbols. *Equations?*

I shook my head. "You remember I left school when I was twelve, right? And Ember's math lessons never really stuck."

He snorted. "I *didn't* leave school when I was twelve and I don't understand most of this. It's far too advanced. See this, though." He pointed. "And again here and here."

It was the same set of numbers repeated over and over. *87543621.*

When Georgie made her maps, the same object appearing more than once meant it was important. Only I couldn't understand *how* this was important.

"Have you seen those numbers before?" Connor asked.

"No! And—what are the equations supposed to mean? That there's a future where Ember's hanging out with a math professor?"

"I don't know. I was hoping you might recognize the numbers."

"Well, I don't." I rubbed at my eyes. They were scratchy and sore.

He glanced at me. "You're exhausted. You should sleep."

"I *can't* sleep. You know that."

"You could take the herb."

One of the herbs that grew in the forest put me into a sleep where I didn't dream and therefore couldn't Sleepwalk. Unfortunately, I couldn't use it for sustained periods, because if I did I would start hallucinating. Apparently, I needed to dream. It would do no harm to take it for one night, though. Only . . .

"If I take that herb, you won't be able to wake me up if Georgie has any more problems."

"Then at least go sit down. I'll keep working on this."

I scowled at the mysterious equations. But if anyone was going to figure out math, it would be Connor, not me. And I *was* tired, so much so that it was an effort to keep myself upright. The day had been full of shocks and changes, and it had drained my strength. I trudged back into the other cave to find Daniel had taken my place at Georgie's head. He didn't even look up as I sat at Georgie's feet, just kept staring down at her sleeping face. It must have scared him when she freaked out. It had scared me, too.

Outside it began to rain. I could see it falling through the holes in the wall, and the scent of it filled the cavern. Nicky padded in to lie at my side, resting his black head on my lap. I patted his ears, leaning back and listening to the steady sound of the rain as it grew stronger and stronger.

I don't know when I made the terrible mistake of falling asleep.

THE NIGHTMARE

There were faces staring down at me. Every one made ugly by hate.

Voices screamed, *Monster!*

I tried to say *no*. I couldn't. They'd broken my voice. They didn't want to hear me speak.

They didn't want to hear me scream.

My gaze fixed on one face. A girl. I knew her. And the others, although I couldn't remember exactly how. But I remembered how I felt. I tried to form the words, so they'd realize I wasn't a threat.

I love you.

The girl seemed to understand the shapes my mouth

had made. For a moment, I thought she would stop the others. I thought she would tell them that I wasn't a monster.

Then she snarled and turned her face away.

That was when I knew. She had never loved me. None of them had.

If I could have spoken, I would have said, *You don't need to take my life. You have already destroyed me.*

And, suddenly, I knew this wasn't real. It *couldn't* be real, because it was impossible that I was unloved. I had an entire Tribe to care about me. This had to be a dream.

And in my dreams, I could do anything.

I surged to my feet, ready to fight back. But my attackers vanished. I was somewhere else, somewhere dark and safe. A cocoon. Only I didn't want to be here. I wanted to find the people who had been hurting me. *Where did they go?* Then I remembered. There was a far-away place where enemies of mine were gathering. My attackers would be there, I was sure of it.

To get to them I had to break out of the cocoon.

I channeled strength into my hand, then drew back my fist to punch my way out. Only I couldn't move. An invisible force was holding my body still. Someone was trying to stop me.

A strange winged being was standing to my left. An enemy. He had to be; no one else would get in my way. Except his power was no match for mine. I threw off the pressure that was keeping me in place and lunged. He leaped back. And something flung itself between us.

I staggered as two big paws thumped against my middle. A dog? The hound barked. "Woof. Woof. WOOF!"

On that third bark, it all changed.

I wasn't in a cocoon anymore. I was in a cave. Connor was standing in front of me, his back against the wall. And Nicky was trying to jump up and lick my face.

Reaction set in, and I started to tremble. I pushed Nicky away gently and bent over, resting my hands on my knees as I waited for the aftermath of Sleepwalking to pass. The shakiness and nausea would subside soon; feeling horribly emotional would last a little longer. When I could speak, I hissed at Connor, "You let me fall asleep?"

"You were tired. Ashala —"

"Did I hurt you?"

"No."

I didn't believe him. I knew he'd lie to me about this.

And while the details of the nightmare were fading, I remembered wanting to attack a winged being, which had to be Connor. I straightened, looking him over. He seemed to be all right, but there wasn't enough light in here to be certain.

I staggered into the next cavern, knowing he'd follow, and grabbed a solar lamp. Then I held it up, peering at him in the glow. *Still* not bright enough. I scowled. Connor took the lamp away, reaching for my hand. "Come with me."

He led me along the passages, Nicky bounding ahead of us, until we reached one of the caverns that opened onto the forest. Connor put the lamp on the ground and strode over to stand where the daylight streamed in. "I'm fine. See?"

I circled around him, checking for bruises and studying the way he was holding himself. He really was fine. I heaved a long, shuddering sigh of relief. And yelled, "What were you thinking? I could've killed you!"

"You didn't."

"You should have woken me up. Or run! Or, or, just got out of the way. Why did you even try to stop me? I was Sleepwalking; nothing would've hurt me."

"No, but I think you were about to smash through a wall. You could have brought the entire cave down."

Oh. I'd been in danger of destroying something that was part of the forest I'd sworn to protect. Not to mention probably killing Connor and Nicky, if they couldn't get out in time. And they hadn't been the only ones in the cave. "Where's Georgie? And Daniel? I didn't do anything to them, did I?"

He shook his head. "They went to breakfast before you started Sleepwalking. You've been asleep all night, Ashala."

That was *morning* light coming in from outside. I'd slept for hours. Anything could have happened, and almost had. Pictures of rocks tumbling on top of my beloved tuarts, and of Connor and Nicky crushed, spun through my head. Guilt rose up to overwhelm me.

"I'm sorry," I whispered to the caves, to the trees, to Nicky, to Connor. "I'm sorry, I'm sorry . . ."

Connor swept me into his arms, and I clung to him and sobbed. Eventually, my tears ran out, but I didn't let go. I couldn't. Whatever had remained of my determination to keep him at a distance had been smashed by that awful nightmare, by the memory of being in pain and utterly alone. He stroked my hair, and I pressed closer to him.

Then he ruined it all by saying, "Ashala. You have to deal with why your ability isn't working."

I staggered back. I couldn't face this now, surely he knew that! "I don't *know* why—"

"Yes, you do."

"No," I snapped, glaring at him. "I really don't."

He sighed. "Let's try it this way. Why didn't you have any bad dreams when you were with the wolves?"

"Who says I didn't?"

He raised an eyebrow, looking skeptical.

"Okay," I admitted. "I didn't. But I didn't Sleepwalk, either. So it doesn't mean anything."

"You Sleepwalked. The third night you were with them."

"I did not!"

"You came out of the den," he said patiently, "and ran into the sky. You kept getting higher and higher—I was about to pull you to the ground when Pack Leader came out after you. He barked, and you went back to him."

That was impossible. Except . . . I did have a vague memory of a dream when I'd been chasing after a glowing ball hanging high above me. The moon? I'd really wanted that ball, only before I could reach it, my big brother had called me inside to bed. *Pack Leader.* It hadn't registered before that I'd been Sleepwalking; the whole experience had merged into my time as a wolf. But Connor had known.

"What were you doing there?" I asked.

He looked exasperated. "What do you *think* I was doing there?"

I stared down at my feet and mumbled, "Making sure I was all right."

"Yes. But I realized the wolves understood how to take care of you. And you returned to Pack Leader when he called—you could tell a friend from an enemy, so you weren't having a nightmare." He drew in a breath and said, "Ashala. Why no bad dreams when you were with the pack?"

"I don't know!"

But the knowledge was there. I could feel it, lurking beneath the surface of my consciousness. A truth that I didn't want to face. Nicky came over to sit beside me, leaning against my leg, and I reached down to pat him. It dawned on me that I'd seen him as himself in the nightmare, which was weird, because normally everything changed into something else when I Sleepwalked. I had no idea why he'd remained the same, but I was glad he had. Otherwise I wouldn't have known he was a friend, not in a nightmare where everything became twisted and askew. And Nicky had helped me. Like Pack Leader had helped me. Like Connor was trying to help me.

It really was about time I started helping myself.

"I guess I didn't have bad dreams because I wasn't responsible for anything when I was with the wolves. I wasn't in charge."

"And that made you feel better. Because you don't want to be the leader anymore?"

"No. Because... because I'm not fit to be the leader."

Connor nodded as if that wasn't a surprise. "You can't let go of it. Evan's death."

"I *killed* him. I was Sleepwalking and I killed him and — no, I can't let go of it."

"He would have killed you. He did kill me." His lips twitched. "For a while."

I eyed him sourly. I didn't find anything remotely amusing about him dying. If I closed my eyes, I could still see the shot from the streaker blazing up into the night sky. Connor had died, and I'd been left alone with Evan. He'd had the streaker pointed right at my head. I'd been at his mercy.

Except then I'd Sleepwalked, which should have been impossible, since I wasn't sleeping. But when

I got very upset I could go into what Ember called a "dissociative state," which was enough like being asleep while awake for my ability to activate. It had only ever happened twice — after I'd lost Connor, and before that, when my little sister had died — and both times I'd been half crazy with grief and rage. "It's not so much that I killed him," I said softly. "It's that I could probably have found another way to stop him, if I'd tried. I never tried. It didn't even occur to me to try. Because I hated him, and I *wanted* him to suffer, for what he'd done to you."

"And your ability has been malfunctioning ever since. You were angry and you struck out in anger, and I don't think you were wrong, by the way. Now you're so scared of doing it again that your ability's going haywire."

I worked my way through that. "Are you saying that I'm losing control because I'm afraid of losing control?"

"That's the way fear works, Ashala. The more you try to run away from it, the more you create what you're afraid of. You need to learn to trust yourself with what you can do."

Trust myself. As if it was that easy after Evan. The nightmare came back to me, the sound of voices screeching "monster." I had something monstrous in me. The people I loved inexplicably didn't see it. I did.

"How can I trust myself when I'm a killer?" I whispered.

He threw back his head and laughed.

"This isn't funny, Connor!"

"I'm sorry," he replied, sounding completely unapologetic. "But you're not a killer, Ashala. And if anyone should know that, it's me. I was raised to be one."

I frowned, troubled that he'd still think of himself that way. Connor's dad had tried to shape his son into a weapon aimed at the man responsible for Connor's mother's death—Terence Talbot, then the Prime of Gull City. Talbot had been an Assessor before he was Prime, and he'd botched an Assessment, scaring a Rumbler into starting a quake that had destroyed a large part of Connor's hometown. I knew that Connor probably *would* have killed Talbot if he hadn't died of a stroke; he'd wanted revenge for his mother, and I understood that, all too well. But I also knew that Connor had never truly been a killer, in his heart. And he was nothing like his cruel, violent father.

"You're not what your dad tried to make you."

"I know." He gave me his dazzling smile. "You showed me that, when we met and shared memories.

I think you're the only person in the world who could have seen my past and still looked at me as if I was . . ." He stopped, shrugged. "Someone you wanted in your Tribe. Someone you could love."

"Of *course* I —"

"Ember didn't agree with you. She thought I was dangerous."

"She changed her mind about that." *Sort of.*

"She was right, Ashala. Except all Illegals are dangerous. Not only because we have abilities but because we live in a world where to have an ability is to be feared."

"So what?"

"So hurt people don't always make the best decisions. But you're the one who sees that we are each more than our pain." He reached out to link his hands in mine. "You're just not very good at doing it for yourself."

Ember had said, on more than one occasion, that I changed people, simply by seeing the best of what they could be. But I wasn't even sure I knew the best of what *I* could be. Whatever it was, I felt a long way away from it right now. "Connor, I don't know. . . . I can't . . ."

"It's all right." He leaned in to press a kiss to my

forehead, and stepped away. "Come on. You need to see the Tribe."

The two of us made our way, hand in hand, through the cave system, with Nicky running alongside. We emerged into the cool morning air and made our way through the trees, angling up to the area everyone called the Overhang. It was a big flat area of granite, with another rock projecting over the top. The Tribe used it as a place to eat in autumn and spring when it was too wet to sit among the trees but the weather wasn't bad enough to keep us in the caves.

Everyone was there, gathered around a fire with steaming mugs of tea in their hands. Nicky bounded in and was greeted with hugs from the children. He settled with the other Tribe dogs, while I hung back a little. I was suddenly nervous at seeing everyone after I'd run away.

I needn't have worried. They acted as if I'd never been gone. Georgie and Daniel made space for Connor and me to sit beside them, while Keiko poured tea from the pot bubbling on the fire and handed me a cup. Micah gave me a piece of bread he'd toasted on a stick over the flames, and Penelope passed me the pot of honey and a knife. I slapped honey on the toast, and into the tea to sweeten it, and began to eat.

Conversations rose and fell in a soothing, familiar rhythm. No one appeared to be paying any special attention to me. But my cup of tea was continually refilled, and I'd barely finished one piece of toast when another arrived. And they all found the time to tell me something, filling me in on a thousand small moments that I'd missed. Micah had finished building a fence to enclose our newly expanded food garden. Benny had come up with a new bread recipe, and Jin had succeeded in growing a bumper crop of potatoes. Penelope was excited about a new variety of aloe. She was our only Mender and she tried to use forest plants for treatments as much as she could, to avoid exhausting her ability on minor hurts. Andreas and Jo had finished making clothes for the youngsters who had outgrown theirs. And everyone had been practicing their abilities as I'd told them to — Mai had gotten faster, Stefan could now lift boulders half his size, and Rosa could summon more water than she'd ever been able to before.

They needed me, I realized, in the same way that I'd needed Pack Leader. And I needed them. I'd been going crazy trying to protect everyone, to keep them all in the nest, just as Jaz had said. But that wasn't how a wolf acted. There was always danger in the world, and wolves knew it. The promise of the Pack was simply to always be there, to defend the Pack or die trying. I called out to them all in my head. *I am your Pack Leader, and I am here.* I could almost hear the echo of it, flowing back to me from them. *We are your Tribe, and we are here.*

Connor was watching me intently. "Do you see?" he whispered.

I nodded, blinking back tears. *Love is the only thing more powerful than hate.* Georgie had told me that once. And she'd been right, it was. It was even more powerful than the monstrous, angry part of me. Because I felt so much bigger than that, here. So much more. How could I have failed to understand that it was through their eyes that I saw the best of what I could be?

I'd been running away from the very thing that would stop me from becoming what I feared.

I whispered back, "I've been an idiot."

"Yes. I know."

I laughed and leaned against him, munching on toast and enjoying being with the Tribe. Eventually breakfast was done and they all began to disperse, drifting off to their various tasks. Georgie and Daniel were the last to go. He was taking her to see the autumn lilies blooming. I didn't care where they went, as long as

Georgie was kept away from her futures for a while. And I knew I could trust Daniel to make sure she was occupied with earthly, everyday, here-and-now things.

As the two of them disappeared into the trees, I jumped up and reached out to pull Connor to his feet. Then I threw myself at him. He laughed, staggering back a step before he steadied himself, and kissed me. Sensation and emotion looped back and forth between us until I wasn't certain where he ended and I began.

The kiss left me breathless and wanting more. But I couldn't lose myself in him for long, not when we were no closer to finding Ember. And I didn't need to tell him what I was thinking. Sometimes he knew me better than I knew myself. He bent to kiss me again, a lingering promise of more. *Later.*

And he said, "Let's go search Ember's laboratory."

THE LABORATORY

I stood in the entrance to Ember's laboratory with Nicky at my side, watching as Connor switched on the solar lamps positioned around the cavern. The three of us were deep in the cave system, enclosed by warm air and musty darkness and layers of rock. Connor finished with the lights and I examined the room, trying to figure out if anything had changed. It took a while, because Ember's lab was big and cluttered. There were long benches scattered with papers. Shelves holding bits of machinery and books. And cupboards that I knew were packed with yet more of her things. Micah had crafted the furniture from bits of fallen wood, and each piece was carved with intricate designs of trees and birds and animals. Ember loved those carvings, just as she loved working down here, in the quiet embrace of the earth. Only she wasn't here anymore. And so far as I could tell, there was nothing to indicate where she'd gone.

"Everything looks the same." I felt a bit crushed. I didn't know what I'd expected. No, I did. A note. A clue. Anything that would help me find her.

Nicky ran over to one of the cupboards. He turned in a circle and sat, wagging his tail. *Is he trying to tell me something?* Hurrying over, I yanked open the doors.

The only thing inside was herbs.

I looked at Nicky. He had his head held up and his chest puffed out, like he'd done something incredibly clever.

"You know," Connor said, "it's possible that's not the smartest dog in the world."

"He *is* smart!" I protested. "Maybe he got the wrong cupboard."

I went to the other one. *More herbs.* Plus a pile of rhondarite collars that we'd taken off the detainees rescued from the center. Rhondarite blocked an ability for as long as it touched someone's skin, and I hated the stuff. I'd wanted to destroy those collars, but Em had thought they might come in useful one day.

With a sigh, I closed the cupboard doors. "If there's some clue, it must be buried among all her stuff."

Connor cast an appraising glance at our crowded surroundings. "We'd better start searching."

He strode over to a set of shelves and began to sort through the contents. I glanced around helplessly, unsure of where to start. Then my gaze fell on the bench where Ember had been sitting the last time I'd seen her here. I wandered across to it, trying to imagine what she'd been thinking and feeling as she worked on her projects. There were two things on the bench—a black box and a streaker. I'd brought both back from Detention Center 3. I picked up the streaker, holding the cold, smooth weight of it in my hand. *No, not a streaker anymore. A stunner.* Ember had altered the weapon so that it would knock someone out without permanently harming them. She'd wanted me to be able to defend myself, and she'd known how I felt about killing. She'd finished the stunner two months ago now. *Not that long before she left.* I wondered if she'd known then that she was going. Had the weapon been her idea of a parting gift?

It was a horrible present, and no substitute for her

being here. I tossed it back onto the bench, turning my attention to the box instead. This was the machine that Miriam Grey had used to pull memories from my mind when I was trapped in Detention Center 3. Except it wasn't only a machine. When it had been inside my head, I'd seen it as a dog, a huge, half-metallic hound that was as much a prisoner as I was. I'd brought the box with me when I fled the center, and asked Ember to build it a mechanical dog body. She hadn't been able to do it yet.

Nicky padded over and pushed his head against my leg. *Maybe he and the box-dog could play together, once I get Ember back.* . . . I patted the top of the box and whispered, "I won't leave you like this, boy. I'll find her. Promise."

From across the room, Connor spoke. "Ashala. What exactly did Ember say about angels?"

"What?" I turned to face him, bewildered by the unexpected question.

He was standing by the shelves, holding a piece of paper in his hand. "You were asking me about angels before, remember? Because Ember told you something. What was it?"

"Nothing important." I walked over, eyeing the paper hopefully. "Is that a note? From Em?"

"No." He pressed it flat against his chest. "What did she say, Ashala?"

Whatever was on that paper, he obviously wasn't going to show it to me until I answered. *Time to confess.* "It wasn't Em. It was Grandfather, and he said, 'Beware the angels.'"

"Why didn't you tell—" He stopped and shook his head. "Because Georgie says I look like an angel. You thought he was talking about me."

"I didn't think he meant I should be afraid *of* you," I explained hastily. "I figured he meant I should be afraid *for* you, in case I hurt you again. . . ."

"I don't need you to protect me, Ashala!"

"I know. I've been an idiot, I told you that before. I'm sorry." And I was. But I could still feel, deep inside, that overwhelming, irrational urge to protect him from all harm. I wasn't over that yet. I wasn't sure how to get over it.

He stared at me a moment longer. Then he nodded, accepting the apology, and handed me the paper. "Read that."

I scanned the page. Ten lines, in Ember's hand-writing. *The angel rhyme.* Except . . . "It's out of order." Every schoolkid knew that poem, and it was supposed to run from one to eight:

Count the angels one by one
We'll get to eight before we're done
One to lead
Two to fight
Three to make all great wrongs right
Four for music, dance, and art
Five to nourish land and heart
Six to invent
Seven to remember
Eight to bring the rest together.

This version of the poem, though, had the numbers out of order.

Eight to bring the rest together
Seven to remember
Five to nourish land and heart
Four for music, dance, and art
Three to make all great wrongs right
Six to invent
Two to fight
One to lead.

I caught my breath. "It's the same as Georgie's numbers! Eight, seven, five, four, three, six, two, one. But what does it mean? That Ember's somewhere with angels?"

"Or that she'll return here," Connor said. "This is where the poem is." I brightened, and he added gently, "Or perhaps not. Georgie's futures are always difficult to interpret, and I couldn't work out what those equations she wrote down were about. None of this really makes sense yet."

That was true enough. Still, the poem was a clue, even if we didn't know what it meant. I glanced around the lab, which now seemed to be bursting with possibilities. "Let's see if we can find something else."

We went on searching. After half an hour, I hadn't found anything else useful. Plus, Nicky was driving me crazy. He couldn't leave that cupboard alone. He tried to push me toward it, and when that didn't work, he sat in front of the thing and barked.

I told him to stop, and he did. But I could feel his big dark eyes watching me mournfully. "It's only herbs, Nicky," I said as I sorted through yet another pile of papers. "There's nothing there."

There was a banging sound. I spun around to find Nicky throwing himself against the cupboard.

It began to topple.

"Nicky!" I dived for him as Connor captured the cupboard in the air, stopping it halfway to falling. Grabbing hold of Nicky's collar, I dragged him out from underneath, pulling him across the room. "Are you hurt?" I knelt down at his side, checking him over. To my relief, he seemed to be okay. "That was a really stupid thing to do!"

"Actually," Connor breathed, "I don't think it was stupid at all."

I glanced up. He was staring at the half-fallen cupboard, looking a little stunned. "Ashala, I think . . . I think there's something behind it."

The cupboard floated sideways, righted itself, and settled on the ground. I gaped at what it had concealed.

A door. A heavy, dull, *impossible* door, set into the cave wall.

Nicky barked, as if to say, *I told you!*

I scrambled to my feet. Connor got to the door first and tried the handle. It didn't open. I arrived right behind him and ran my fingers over the cold, pitted surface. It felt a bit like metallite, one of the building materials churned out by the recyclers. But metallite was black. Smooth. This was . . . something else.

"I think this could be the entrance to a bunker," Connor said.

I struggled to string thoughts together. "You mean, like where people hid out? To survive the Reckoning?"

"This door is old. Whatever it's made of didn't come out of a recycler."

"Yeah, I can see that! But there's never been any sign of anyone living in the caves except us."

"Are you sure? How well do you know the cave system?"

"Well!" Then I thought about it. "Pretty well. I mean, it's huge; I've never explored it all. And Ember knows it best." Ember's ability meant she never forgot anything, so she could wander as far into the caves as she wanted without getting lost. "I always thought she'd tell me if she ever found anything interesting."

"You had *no* idea about this door?"

I shook my head. "When we first began using the caves she had a different lab. She shifted here later, because it was bigger, and she'd already put that cupboard there the first time she showed me this room." I glared at the door. "How could she have hidden this from me?"

"A better question might be, how did the dog know about it?"

We both looked at Nicky. He'd rolled on his back and was lying with his paws in the air. "I thought you said he wasn't very smart."

"I've changed my mind." He bent to scratch Nicky's belly. "I wonder if Ember can give memories to animals, the same as she can to people?"

"You think she made him remember stuff?" It would explain how he'd known about the door. Then something occurred to me, and I frowned. "But if she made him remember the door . . . and that poem wasn't very well hidden, either . . . does that mean she *wanted* us to find this?"

He straightened and shrugged. "Maybe."

"Then none of this will lead me to her! She wouldn't leave me anything that tells me where she is, not when she doesn't want me coming after her." I kicked the ground in frustration. "It's all useless."

"It might not lead us directly to her, but everything new we learn about Ember—about what secrets she's been keeping—helps us to narrow down where to start looking."

He had a point, I supposed, although it wasn't a very satisfying point. I wanted more information than what we'd found, much more. Like the identity of the false Serpent. Or the names of those mysterious "bad people" Ember was worried about. *Or a map with a big* x *on it to show where she is . . .*

"You know," Connor said thoughtfully, "if Ember

did send the dog to show us the door, we should be able to open it. I can't see why she would have gone to so much trouble otherwise."

"If you're thinking there's a key hidden around here, you're wrong." I waved at the door. "In case you haven't noticed, there's no keyhole."

"What I'm thinking is that a set of numbers can be used for a lot of things," he replied. "Including codes." He crouched in front of the door, studying the handle. "Bring a light over here so I can see, would you?"

I grabbed a lamp and held it above him, watching as he ran his fingers along the handle's metal base. After a moment, he muttered, "Aha!"

He pressed the sides of the base, and it slid downward.

There was a tiny keypad underneath. Nine numbers, set in a square.

Connor grinned up at me. "I'll bet you anything in the world this unlocks with an eight-digit code."

"Try it!"

He entered the numbers: 87543621. Then he rose and reached for the handle. So did I. My hand covered his, and we turned it together.

The door opened.

THE CACHE

I held up the lamp, peering into what seemed to be another cave. I could make out the shapes of shelves against the walls, but not much more than that. The light faded to nothing before it reached the end of the space, as if the darkness were eating the light. *Don't be silly.* It was just a really big cave.

A big, hidden, spooky cave.

I whispered to Connor, "We need more light."

"Yes, we do." He bent to speak into my ear. "Why are you whispering?"

"I don't know! It just feels as if I should."

Connor grabbed a lamp, and the two of us walked

into the cavern, our footsteps echoing in the vast space. But there was something wrong about the sound of that echo; the reverberation was a little off. I stopped and swung my light up to find that the walls, floor, and ceiling were unnaturally smooth and seemed to be made of the same material as the door. Someone had built this place. "I guess you were right about it being a bunker."

"Yeah." Connor shone his light across the shelves, which were filled with containers. "Or—some kind of storehouse, maybe?" He paced to the end of the room, and I watched, heart pounding in anticipation, as the glow of his lamp shone over the room.

There was a table in the center of the space. There were more shelves. And there was nothing else.

This really isn't what I was hoping for. I went over to a container and pushed open the lid to discover a collection of tools inside. Holding up a hammer, I said, "So Ember basically hid a giant cupboard."

"There must be something significant in here." I could hear a hint of frustration in Connor's voice; he'd been expecting more, too. "We'll just have to go through everything." He looked down at the lamp in his hand. "Which means . . ."

I finished the thought. "We still need more light."

The two of us went back and forth, gathering up lamps and placing them around the cavern. Nicky came padding in, and I stopped still, watching him in case he wanted to show me something. Except all he did was flop onto the ground with the satisfied air of a dog who felt his work was done.

I went over to the shelves nearest to me and got to work opening containers. Connor did the same across the other side of the room. Aside from ordinary stuff like tools, all I kept finding were bits of machines. I had no idea what the parts were for, because advanced technology was something everyone learned about in upper school, and I'd never gone. Besides, machinery didn't seem very relevant to finding Ember. I left it for Connor to figure out, and went on searching.

Finally I came across a container filled with papers and hauled it over to the table so I could rifle through the contents. "I've got a bunch of Alexander Hoffman's writings here. Only it's a bit weird."

Connor turned. "Weird?"

"It's handwritten, but it's not Ember's writing. And why would she need any of this when she's got the collected works of Hoffman in books?"

"Let me see that." He strode over to pull a piece of paper out of the container.

"The paper looks strange, too," I pointed out. "All white and shiny."

Connor examined it with a focused, intent expression. Then he muttered, "I can't believe it."

"Can't believe what?"

"It looks strange," he told me, with an air of suppressed excitement, "because the paper you're used to seeing comes out of a recycler. And this paper isn't recycled. It's old-world, Ashala."

I snorted. "It would have rotted to dust by now! Everyone knows the only old-world paper that still exists is the stuff Hoffman preserved, and that was all in . . ." My voice trailed off. I stared at Connor. He stared back steadily, waiting for me to put it together. "Connor, you're not saying—you don't think this place is—it *can't* be."

"I know." He looked around and gave an incredulous shake of his head. "But I think it is."

"A *Hoffman cache*? There's only been eight of them ever discovered!"

"Nine. Now."

I leaned against the table to support my shaking legs. *Not a storeroom. Not a bunker.* Connor thought we were standing in one of the legendary repositories of technology and knowledge that Alexander Hoffman and his followers had hidden around the world. "Are you sure?"

"You'd need a team of experts to be sure. But—there's the paper. You said it yourself, the only old-world paper that still exists comes from caches."

That was true. No one had ever been able to work out how Hoffman had managed to preserve paper, but he'd found a way. And he'd left his words, along with the technology he'd invented, as a gift to humanity so that people could rebuild once the Reckoning was finally over. I breathed, "The machinery . . . it must be . . ."

"All the things that Hoffman put in his caches." He dropped the paper, striding over to the shelves he'd been sorting through, and reached into a container. "See this?" He held up what looked like a big mess of wires. "I think it's a recycler component." His eyes were sparkling with enthusiasm—Hoffman might not have meant a lot to Connor, but he obviously loved having access to all this technology. "And," he continued, showing me yet another mysterious piece of equipment, "I'm almost certain that this is part of a solar generator."

This really was a cache. I picked up the paper Connor had dropped with a trembling hand. It was

"Instructions for a Better World," and I read the familiar directives with a sense of awe. *1. There are no gods. Only an inherent Balance between all life, and to preserve it, we must live in harmony with ourselves, with each other, and with the earth. 2. Advances in technology can never compensate for failures in empathy . . .*

"Hoffman touched this," I whispered.

"More likely one of his many devoted followers. I can't imagine Hoffman patiently writing out copies of his words for all the caches."

I frowned at him. He threw me an unrepentant grin, and after a moment, I smiled back. Then I thought of Ember, and my smile faded. "Em must have known what this place was. And she hid it." I looked around, feeling a bit depressed. "Do you think it's *all* part of the cache?" Because if it was, then it was amazing—but it wouldn't help me find Ember.

Connor shrugged, his gaze darting across the shelves. "There's a lot of containers in here. We won't know for certain until we check them all." He obviously couldn't wait to get back to the search. With his quick, puzzle-solving mind, the bits of tech probably looked like the pieces of a satisfyingly complex jigsaw to him; he must have been dying to try to assemble some of it. *Glad one of us is enjoying this.* I put down "Instructions for a Better

World" and stalked back to the shelves. "Let's see what else is here."

After another hour of searching, all we'd discovered was technology we didn't understand, and yet more of Hoffman's writings. It was frustrating, the more so because in any other circumstances I would have loved being in here. I mean, a *Hoffman* cache! It was an incredible find. Right now, though, the only thing I could think about was Ember. Nothing we'd uncovered so far would lead me to her, and everything showed me that I didn't know her the way I'd thought I had. *I'm not getting closer to her. I'm getting farther away.*

I'd been lied to by a Tribe member once before — Briony, who'd betrayed us to Neville Rose and died trying to escape from Detention Center 3 after Rose had turned on her. But Ember wasn't Bry. Whatever she was up to, she wasn't plotting against me, I was positive of that. In fact, she seemed to be trying to protect me. I only wished I knew from what.

Connor's voice broke into my thoughts. "Ashala. I think I've found something."

I looked up. He hurried over to the table, holding a long rolled-up paper in his hand. I arrived at his side as he spread the paper out, putting lamps on the corners to keep it in place. It was—a blueprint? A really complicated blueprint, for some kind of machine.

I rolled my eyes. "We're looking for things to do with Ember, remember? You can play with all the tech later."

"This *is* about Ember. This is—Ashala, this shouldn't be here. Nothing like this has ever been found in a Hoffman cache."

That was more interesting. "So what is it?"

"It's a design, for a kind of computer."

"Like my black box?"

"Yes . . . and no. This is more advanced than that. It's more advanced than anything. And I think Hoffman invented it—see his signature, there in the corner?"

I stared down at the loopy writing. *A. Hoffman.* "I still don't see what this has to do with Em, Connor."

"Did she ever talk to you about something called artificial intelligence?"

"Artificial *what*?"

He drew in a breath, and explained, "In the old world, before the Reckoning, people were starting to develop computers that were like human brains. Computers that could think."

He gestured to tiny lettering at the bottom of the page, words all stacked up on top of one another.

Artificial
Intelligence
New
Gaia
Lifeform

Gaia . . . I'd heard that word before; Ember had told it to me once. "Isn't Gaia an old-world name for earth?"

He nodded. "Hoffman might have been trying to build a life-form that could survive the Reckoning. Remember he didn't know if anyone would live through it. And watch this!"

He pressed his hand flat over the words until only the first letter of each was showing, and demanded, "What do you see?"

For a second I just stared, confused. Then I got it, and choked. "A-I-N-G-L. *Angel?*" I put my hands to my head, which was spinning. *Beware the angels.* "Beware the *aingls?* Grandpa was warning me about *computers?*"

"Yes. Maybe." Connor tapped the paper. "This is just a blueprint. Hoffman might never have built an aingl. But if he did, they could still exist. Because he certainly knew how to make things last."

"That's — this is . . ." I stopped speaking, trying to

sort through the implications. Connor had said the aingls were advanced. But under the Benign Technology Accords, advanced tech could only be developed for projects of public good, and was strictly controlled by the Primes of the seven cities. If aingls existed, the governments would want them. Or maybe the government already had them and wasn't telling anybody.

I paced, thoughts tripping over one another in my mind. *The numbers, and the poem . . . If aingls exist they're tied up with where Em is, or where she will be . . . and the bad people Em was worried about, could they be from the government?* I couldn't make everything fit together yet, but one thing was clear. Ember could be in terrible danger. And she'd gone off alone, without telling me where, or even why, really. I'd been confused by her behavior, and hurt; now I was just mad. I took a breath and yelled, "You should never have hidden this from me, Em!"

My shout rang out through the caves. Nicky raised his head and gave a soft woof. As if he agreed with me. Or just wanted to join in the noise.

"Feel better?" Connor asked.

"No," I answered grumpily.

He reached out, and I went to him, wrapping my arms around his chest and pressing my cheek against his shoulder. He held me tight, and I closed my eyes — shutting out the room, Ember's secrets, all the things that had to be done — until there was only Connor and me. "She's in real trouble."

He didn't lie to me. "Yes. Whatever she's mixed up in, it's much bigger than we thought. More complicated. More dangerous."

I clung to him for a moment longer. Then I let go and stepped back, baring my teeth in a wolf snarl. "We've dealt with dangerous before."

"So we have." The fierceness in his face matched my own. *He is here, I am here.* . . . I looked around the room. "Let's finish searching this place. Then I'm going to talk to Grandpa again. And I'll try the crows, and we'll go to the city — whatever it takes."

One way or another, I was going to find Ember. Yell at her. And save her.

Not necessarily in that order.

THE REALIZATION

The search dragged on, into hours, then days. There was a *lot* of stuff in the cache. We found more bits of tech, and a heap of Alexander Hoffman's writings, plus sets of schematics for some of his inventions—but nothing else about aingls, and nothing that would lead us to Em.

After three days, we'd finally managed to get through it all, and I went to talk to Grandfather. He wouldn't come out, no matter how much I pleaded or how loud I shouted. I tried the crows as well. They weren't talking, either, not even to the Chirpers. The only leads I was left with were the aingls—which didn't seem to be getting me anywhere—and the fact that Ember had been chasing after the false Serpent. Connor and I were going to have to go to the next anti-Citizenship rally in Gull City, which was over a month away. And since there was nothing I could usefully do to find her in the meantime, I returned to forest life with the Tribe.

I'd broken the news to them that Ember was missing, just the bare details that she was gone and I wasn't sure where. Everyone was worried. They needed the reassurance of my presence, and I needed to lead my Pack. I slipped back into the daily routine of doing chores, sorting out any disputes that flared up between Tribe members, and simply being around to listen to people's troubles and triumphs. Nicky trailed around after me, except when he was off hunting his meat with the other dogs, or shamelessly lapping up attention from the rest of the Tribe. He couldn't seem to get enough love, that dog; he soaked it up like his heart was a sponge. Georgie stayed nearby, too; she'd clearly missed me while I'd been gone. And I wanted her close, to keep her away from future-gazing. She'd immediately volunteered to look again after I'd told her and Daniel about the aingls, in case she could See anything more than numbers and equations. I'd forbidden it.

Ten nights after I'd returned from the wolves, I lay huddled in my sleeping bag in the big cavern the Tribe used for winter camp. Nicky was at my feet, and everyone else was snoozing around me, with the exception of Daniel and Connor. The two of them were spending the evening in the cache. Daniel seemed to find the tech as fascinating as Connor did, even though he didn't understand it any better than me. The last time I'd visited them, I'd found Connor explaining various bits of machinery to Daniel as the two of them organized the parts into categories; they were going to try to build a recycler if they had all the right pieces. Neither of them had been very impressed when I'd picked up a couple of the parts and started to juggle them.

We really did need a list of everything in the cache, and I was glad Connor had someone who was happy to help him go over it all. I'd had more than enough of the dark, silent room. I was much happier out here, surrounded by familiar, comforting things: the steady breathing of Tribe members and Tribe dogs, the flickering flames of our campfire, and the woodsy scent of smoke rising up though a hole in the roof of the cave. *And the stars.* I could just glimpse a small patch of night sky, out through the mouth of the cavern. In the old world people used to make wishes on stars;

119

Em had told me that. I could see six stars from where I was, so I made the same wish six times over. *Let her come home safe.*

I yawned and let my eyes close, blacking out the sky. It wouldn't take me long to doze off. I'd taken the herb that guaranteed a sleep without dreams. I'd been using it ever since the nightmare. I didn't want to be worrying about my ability on top of everything else, but I was going to stop soon. I'd *have* to allow myself to dream sooner or later, and not only because of the danger of hallucinations if I used the herb for too long. The only way to know for sure if I'd resolved the fears that were causing my ability to malfunction was to allow myself to Sleepwalk. But I didn't want to try it yet, not when things were just getting back to some sort of normal. *I'll stop taking the herb tomorrow night. Or the next one. Or the one after that . . .*

I drifted into sleep. I should not have dreamed.

But I did.

And in my dream, I was a monster.

I had to find prey. I was being driven to hunt by pain that roared through my body. If I could find prey, the pain would end. For a little while. Then it would return, but that was only right. Monsters deserved to suffer.

120

I roamed back and forth, searching. I was surrounded by structures, some tall, some short, but all made of the same white material. Suddenly, I knew where I was. This was Detention Center 3. There was the cell block where I'd been imprisoned. There was the hospital where Dr. Wentworth had saved my life, more than once. There was Neville Rose's secret rhondarite-processing plant, and the high composite wall that surrounded the whole place. Only it was wrong. Everything was shining, new, complete. This wasn't how the center looked now. Much of it had burned, and they hadn't rebuilt the ruined section.

This wasn't real. It couldn't be real. I was having a bad dream.

The moment I understood that, everything changed.

I was in a den where wolf pups slumbered. Some were curled up; others lay on their backs with their little paws in the air. There was a black dog, too, sleeping along with the rest. They were all so helpless, so vulnerable. *I can't be here! I am a monster.*

I ran. Out of the den and into a strange landscape, one made up of flowing green creatures. They reached out to me, calling me into the protection of their long, thin arms. I ran from them as well. Didn't they understand how dangerous I was? They shouldn't have been offering me shelter.

Something slammed into me from behind, knocking me down. I tried to get back up, but the weight on my back was heavy, pinning me to the earth. A voice whispered, *You are good.*

Those words were alive; they tore through my body and set me on fire, but I did not burn. *I am good? I am good.*

The weight on my back shifted, and there was a sound, right in my ear — "WOOF!"

And I woke up.

It was dark and I was sprawled in the dirt. Someone was lying on top of me, panting. Someone with really smelly breath.

"Nicky? Get off!"

He bounced away, and I sat up. I was in the forest, surrounded by towering tuarts and the twisting shadows cast by moonlight. Hunching over, I rested my head on my knees and closed my eyes, waiting for the shakiness and nausea to pass. *I Sleepwalked?* But I shouldn't have been able to dream!

Nicky came back to flop at my side, tail wagging, and I rested a trembling hand on top of his head, trying to sort through what had happened. I'd been having a crazy nightmare about hunting things in Detention Center 3, of all places. Except I'd realized it was a dream, which meant my ability had activated.

But even though I'd been Sleepwalking during a nightmare, I'd known the Tribe wasn't a threat. I'd seen them as pups. I'd known Nicky wasn't a threat, as well, or the forest. In fact, I'd tried to protect them from my monster-self.

I could tell a friend from an enemy when I Sleepwalked.

My ability was working again.

I raised my head, a huge grin breaking across my face. Nicky nosed my leg, and I petted his ears. He'd helped me, and maybe the forest had, too. *I am good.* Had that been the trees, reaching out to me with those words, that reassurance? *The Tribe makes me the best of what I can be; the Firstwood makes me the best of what I can be. . . .*

"Guess what, Nicky? I think I'm all better!"

Somewhere among the trees, someone said, "That's great, Ash!"

I gaped as Georgie came walking out of the trees, wearing her gray winter coat and carrying a blanket over her arm.

"What are you doing here?" I demanded. "And

don't say you always know where to find me!" That was what Georgie usually said when she unexpectedly turned up wherever I happened to be.

She draped the blanket over my shoulders and dropped to sit at my side. "I followed you. When you started to Sleepwalk."

Oh. I hadn't sensed her in the dream; she must have been far enough behind me to not become part of it. "That was dangerous, Georgie."

"No, it wasn't. Because you're all better."

"Yes, but you didn't know that! And . . ." I frowned. "Actually, I might not be totally better, because it was weird that I could Sleepwalk at all. I took the herb, the one that makes me sleep without dreaming —"

"No, you didn't," she interrupted cheerfully. "You took the *other* herb, the one that just makes you sleep."

I shook my head. "I'm really careful with those herbs, Georgie; I wouldn't have mixed them up."

"You didn't. I switched them."

"You *what?*"

"You needed to dream, Ash. That's how you work things out. So I switched the mixture."

"Since when?"

"Since you first starting taking it. After you came back from the wolves."

Which meant I could have Sleepwalked at any time over the past nine nights. "Georgie, that's — if I'd known I might use my ability, I would've slept away from the Tribe, so no one would get hurt if it went wrong. You should never have taken such a risk."

She smiled her sunny smile, teeth shining in the moonlight. "If I hadn't, you wouldn't be better. And you wouldn't know the thing you didn't know before."

"I don't know anything that I didn't know before!"

Georgie didn't respond to that, just sat there. I could feel the pressure of her expectant gaze. She was waiting for me to realize something. And it dawned on me that I *did* know something new. Something that I'd been slowly coming to understand over the past days — no, weeks. I was at the end of a process that had begun with the wolves. Because the Pack had taught me something about letting go and not looking back. Wolves mourned, but they didn't regret. And since I'd returned, I'd been given a message, over and over — from Connor, and Grandpa, and Jaz, and Nicky, and the Tribe. I'd heard what they'd been saying, and I'd even understood it, sort of, in my head. I hadn't felt it in my heart before now.

I gave voice to my new realization. "I killed a man. But I am not a monster."

Saying that out loud seemed to shake something loose inside me. I took in a gasping breath, wiping at suddenly misty eyes. *I killed a man, but I am not a monster.*

"Ash?" Georgie sounded alarmed. "Why are you crying?"

"It's all right. They're happy tears." I smiled at her through them. She smiled back, reassured, and bounced to her feet, holding out her hands. "We should get back to camp. It's freezing out here."

I let her pull me up. The two of us began to make our way back to the caves, Nicky padding along by my side. We were moving slowly — I was still a little shaky, and besides, I was enjoying the walk. Georgie was right that the air was icy, but I didn't feel cold.

I am good. In the dream, those words had set me alight.

They warmed me still.

THE IMPERSONATOR

A day later, and I was sitting on the shore of the lake.
I was alone for the afternoon — Nicky was out hunting,
Georgie had joined in a honey-harvesting expedition,
and Daniel and Connor were in the cache. I'd decided
to see if I could get Grandpa to come out, but I hadn't
had any luck so far. I was considering splashing around
in the shallows to get his attention, when Jaz's voice
came thundering into my mind.

ASH! YOU THERE?

I winced. *There's no need to shout.*

Pepper's caught someone.

What do you mean, she's caught someone?

An Illegal. On the grasslands, trying to get to you.

A potential Tribe member. *New recruit? How far away—*

No, you don't understand. This guy says he has a message. From Ember.

What? WHERE IS HE?

A moment of silence. Then: **There's no need to shout. . . .**

Jaz!

You're losing your sense of humor, Ash. Pepper's bringing him to the Traveler.

"The Traveler" was the saur name for the big river that meandered out of the forest and cut across part of the grasslands. *Meet at the usual place?*

Yep.

Which meant Pepper was heading to the point where the river broke into two smaller streams. *I'm coming. Did you warn Pepper to be careful?* I'd mindspoken Jaz about the aingls, but we'd agreed to keep it quiet until we knew more, and as far as I knew he hadn't told any of his Tribe. *We don't know who this guy is, and Em's mixed up in some serious stuff. . . .*

Pepper's fine, Ash. Wanders-Too-Far is with her.

Good. Pepper would be safe enough with a saur around. *I'm on my way.*

She'll be waiting.

. . .

Half an hour later, and Connor and I were hurtling through the air above the trees. Questions tumbled through my mind as we rocketed toward the grasslands. Who was the Illegal? A friend of Ember's, maybe? *Or . . . not a friend.* But he must have known her somehow. And what was the message? Did she need help? *Is she coming home?*

It seemed to take forever before the two of us began to drop back down to earth. Only we were descending into the Firstwood, not over the grass. The moment my feet hit dirt, I spun to face Connor.

"What's wrong?" I demanded.

"Nothing," he answered. "We were about to be in sight of the fork in the river, and we don't know who this Illegal is. Better that he has no idea what any of us can do."

That was smart. *In fact . . .* I glanced around. "Let's go past the ridge. We should be able to spot them from there, get a look at this guy before we meet him."

The two of us hurried on through the forest, following the curve of the Traveler's banks until we neared a long outcrop of rocks. I scrambled up to the top, Connor right behind me. He and I lay flat, gazing out through the trees and across the grasses beyond to where the river broke in two. Pepper was there, dressed in the same yellowy color Jaz had been wearing, her dark pigtails bouncing as she skipped along the water's edge. Behind her, stalking back and forth, was a huge black saur. *Wanders-Too-Far.* And then the stranger.

He was standing with his hands in his pockets and a large backpack at his feet, and he didn't look much older than me. Other than that, all I could tell from here was that he was brown haired, broad shouldered, and wearing a mix of colors—Jet City–black pants, Cloud City–white shirt, and Fern City–green jacket.

"Have you ever seen him before?" Connor asked.

I stared hard at the distant stranger. "I don't think so. And certainly not dressed like that." It was unusual to see anyone combining different-colored clothes. Generally, everyone wore the shade that belonged to the place where they lived; the only people I'd ever seen mix colors were the ones who moved between the cities on a regular basis, like traders. "Do you think he travels around a lot?"

"Maybe. Or maybe he wants us to think he does."

We exchanged glances. I wasn't prepared to assume anything was as it seemed, given what Ember was involved in. This guy could be dangerous.

"I'll ask him questions," I said. "You watch his reactions. And look intimidating and scary."

His lips twitched. "I think I can manage that."

As we emerged from the trees, a voice spoke in my head. Not Pepper. *Wanders-Too-Far.*

Makes-the-Lightning and I have caught someone.

"Makes-the-Lightning" was Pepper's saur name — appropriate enough, since she was a Skychanger. *I know, Wanders. Good job.*

Tramples-My-Enemies said to watch the white building. But nothing was happening there. So Makes-the-Lightning and I went exploring instead.

It sounded as if Pepper and Wanders hadn't been obeying orders, which wasn't a surprise. Wanders had always been a bit of a maverick, and while Pepper adored her big brother, Jaz, she did tend to act first and ask permission later. *It's good you found him, Wanders, but you know, it's really important that you keep up the patrols of the center.*

The others are patrolling. None of *them* found anyone.

I suppressed a smile. We were getting close to where everybody was, and I didn't want to look friendly in front of the stranger. Pepper ran over, giving me a cheerful wave before bouncing to a halt in front of Connor. "Hi, Connor."

He pulled one of her pigtails. She giggled, and I had to bite back another smile, imagining her fury if anyone else had tried that. Pepper adored Connor, mostly because he occasionally used his ability to make her fly.

She jerked her head back at the stranger. "This is Jules. He says he has a message from Ember. But"—she sniffed—"I dunno."

The new Illegal grinned a crooked grin at her. "What, you don't trust me, short stuff?"

She turned to scowl at him. "I told you, don't call me short stuff."

I could tell from the tone of her voice that she wasn't really mad, which was . . . interesting. She seemed to like this guy, and in general, Pepper only liked people outside of the Saur Tribe if they'd managed to earn her respect. I examined Jules, trying to work out what she'd seen in him.

Close up, he looked—well, kind of disreputable. His clothing and hair were rumpled, there was the shadow of a beard on his face, and he gazed out at the world with an air of mocking nonchalance. Everything about him seemed to shout out that he didn't follow the rules, which was weird, given that most Illegals did their very best to appear to be law-abiding Citizens.

Jules folded his arms, studying me in return. "So you're the great Ashala Wolf." He nodded to Connor. "What are you, the boyfriend or the bodyguard? Or both?"

Connor gave him an icy stare. It was his enforcer stare, the one that said, *I know what you've done, and you will never get away with it.* I hadn't seen him use it in a while, not since we'd fled Detention Center 3, but it certainly had an effect on Jules. The impudent gleam in his hazel eyes faded a little, and he shifted on his feet. He wasn't scared, exactly, but he was a little warier than he'd been before.

Good.

"Where's Ember?" I demanded.

He held up his hands. "Whoa, hold up, wolfgirl! I don't know where she is. Got a message from her, though."

Was that a tattoo on his wrist? I grabbed his arm, pushing back the sleeve of his jacket to reveal the mark of a seagull in a circle. A Gull City Citizenship mark. "I thought you were an Illegal!"

He pulled free of my grip. "Don't tell me you've never heard of an Illegal getting past an Assessment."

Pepper rolled her eyes. "I wouldn't have brought him if he didn't have an ability. Show her what you can do, Jules!"

The air surrounding Jules started to shimmer. I took a hasty step back, and Connor flung himself between Jules and me.

"He's not going to hurt her," Pepper said. "Watch."

Jules's entire body seemed to ripple. Then he solidi-fied. Only he wasn't Jules anymore.

He was me. A perfect copy, right down to the clothes I was wearing.

Connor made a choking noise. My jaw dropped, and I stepped out from behind him to examine — well, myself. It was positively spooky, staring at me that wasn't me.

Pepper's voice spoke in my head. **Awesome, isn't it? He calls himself an Impersonator.** She added, out loud this time, "He does the voice as well. Say something to her, Jules."

He smiled — *my* smile — and turned in a circle, say-ing in *my* voice, "How do I look?"

This was just disturbing. "Stop that! Quit Imperson-ating me."

"Are you sure?"

"Yes!"

He shimmered again, blurring into a mess of colors, and then into himself. "Impressed, darling?"

"No," I replied. But I was, and I was pretty sure he knew it.

If you don't want him for your Tribe, Ash, can we have him for ours? Pepper asked.

No! He knows something about Ember, and besides, he might be dangerous.

The Saur Tribe is way more dangerous than he is.

Wanders chimed in, **If he causes any trouble, I will eat him. Or Tramples-My-Enemies will. Or Gnaws-the-Bones. Or—**

"Tell me, Jules," Connor said, "exactly how is it that you know Ember?"

He'd spoken to cover the quiet, I realized. I called out to Pepper and Wanders, *No more mindspeaking!* It was distracting, and I didn't want Jules noticing anything weird, especially not when the saurs' telepathic powers were a closely guarded secret.

"Ember and I met about a month and a half ago," Jules answered with a grin. "And spent a memorable couple of weeks together."

I didn't like that knowing smile, I didn't like his ability, I didn't like him. Then my brain caught up with my emotions. *A month and a half.* And Ember had been gone close on seven weeks now. If Jules was telling the truth, she'd run into him soon after she'd left the Firstwood. And she'd sent him back here.

"What's the message?" I asked.

He reached into his jacket pocket to produce a folded piece of paper. I snatched it from him but didn't open it up; I wasn't going to read Ember's message in front of Jules.

Only he wasn't finished. He took out something else—a gray river stone, hung on a cord. He dangled it in the air and drawled, "You'll find the password for this rock in the note."

Connor drew in a sharp breath. I stopped breathing for a second. Then I gasped and grabbed for the river stone, my mind whirling. *Jules knows what Em can do.* How desperate must she have been to send this guy here, to trust him with knowledge about her ability? Most of the Tribe didn't even know the full extent of her memory-manipulation power. She didn't like the way people reacted if they knew she could mess with their minds.

Pepper tugged at my arm. "I don't understand! What password? And what's so special about some rock?"

"This is Tribe business, Pepper," I answered, keeping my gaze on Jules. "My Tribe, not yours."

She muttered something but didn't argue. Tribe business meant she had to stay out of it, just as I asked no questions if Jaz told me something was Saur Tribe business.

Who was Jules to Em? The only possible reliable source of answers I had to that—and to all my other questions—was the river stone. I glanced around, spotting a nearby hill. I'd be out of sight once I was on the other side of it. *Good enough.*

I glared at Jules. "I'm going to leave for a while. You stay right here. And," I added, baring my teeth, "in case you haven't understood how things work, the only reason you're safe on the grasslands is because you're with us. If you try to run, if you hurt Pepper, if you so much as twitch—that saur over there is going to eat you."

Never one to miss a cue, Wanders tipped back his head and let out a long, bloodcurdling wail.

Jules paled. "I get it. I'm not going anywhere."

I nodded and stomped off through the grass, Connor following behind me. The moment we'd circled behind the hill, I stopped, kicked at the dirt, and hissed, "Em gave a memory stone to that guy? What was she thinking?"

"I don't know. Is there anything in the note?"

I opened it up, staring down at Ember's familiar handwriting.

Ash,

If you're reading this, then Jules made it to the Firstwood with the memory stone. You might not like him at first. Try not to judge him until you've seen him through my eyes.

There're a lot of memories on the stone this time. I've put them together like a story. It's the story of where I've been since I left the Firstwood, and why I went. By now you'll know there're things I haven't told you. Whatever you think of me, please believe I've done all this to keep you safe.

The password is the name of the boy made of wood.

Love you

Em

I read it again, checking to see if I'd missed something. Then I held it out to Connor. He scanned the contents and reached the same conclusion that I had. "It doesn't tell us anything."

"No, it doesn't." Which meant there was only one way to get some answers. I stalked over to sit at the base of the hill, cupping the stone in my hands. But I didn't speak the word I needed to activate it, not yet. I needed some time to prepare. Experiencing a bunch of memories would be overwhelming, so I really had to calm down a little before I did it. I breathed, slow and deep, trying to let go of my emotions — my irritation at Jules, my anger at Em for hiding things and my fear for her safety, and my dread at what I would see in the stone. The "not-nice things" that she hadn't been able to tell me in person.

When I was ready, I held the stone up to my mouth. *The boy made of wood.* Another one of Ember's stories. An old-world tale about a puppet who'd wanted to be a real child.

"Pinocchio," I whispered.

Electricity rushed into my arms and then my head, and I was dragged into someone else's memories, someone else's life. I was not Ashala, not anymore.

I was Ember.

THE MEMORIES

THE RALLY

There are a thousand ways to disappear.

Eight days ago, I'd disappeared from the Firstwood, and I'd done it without anyone knowing that it might be a very long time before I returned. Tonight, I had disappeared into the crowd. I was standing on the beach, surrounded by the gentle rush of the waves and the salt tang of the air, and like everyone else I carried a small lamp in my hand. Between us all, we had turned the shore into a constellation of lights, mirroring the stars above. *Ash would love this.* But I couldn't bear to think about what

I'd left behind, so instead I studied what was happening around me.

We were gathered in front of a makeshift stage, which was lit up by spotlights. It was empty at present, except for a few people stationed around the edge. They were presumably there to make sure nobody overran the speakers in excitement, although from the relaxed way they were standing it didn't seem as if they were really expecting trouble. Nor was there any reason why they should. After Belle Willis had been elected Prime, the enforcer presence at these rallies had ceased, and no one else was likely to cause a problem. People were respectful of one another, and of boundaries; a lesson learned from the excesses of the old world, where there had been no rule that someone had not been willing to break in pursuit of their own ends.

I was pleased to see that a lot of the crowd were displaying red question marks; some wore it on buttons, and others had it painted on their faces. The Question was a tool of the reform movement, and it was simply this: *Does a person with an ability belong to the Balance?* It was designed to make people query the justification for the Citizenship Accords, and it was working. Change was inevitable. It was flowing in like the tide. I only wished that meant no one would try to stop it.

There was a stirring around me. A dark-haired man was striding to the center of the stage. He wasn't the false Serpent. I'd never seen him before, but I recognized the barely contained energy of his quick movements from the way Ash had once described him. This had to be Jeremy Duoro, who, along with Belle Willis, had helped to expose the many crimes of Chief Administrator Neville Rose and Dr. Miriam Grey. Willis and Duoro had been members of the Inspectorate back then, a committee set up to monitor detention centers. Now she was the Prime, the head of the Gull City government, and he was one of her advisers, in addition to being a leader of the reform movement.

The crowd quietened as he began to speak. "There are people who would tell us," he called out, "that those born with abilities are not part of the Balance. They are *wrong*. My name is Jeremy Duoro, and I say that the answer to the Question is yes!"

People raised their lamps, waving them back and forth in what was evidently a sign of approval. I waved mine as well, blending in with the rest. "For too long," Duoro continued, "we have been told that treating Illegals as we do preserves the harmony of this world. But let me tell you about true disharmony. Let me tell you what I witnessed in Detention Center Three."

He began to tell the story of the events that had taken

place at the center six months ago, his voice shaking as he spoke of how sixteen detainees had been so terrified of Rose that they'd fled onto the grasslands and been horribly devoured. He sounded haunted by those deaths. *Poor man.* But we could never allow anyone to know that those children were alive and well and living with the lizards who'd supposedly eaten them. I let his words wash over me as he described the way he and Willis had seized control of the center from Neville Rose and provided the world with proof of Rose's crimes. They hadn't done it alone, although neither Willis nor Duoro was fully aware of the many ways in which Ash and Connor had helped them that night.

Duoro was still talking when someone else climbed onto the corner of the stage. Tall. Red haired. Forty or so, and dressed in Gull City blue. I stared, blinked, and stared again. A rumor had drawn me to this place, a description of the Serpent that seemed too familiar to be a mere resemblance or coincidence. I hadn't been sure it was him. Until now.

Jeremy Duoro finished speaking to enthusiastic applause. He hurried over to the newcomer and they shook hands. Then Duoro moved to the side, and the red-haired man walked to the front. He stood, waiting for absolute silence. When he had it, he roared, "I am the

Serpent, and together we will change the world!"

The crowd surged, pressing me forward as he launched into a speech. I was wedged in, unable to get any closer to the stage than I was already. But I didn't need to be. Everything about him was familiar. The deep, gravelly tone of his voice; the way he gestured with his hands to emphasize a point.

I'd thought him gone forever. I'd been wrong.

I had to free myself from all these people. I shut off my light and began to push and shove my way out. By the time I escaped from the crowd, the "Serpent" had concluded his talk. People were cheering and waving their lamps, and I took advantage of the distraction to scurry into the night, circling around until I neared the stage. Then I darted into the sand dunes, crouched down, and waited.

Everyone slowly grew quiet and still again as someone else came on, a mother whose child was in detention. The Serpent was still onstage, but he was lingering at the back, standing in the darkness where the spotlights didn't reach. All the speakers were supposed to stay and take questions from the audience, but I knew he wouldn't take the chance of remaining here for that long. *He'll want to slip away unseen.* Things might be changing, but he was playing the part of a self-confessed Illegal, which meant he was breaking the Citizenship Accords by being out of detention.

When he leaped down onto the beach, I followed at a cautious distance, keeping watch to make sure that no one had noticed either of us. I trailed patiently after him as he moved off the shore and into the city. I didn't call out; I wanted to be sure we were alone before I approached him. The two of us wandered past gleaming composite buildings, into the older part of Gull City where the houses were composed of cobbled-together materials left over from the old world. These were the first structures, built before the recyclers functioned. Some of the other cities had torn down houses like these; Gull City had kept them, as a testament to tenacity and survival.

It seemed only right that we meet again in such a landscape.

He paused suddenly, standing in the middle of a lane. He'd sensed that someone was behind him, or perhaps he'd known all along and had been waiting for me to show myself. I stepped out from the shadow of a building.

"Dad?" I whispered. "It's Ember."

My father tilted his head toward the sound of my voice.

And then he spun around and shot me.

I was adrift, neither entirely conscious nor entirely unconscious. I fought to piece together fragments of memory and sensation, trying to assemble a coherent picture of what had happened to me. There had been—fire? No, electricity. *Energy weapon.* Except that weapon hadn't been a streaker. Nor had it been a stunner, like the one I'd created for Ash. It was something new, something that had burned the world with orange light.

I struggled back to awareness. My eyes would not open yet, but I was conscious of a steady sense of motion. I was in a vehicle of some kind. How long had I been unconscious? Hours? Days? I had no way to tell. It felt as if it had been a long time, but that was meaningless, especially in my present state, with my brain fogged and my thoughts muffled. *This isn't only the effect of the weapon.* I recognized this feeling.

I'd been injected with liquid rhondarite.

An unfamiliar voice spoke. "You awake yet, Red?"

Someone was here! Panic surged, lending me enough strength to push my eyes open. My vision was a little blurry, but I could see enough to tell that I was staring up at a white ceiling. With a supreme effort, I turned my head in the direction of the voice. There was a stranger, sitting opposite where I lay. All I could make out about him were vague impressions of color: brown hair, black shirt, blue pants. "Who arrrrr . . ."

"Name's Jules. And you're Ember. Runaway, rebel, and Tribe member. You've had quite the criminal career for someone who's only, what, sixteen?"

"Seventeen," I whispered. To my intense relief, my vision was returning to normal. I blinked, clearing away the last of the blurriness, and gazed at the stranger, who was sitting on a narrow bed attached to the wall. *So I'm in some sort of white room . . . with two beds . . . that's moving . . . I'm in a twin sleeper compartment, on the Rail.*

I'd worked out where I was. But that was no great victory, given that the Rail itself could be anywhere. I studied my captor, paying attention to the small details that could reveal so much about a person. My thoughts were still sluggish, but I knew I had to find a way to connect with him. *Win his sympathy. Lure him into carelessness.*

"Why are you doing this?" I asked. My voice sounded weak. I wished it were an act. "You're an Illegal like me."

He showed me the Gull City Citizenship mark on his wrist. "Now, why would you think that?"

Idiot, Ember. I shouldn't have let on that I'd deduced what he was. That was information that could have been hoarded away and used later, when it would gain me the most advantage. My mind, usually my greatest weapon, was misfiring under the influence of the rhondarite.

He was waiting for a response. *Do I tell him how I knew?* There seemed no harm in it. I hoped there was no harm; I was finding it difficult to calculate consequences at present. "My father wouldn't shoot me. And there's a burn on your hand. Kind of thing you might get from using an experimental weapon." It was taking a surprising amount of energy for me to form words, but I managed to put together five more. "You're some kind of shifter."

"I prefer the term Impersonator." He looked down at his hand. "You don't miss much, Red."

No, I didn't. At least, not usually. At the moment there were no thoughts at all in my head, just a gray, exhausted blurriness. The effort of holding a simple conversation and putting a few clues together had been too much for me. My eyes drifted shut.

Jules snapped his fingers in front of my face. "Stay with me, darling. Come on, tell me something. What's your favorite color?"

"Green," I answered, blinking up at him.

"Favorite Hoffman quote?"

"Don't have one."

"Everyone's got a favorite Hoffman quote."

I sighed. "All revolutions begin with a question."

He chuckled. "Guess a rebel like you would pick that one."

His voice was growing fainter, as if it were coming from a long way away. He shook my shoulder. "Red. Red! What's your dad's name?"

That got my attention. "Why do you want to know?"

He shrugged. "I impersonate a lot of people. Sometimes I like to know their names."

"Timothy," I mumbled, choosing a name at random. "Timothy Collins."

He peered down into my face and shook his head. "You're not coming out of it, are you?" Reaching into his pocket, he held up a small bottle filled with amber liquid. "How much more of this do I need to give you to wake you up properly?"

He has the neutralizer! I would have snatched it from his fingers, if only I could have moved. "All of it," I lied.

Jules grinned at me. It was an odd, crooked smile; one half of his mouth seemed to lift higher than the other. "You wouldn't be lying to me, would you? Because I know that if I give you too much, you'll recover all the way. And that wouldn't be good for me, as I understand you could make me forget my own name." He eyed the liquid. "I'm giving you a quarter of it."

Jules leaned over, tipping the vial to my mouth, and I gulped down everything I could. But it was only a small taste, not enough to purge my system of rhondarite. I gazed longingly at the vial as he took it away and rose to his feet, crossing to the compartment door. "I'll come back later and see how you're doing."

"You have to give me more," I pleaded. "I promise, I'm not lying to you."

"Yes, you are, Red." He paused in the doorway, looking over his shoulder at me. "In fact, you lied to me twice. Three times, if I count the right dose of the stuff in the bottle."

"I didn't . . ."

"Seventeen years old?" He snorted. "More like three *hundred* and seventeen. And your 'father' was named Alexander Hoffman."

Shock forced my eyes wide open. He winked, enjoying my astonishment. "Oh yes, darling. *I know what you are.*"

He left, locking the door behind him. I fought to stay awake.

But I couldn't prevent myself from slipping back into unconsciousness.

There was blackness for an indeterminable length of time. Then awareness broke over my mind like the light of the dawn. *How does he know? He can't possibly know!* Except he did, and it was stupid to lie here wasting time on shocked disbelief. Instead I directed my attention to a more useful question. How *much* did he know?

That I was built, not born, for a start. Constructed by the man I thought of as my father, Alexander Hoffman. I wondered if Jules imagined me to be impervious to pain or incapable of emotion. I wasn't. I wasn't even completely synthetic—much of me was made up of the bio-fibers my father had invented, organic strands that carried feeling and sensation through my body. When Dad had begun to make his children—his aingls—he'd thought the human species might not survive the Reckoning, and he'd wanted to preserve the essence of humanity, not just the memory of it. So while he'd built the eight of us to outlast the ages, he'd ensured that we could experience our existence in much the same way as ordinary human beings. Dad had always said we were human in all the ways that mattered.

Certainly human enough to be hurt.

But I didn't believe Jules intended to do that, unless

it was to stop me from escaping, and I had no plans to try that at present. He *had* to be working for one of my brothers or sisters. There could be no other explanation for the face he'd worn at the rally, the sophistication of the weapon he'd used, and the knowledge he had about me. For reasons that weren't clear yet, a member of my family had gone to a great deal of trouble to lure me out, and I wasn't going anywhere until I discovered what was going on.

I sat up. The movement made my head spin, forcing me to shut my eyes as I waited for it to pass. The neutralizer had done its work and purged some of the rhondarite, but I was still woozy. *I loathe rhondarite.* On Illegals, it worked by interfering with the neural connections that were necessary for abilities to activate. On me, it worked because I was one big mass of connections. Not only did rhondarite prevent me from altering memories, it made it hard to process sensory information, turning me into a mentally and physically uncoordinated shadow of my usual self.

The dizziness faded, and I opened my eyes again, taking a quick inventory of my surroundings. It was a standard twin compartment: two beds, tiny bathroom squashed into the corner, narrow window, and all of it bland and white. I reached over to pull up the blind on the window and discovered that it was night outside. I could make out the outlines of a few features—hills, trees—but nothing identifiable enough to tell me where I was. The Rail ran around the entire world, linking the seven cities together. Jules could be taking me anywhere. Although it did seem a little risky on his part, to be holding me on a train where I could attract the attention of the other passengers . . . *ah*.

The rhondarite was still slowing me down. I had to be in one of the *government* carriages, reserved for the use of employees of the cities, and I'd bet there was no one around except for Jules and me. It would have been easy enough for him to gain access to the carriage by masquerading as someone else. Either that or he'd had access organized for him by whoever he was working for.

I leaned back and breathed deep, letting my gaze grow unfocused as I began to process everything I'd seen and heard since the rally. I needed all the information I could gather.

I'd been sitting there for a while when Jules came back in.

"Finally woken up, huh?" He handed me a flask and threw himself onto the bed opposite mine. "I can get you something to eat as well, if you want."

"I'm not hungry," I told him. *And you're showing off.* He

was demonstrating that he understood I consumed food and water, converting them into energy like any organic human being. Except I wouldn't be able to absorb food for some time, not until my system had gotten rid of more of the rhondarite. But I had no reason to share that information with him.

I took a cautious sip from the flask, and then—once I was certain it was only water—a few big gulps. Jules was watching me, arms folded and shoulders resting against the wall.

"You work for Terence," I said.

I'd hoped to surprise him, and I did; he jumped slightly. He recovered fast, his features settling into what appeared to be a habitual expression of detached amusement. "What makes you think that?"

You have access to a weapon advanced enough to paralyze me. You know I'm synthetic. And someone must have shown you an image of my father. But none of those reasons were the one that truly mattered. "I haven't seen my father in a long time. To pretend to be him, to draw me out, and to *shoot* me, wearing that face—it was a cruel thing to do. The sort of thing Terence would think of. Because he can be cruel."

Jules shrugged. "He's always been very good to me." But there was a faintly bitter, ironic edge to those words.

Thought so. My brother Terence wasn't nice, he didn't ask the people who worked for him to do nice things, and he wasn't nice to them. Terence used Illegals because they could do things no one else could, but he hated people with abilities.

"So, is your dad a machine, too?" Jules asked. "Because Alexander Hoffman can't possibly still be alive."

He didn't want to talk about Terence, at least not yet. *So let's talk about something else.*

"How about we trade question for question?" I suggested. "You answer honestly, and I'll answer honestly."

"And how will we know we're each being honest?"

I offered him a wide, sweet smile. "I guess we'll just have to trust each other. Darling."

He laughed softly. "Okay. I'll play. Is your dad a machine?"

We're not machines. Only we were, to Jules. Automatons without feeling, and he had some justification for thinking so. I considered how much to share about Dad. There seemed no harm in giving him a few extra scraps of knowledge, not when he already knew so much. "My father was originally completely organic—"

"You mean human."

No, I mean organic. Because I am as human as you. But I let it go. "He found a way to become—something

155

else. To live a long time." And that was all I planned to tell him about my father. "Where are you taking me?"

"Mangrove City."

So that's where Terence is living these days. I hadn't seen him in over eight years, not since before I went to the Firstwood and he'd had that last, spectacular argument with Dad. My father wanted the Citizenship Accords abolished; Terence didn't, and they'd fought, a lot.

"Why are you pretending to be an Illegal?" Jules demanded. "What's the point of it, when you could go anywhere? Do anything."

"Be one of the privileged, you mean?" I shook my head. "I couldn't. At least, not and live with myself. This world, the way Illegals are treated — it's wrong, and I am going to help to change it."

"Very high-minded," he mocked. "Going to tell me you're kind to puppies and small children next?"

"I'm telling the truth," I snapped.

"So you say."

"If you don't believe me, why don't we stop this?" I challenged him. "Then the two of us can sit here in absolute silence. Or you could leave."

He looked away, a tacit admission of defeat. Jules didn't want to stop talking, because he was trying to understand me as much as I was trying to understand

156

him. More, perhaps, because I was fairly certain he wanted something from me. I couldn't think of any other reason for him to have given me the neutralizer.

"My turn, Jules. How did you know what I am? And," I added quickly, "don't try to tell me Terence told you, because I know that he never would have."

"No, he wouldn't," Jules agreed. "Not *me*."

It was interesting, that emphasis on the last word, as if there was another person Terence might have told. I filed it away, to be pursued later, as he continued, "I found out by hearing things. Seeing things, here and there."

In other words, he'd put it together, slowly and in pieces. He must have been with Terence for a long time to have learned so much. *He's smarter than he likes to pretend.* And more ruthless than he appeared. He had to be, to have survived Terence for any length of time.

"Terence talks about you," Jules said. "Not about what you are, but about his rebellious baby sister." He uncrossed his arms and drew up one knee, leaning forward to rest his arm across it. "He says you hate him. Do you?"

I opened my mouth, and closed it again. I was doing my best to tell him the truth, to win his trust. But the answer to that question wasn't as simple as a yes or no. In fact, I wasn't entirely sure I knew how I felt.

I began to talk. "I loved him a long time ago, when he was different. He's filled with hate now, and fear, and paranoia."

"I already know what he's—"

"Will you listen? You asked. I'm trying to explain." Jules was silent, and I continued, "My brothers and sisters and I were supposed to embody the best of humanity. Except I think that the most human thing about Terence is his ability to justify hurting people. There's something about that which is so . . . tragic." I paused, searching for words. "When I think of him, all I feel is pity. Which is a *horrible* thing to feel for your big brother."

I stopped. There was nothing else to say, and even if there had been, I didn't want to speak about this anymore. It made me sad, and that was something I tried to avoid, because I could be sad in a way that was deep and bleak and endless. Jules was staring across the compartment at me with a faint frown. *Not sure what to make of me, are you?* I wondered what he'd say if I told him that, most days, I wasn't sure what to make of myself.

"What do you do?" I asked quietly. "For Terence, I mean."

"Acquire things. Information, mostly."

"You're his spy."

"Spy. Thief. Tester of loyalties—you'd be *amazed* what

158

people will confess when they're speaking to someone they believe is a friend."

He'd probably intended to sound sarcastic. He sounded savage.

"You've met the worst of us," I said. "I'm sorry for that. We're not all like him, you know."

"Yeah. I get that you've been trying to show me that. Ember-the-Rebel, friend to Illegals everywhere. *Maybe*. Or maybe you just enjoy playing at being a renegade. Especially when you know you can walk away if things ever get too serious."

"And maybe you stay with Terence because you like the danger," I shot back. "The adrenaline rush of outsmarting him and getting away with it. Exactly how often do you deliberately fail at something he's asked you to do?"

"Why on earth would I do something so deeply stupid?"

"To prove that he doesn't own you, of course. And to show the world that you're better than you might seem."

"You think I'm some kind of lost soul underneath my hardened exterior?" He shook his head and grinned. "Are you going to save me, sweetheart?"

I stared at him until the gleam of cynical humor in his eyes softened into something less certain, and more real. Then I answered, "Yes. Isn't that why you woke me up?"

He looked away, jaw clenched. There was a long silence. *Come on, Jules. Ask me for what you really want. Ask me how to get away from Terence.*

He didn't. He stood up abruptly and went to the door. "You should probably get some sleep. Or whatever it is you do."

Jules left without a backward glance, and I heaved a disappointed sigh. I hadn't persuaded him to trust me yet. I would, though. I wanted Jules for the Tribe—with his ability and his knowledge of my family, he'd be an invaluable asset to Ash. And I wanted the Tribe for Jules, because he needed a family, and a home. *You've been damaged by my brother, Jules, and that makes you mine to fix. Mine to save.*

I closed my eyes and waited for his return.

THE OFFER

I slipped into my version of sleep, a regenerative cycle that allowed my systems to recover further from the effects of the weapon and the rhondarite. When I woke, the sun was rising outside, casting enough light into the world for me to make out rolling green hills and the beginnings of dense forest. We were somewhere near Fern City. I knew this landscape, because Fern City had been my home once, back when it was little more than a collection of huts. We had about a week and a half to go before we reached Mangrove City.

Jules came back in. He handed me a protein bar, which I didn't unwrap; I still couldn't eat, and besides, government-ration protein bars were notoriously unpalatable. He sat on the other bed, saying nothing and looking unsure of himself for the first time since I'd met him.

Finally he said, "Terence warned me you could make me forget."

"I wouldn't—"

He shook his head quickly. "That's not what I mean, darling. Terence can't make anyone forget, because if he could do something like that he absolutely would. But he doesn't. Which means you can do things that he can't."

Which means I might be able to help you. "How long have you been trying to get away from my brother?"

"Pretty much since the day I met him," he answered, with a twisted smile. "Six years ago, now. I was thirteen— he got me out of detention, organized me a tattoo. And I knew, right from the start, I *knew* that he was no good. But I thought, some crazy guy wants to let me out of this

161

prison? I'll take that bet." He was silent, then added, in a voice so soft I almost didn't hear it, "I always thought I'd be able to run one day."

"You saw someone else try, didn't you? And they died. It began with sweating and trembling, then fever and pain."

"You know all about it, huh?"

I nodded. The toxin had been invented by my sister Delta. She'd told me about it at one of our rare meetings, and she'd been so excited, as if she'd found Terence the perfect birthday present. I hadn't been successful at talking her out of giving it to him. And she was still making toys for Terence. Only Delta could have designed the weapon that had incapacitated me.

Jules shuffled back on the bed, to rest against the wall. "I always figured all I had to do was get far enough away and never stop running. But the woman, the one who died—I could've sworn Terence had no idea where she went. He still got the poison to her somehow."

I sighed and explained the awful genius of my sister's invention. "He didn't poison her after she left. He'd already done it, years ago."

He jolted out of his slouch, staring at me. "What do you mean?"

"Terence never allows anyone to leave him for an

162

extended period, does he? No longer than—what, a month? Two?"

"Usually five weeks."

"That's because he has to give everyone the antidote. It's undetectable—it could be in anything you eat or drink. He doses you with the toxin on the very first day you start working for him. Once it's in your system, you have to get the antidote at regular intervals, or . . ."

He looked alarmed. "I've already been gone over five weeks!"

My stomach clenched in fear. I scrambled off the bed, reaching across to take hold of his wrist so I could check his pulse. It was a little fast—not unexpected given what I'd just told him—but strong. And he wasn't sweating or shaking. I leaned in and grasped his chin, tipping his face to the light. There was no unusual paleness of the skin, and no discoloration of the eyes.

"You're okay. He must have given you a longer-lasting dose of the antidote whenever you saw him last. I imagine he didn't know how long it would take you to find me."

Jules grinned. "He did think you'd be elusive."

I was close enough to feel his breath on my skin, and I was suddenly, overwhelmingly aware of the beat of his pulse beneath one hand, the stubble on his face beneath the other, and the warmth of his body near mine. I let go and scooted back to my bed. "I can cleanse your system of the poison."

"How?"

"By using—that is . . ." I was finding it strangely difficult to focus. I forced my thoughts into order. "This is going to be hard for you to understand."

"Try me."

"I can control these machines called nanomites. They're small, so small you can't even see them. Not . . . not like me, not self-aware. They'll do what they're programmed to do, and then they'll"—*become inert*—"dissolve."

"You're going to fix me with invisible machines? I'm not even sure that's a real thing!"

"I promise you, it'll work." *This time.* I'd tried to help someone who'd run from Terence once before, years ago, and they had died because I hadn't understood the toxin well enough to be able to program my nanomites to eliminate it. But I'd learned from that awful experience. I knew what to do now.

He eyed me suspiciously. "Invisible machines, huh? Is that what you use to make people forget?"

He'd made that connection fast.

"They can be used for a lot of things. Including freeing you from Terence, just as soon as the rhondarite's out of my system—"

"You want me to hand over the rest of what's in that little bottle?" He shook his head. "So I'm supposed to restore you to health and then just *believe* that you'll help me? With machines, that I can't see. I won't even be able to tell if the poison's gone, will I? Until I die, or I don't."

"I'm not Terence."

"You keep saying that. And I'll give you this, you do a good job of sounding human." He fixed me with a hard stare. "But in the end, you're a collection of circuits, and you don't actually have a heart. Why should I trust you, Red?"

A flood of words rushed into my mouth, waiting to be spoken. *You should trust me because I see the best of what you could be, just as someone once saw it in me... because I will not yield you to Terence, not your body or your soul...*

Because in all the ways that matter, I do have a heart.

I wanted to shout all of that out, as if by doing so I could prove to Jules, and the world, that I was better than I might seem. I didn't. He wouldn't believe any of it.

"You can think what you like of me," I said. My voice was shaking. I steadied it and continued, "But we both know that you're worried that you've become more of a liability to Terence than an asset. Or you would never have risked waking me with that neutralizer, which I am

165

betting you are not even supposed to have." I gave him a fierce smile, a warrior's smile. It was an expression I'd borrowed from Ash. "The way I see it, I'm your only option for escape. So, *sweetheart*, I guess you'll just have to decide if I'm a good bet."

He sat there for a second longer. Then he stalked out, slamming the door behind him.

THE MINIONS

Day passed into night. Jules returned periodically, but only to offer me more food, which I refused. I tried to talk to him; he wouldn't listen. By the time dawn came again, I was beginning to wonder if I should confess that I didn't actually need what was in the bottle to get rid of the rhondarite. In a few more days I would have purged the stuff myself, thanks to a series of secret alterations Dad and I had made to my systems. Except if I shared that information with Jules, he might panic and inject me with rhondarite again. Or shoot me, and either way, I'd lose my chance to save him.

The train began to slow. I shifted to stare out the window. We were rolling past buildings that were made of composite and covered with vines. *Fern City.* Assuming

Jules had left Gull City immediately after the rally, it had been ten days since I'd met him; that was how long it took to get here by Rail. Eventually we pulled into a station crowded with king-ferns, their long stems curling upward into huge, delicate fronds that arched high above the people on the platform. Fern City was perennially overgrown; it was being gradually swallowed by the surrounding Deepwood. The situation was partly my fault, because I'd helped to choose the site for Fern City, hundreds of years ago when the Deepwood was mere saplings. No one could have predicted how fast and how ferociously that forest would grow once the world's ecosystems stabilized in the years following the Reckoning. There was an ongoing debate in the government here about which of two possible alternatives for the future of the city was more harmful to the Balance: maintaining it where it was—which meant constantly cutting back the vegetation—or establishing it anew outside the forest.

I watched the people milling around. Then I heard sounds: a door swinging open and voices. Someone was coming into this carriage. Into the government carriage, to which Jules had no doubt arranged exclusive access. Whoever it was couldn't be a random stranger.

Pulse racing, I hurried to the door and pressed my ear to it. Technically, Jules had been right when he said I didn't have a heart, but the fact that there was an energy core in my chest didn't prevent me from experiencing the sensation of a heart pounding in panic. I could make out a murmur of voices, too low or too distant to distinguish words. Frowning, I concentrated on extending the range of my hearing. Dad had made certain that none of us could push our senses too far beyond normal human capacity, but I only needed a small boost.

The murmurs crystallized into words. A girl, saying, "I *said,* obedience is service."

"And I don't believe in that crap, and never have." *Jules.* "You think I've suddenly become a convert since the last time we met? I don't change, darling."

Someone else spoke—male, and disdainful. "Obedience is service, and service is redemption. You are not worthy to serve."

"Maybe not, but at least I'm capable of having an original idea. Or haven't you figured out there's a reason you minions are never sent on missions that require improvisation?"

The boy started to respond. The girl spoke over him. "Don't let him bait you. We've been sent to retrieve your cargo, Jules. We'll be taking her from here."

"Oh, yeah? Where to?"

"That is not your concern."

They were moving in this direction. I hurried back to the bed, closing my eyes and feigning unconsciousness. My thoughts traveled in circles, running in panic. I couldn't be taken, not yet. Not before I'd helped Jules, and not before I'd sent a message to Ash. But I wasn't going to be able to fight them with the rhondarite still in my system.

The door opened, and Jules spoke. "See? She's totally out, just like I said."

The girl answered, "Perhaps. But we were told to be sure."

There was a familiar sizzling sound, and then nothing.

THE CRASH

I opened my eyes onto blackness, with no grasp of how long I'd been out. I was somewhere dark and enclosed. I felt around the space, my fingers brushing over smooth, hard surfaces.

They'd put me in a box.

This was bad, even for Terence. I imagined myself locked forever in this airless prison. *Don't be absurd.* He hadn't gone to so much trouble to find me only to shut me away, and it wasn't like this would kill me. While I did breathe, it wasn't because I required air; it was yet another refinement my father had introduced to make us as human as possible. I wasn't going to suffocate.

That really should have made me feel much better than it did.

I pushed against the lid. It was unyielding, locked down tight. I wondered if Jules had helped them load me in after he'd let them shoot me. What would he do now? Return to following Terence's orders, and search for another way to escape? Perhaps he thought he could find the antidote and start stockpiling it. . . . *Stop thinking about Jules.* It wasn't useful, and it hurt the heart he didn't believe I had.

Where was I now? There was a sense of motion, almost the same as on the train, but a little bumpier. *I'm in a car? Truck?* It had to be a truck, otherwise it wouldn't be big enough to hold the container that I was trapped in. I was being taken somewhere, by the people who'd come onto the train. *Cloud City?*

There was an old highway that ran to Cloud City, and it would get you there from Fern City considerably faster than the Rail, provided you had a vehicle. It wasn't used much, because all the vehicles were owned by the government and even they tended to avoid the highway. It ran through the Deepwood and was always partially covered with vegetation. The governments of Cloud City and Fern

City had a joint clearing program, but they never did manage to keep up with the growth of the forest. *If we're on the highway, Terence must have a reason for wanting me in Cloud City as fast as possible.* Was that where he was? Had his plan changed, or had he not trusted Jules with the real destination?

I had no way to determine the answers to any of that from inside this box. I glared uselessly up at the lid. My only advantage was that no one would expect me to be awake yet; my body had adapted to the effects of the weapon, counteracting it in the same way I could counteract rhondarite. I didn't know how close we were to Cloud City, but when someone finally opened my container, I wouldn't be completely at their mercy.

Gradually, I became aware of a new sound from outside. A rumbling noise, growing louder and louder. It took me a moment to identify it as another vehicle. A very large vehicle, rapidly approaching. It roared closer, and there was a sudden lurch as something slammed into the side of the truck. The container skidded to the side, and I flung out my hands to brace myself. Tires screeched, and there was another tremendous reverberation.

Then I felt my prison go airborne.

There was precisely enough time for me to comprehend how much landing was going to hurt before the container crashed back to earth. It bounced along, throwing me back and forth. When it stopped moving I lay still, dazed and in an immense amount of pain. My head felt like it had been cracked open, my leg and stomach screamed in agony, and there was a white-hot stabbing every time I breathed, as if a rib was digging into a lung. If I'd been organic, I would have had broken bones, internal injuries, and a concussion. I wasn't actually damaged, but that made no difference to what I felt. Dad had always believed that in order to truly understand human frailty, it was important to experience it.

I endured, biting into my lip to stop myself from screaming until the pain began to ease. As it ebbed, I realized I could hear shouting from outside the box. Were they coming for me? The lid had buckled under the impact of the crash, enough for me to see light in places. I threw myself against it. And again. It gave way, and I tumbled out into the humid air of the Deepwood.

Brushing dirt off my face, I pushed myself to my feet and looked around. I was standing at the bottom of a steep embankment, surrounded by ferns of various sizes, and loomed over by ylang-ylang trees. There was a truck in front of me, turned on its side with its wheels spinning in the air. Someone was lying beside it, half concealed in the dense foliage. I stumbled over and found myself gazing into the blank stare of a slim, freckled boy. My mind registered details: *dressed in enforcer black . . . must have been thrown from the truck when it crashed . . . head cracked open.* One of the "minions," as Jules had called them? But where was the other one?

There was a sizzling sound from somewhere above. The weapon! I crawled up the steep embankment and peered over the top. Another, *much* bigger truck was sitting in the middle of the deserted road. Beyond that was a tall, dark-haired girl, also dressed as an enforcer, pacing along the far side of the road. She was staring into the forest and holding the weapon in her hand.

"How far do you think you're going to get, Jules?" she yelled. "Riley hurt you pretty bad. And when I find you . . ." She picked up a rock from the ground and crushed it, sending it crumbling into dust. "I might not even bother to shoot you."

She was a Strongarm, and Jules was in trouble. I climbed over the top of the rise and crept toward her. I was halfway there when she abruptly raised the weapon, pointing it at something in the forest. She'd spotted Jules, and a hit from that thing would kill an organic being.

"Hey!" I shouted.

The girl spun around, firing without hesitation, and barely missed me. I scrambled for the shelter of the truck.

She raised the weapon to fire again, and Jules came flying out of the forest, slamming into her.

The weapon clattered across the road. I ran for it as she fought with Jules, aiming a punch at his face. He dodged just in time—a Strongarm hit would cave his skull in—and rolled to the side. But his movements were awkward and slow. *He's injured.*

The girl grasped hold of his shoulders and flung him away from her. Then she stalked to his side, standing over him and pulling back her fist to strike.

I grabbed the weapon. "Stop!"

She looked at me. Her lips curled into a contemptuous smile. "You won't hurt me. I know all about you. You *can't.*"

Terence had told her that? Her fist started to descend. Jules stirred, but he wasn't going to be able to get out of the way in time.

"Stop!" *Don't make me do this.* "Please stop!"

She ignored me.

I fired.

Orange energy arced out and tore into her, hurling her back into the Deepwood. It was a clean shot; there was not the smallest possibility that she had survived it. I waited. One second. Two. Three . . . and agony ripped through my body.

The weapon fell from my hand as I collapsed. The only thing I could hear above my own screams was my father's voice, roaring in my mind: *No killing no killing, nokillingno killingnokillingnokilling* . . .

I had to do it! I shouted back inside my head. *It was to save someone else. It was the only way, I promise, I promise* . . .

The racking pain seemed to last for hours before it finally began to ease. Someone was speaking, sounding frantic. "Red. Red! What's happening? Tell me how I can help you."

Jules was crouched over me. I struggled up, grabbing hold of the front of his shirt, and whispered, "Say that I saved you."

"Of course you saved me."

"I'm not like Terence. I'm not. I'm not, I'm not . . ."

He pulled me to him, cradling me in his arms. "You're *nothing* like him. You saved my life, Red."

I closed my eyes and clung to Jules as if he were the only real thing in the world. He continued to speak, repeating the same thing over and over—"You saved me. You saved me." *I saved Jules. I did.* The more I believed it, the more the pain diminished, getting smaller and smaller until it was finally gone.

I stirred, and gazed up at him. He looked so terrified

that I almost laughed. It must have been horrible to go to so much trouble to rescue the one person who could help him, only to have me appear to go crazy.

"I'm all right."

"Are you sure?"

"Yes." I closed my eyes again, resting against him for a single, indulgent moment. Then I pushed him away, forcing myself to my feet. "We can't stay here. Have to get . . . somewhere safe."

Everything was moving back and forth. *I'm swaying.* Jules rose and bent to grab the weapon before putting an arm around my waist and helping me over to the truck.

"I've got somewhere we can go," he said. "Back in Fern City."

He lifted me into the passenger seat and walked around to the driver's side.

"Do you think we should bury them?" I asked as he climbed in. "To hide them, or . . . out of respect?"

He shook his head. "I don't want to hang around here, and I've got no respect for those two. Believe me, neither of them ever shed any tears over killing people. And as for hiding the bodies—take a look. Can you see them?"

I couldn't. The vegetation was too dense. "Also," Jules

added cheerfully, "what with the humidity around here, not to mention all the little critters in the Deepwood that feast on dead things, they'll be gone fast."

That was an absolutely awful thing to think of, if true. I stared at the forest, which seemed to have already consumed them, the way it was consuming Fern City. *I suppose it's not such a terrible thing, to be food for a forest. I wouldn't mind it.*

Jules reached into his pocket and pressed something into my hand. "Here. Almost forgot."

The neutralizer. I wasn't sure how much rhondarite was still left in my system, but it wouldn't hurt to help get rid of whatever remained. I gulped it down, watching as he took hold of the wheel. He was still moving a little awkwardly. "What did they do to you?"

"Riley was trying stop me from causing the crash by extracting the water from my body. It was only for a few seconds."

I'd never heard of a Waterbaby being able to use their ability like that. It was clever, and cruel. "Are you sure you can drive?"

"I've been hurt a lot worse than this." He winked at me. "You'd be surprised at the number of people who don't find me at all charming."

I smiled, and Jules grinned his crooked grin.

Then he started up the engine, swung the truck around, and sent us roaring in the direction of Fern City.

THE JOURNEY

We chugged along the road, swerving to avoid encroaching vegetation. The air was fragrant with the scent of ylang-ylang, and it was warm, of course. It was always warm here; the difference between seasons in this part of the world was between "wet" and "dry," rather than "cold" and "hot." I preferred the cool autumn air of the Firstwood and the eucalyptus tang of tuarts, but it was pleasant to be back in any kind of forest.

The Deepwood was dense in a way that the Firstwood wasn't—it was a jungle, dominated by the massive ylang-ylang trees and crowded out with fan palms, king-ferns, and pepper vines. A forest of dark, secret spaces, inhabited by forest animals and nobody else. I spotted a few crows, now and then. These birds didn't know me as a friend the way my Firstwood crows did, but they still recognized me as a crow, and I had a comforting sense of familiar beady eyes watching me from the trees. I drank in the reassurance of their presence, using it to soothe my weariness and frailty. *I took a life.* I'd had to do it, but I grieved over the necessity of it. I was sad for everything the girl would never be, and for a society that drove people with abilities into horrible places and horrible choices. For all the lost chances, and all the lost people.

If I allowed myself to sink into these emotions, it would end in a kind of madness. *You had to act. And that is all there is to it.* I switched my attention to the road in front of me, and what lay at the end of it. "How far away are we from Fern City?"

"Two days."

I'd been unconscious for longer than I'd thought. At least the journey back to the city would give me enough time to completely recover from the rhondarite, and from the effects of killing someone.

"By the time we get to Fern City, I'll be able to help you—"

"Don't worry about it. You should sleep or rest or . . . whatever it is that you do to recuperate."

"I sleep. But I can't, yet."

"Why not?"

"Um." I considered how best to explain. "You know how it is when you wake up from a nightmare, and you don't want to go back to sleep in case you end up in the same bad dream?"

He nodded.

"If I slept now, I might get drawn back into—what I was experiencing, back there."

"Yeah. What *was* that?"

"Something my father did to us. He made it so that we can't kill, at least not without consequences. If we do, we hurt."

He snorted. "I've seen Terence kill people!"

"Not directly, you haven't." I yawned. "I don't think he administers that toxin himself, and I'm not sure withdrawing the antidote is direct enough to count. Besides which, Terence is willing to endure some pain to accomplish his ends."

"Kind of a big loophole, isn't it?"

"It didn't work out quite the way Dad intended," I acknowledged. "At least, not once Terence realized where the limits were and how he could circumvent them. He has no trouble resolving a death, either."

"You're going to have to explain 'resolving a death,' darling."

"Justifying it. We have to be certain the death was unavoidable. Necessary. Problem is, what we each think is justifiable depends on where we draw our boundaries of right and wrong."

"That was why you wanted me to tell you that you saved me."

"Yes." *I don't want to talk about that moment.* "Where is this place in Fern—"

"What happens if you can't justify it?"

I sighed. "It causes a systemic failure, and we shut down. For all intents and purposes, we're dead."

Jules slammed on the brakes. The truck screeched to a stop. He twisted to face me. "You're saying that you could have *died*?"

He seemed very upset. I suppose the prospect of my death must have come as a shock if he'd thought I was invulnerable, and he probably had. That was certainly the impression Terence liked to give. "Not dead, precisely. More like the equivalent of being in a coma."

"And Isabelle knew that." My confusion must have been apparent, because he added, "The girl who shot you. She knew, and she didn't think you'd risk it. Not for me."

"She was wrong."

"I didn't even know it was possible for you to be hurt!"

I shrugged. "It's hard to permanently damage us. Otherwise, we function as if we're organic, feeling everything a normal human being would."

He paled. "When I crashed their truck . . ."

181

"I wasn't in pain for long."

Jules's hands clenched on the steering wheel, turning his knuckles white. "I'm sorry."

"You weren't to know."

He muttered something to himself. It sounded like "You're really something, Red," but I couldn't be sure.

We resumed our journey along the road, and I curled up in the seat, angled toward Jules. "Tell me about those Illegals."

"You mean the minions? They are what they are. Terence's devoted slaves. He recruits them young and indoctrinates them in his own special brand of insanity."

I frowned. "He's never done anything like this before. And that girl, Isabelle—Terence must have told her I had a problem with violence. He's never shared information about our family like that before, either."

"Belle always was one of his special pets. He has a few, among the minions. The ones who worship him the most. And hate what they are the most."

Obedience is service, and service is redemption. That was what the boy had said, back on the train. It sounded as if Terence had started some kind of cult, which was both disturbing and unexpected. Terence had never been very good with people, and manipulation on this scale required an in-depth understanding of human nature. *The*

amount of time he must have put into thinking this up,
and making it work . . . Although I could see how much
it would appeal to him to have an army of utterly loyal
Illegals. He'd consider that outcome to be worth any
amount of effort. "How many minions does he have?"

"Ten that I've met. I don't think there are that many
more. I was supposed to be one of them."

"You?"

"Seems crazy, doesn't it? But he tried to twist me up
along with the rest, using all the usual crap everyone
says about people with abilities—you know, we're unnatural, we're dangerous, we're unworthy. Basically wanted
me to believe that my only shot at ever being part of the
Balance was to obey his every whim." He shook his head
with mock regret. "I guess I've just always loved myself
too much for it to work."

I laughed, and he added, "Truth is, he didn't try that
hard with me. I think he realized he might have a use
for someone who could operate independently. Except I
always knew he'd kill me for it, one day."

"He's missed his opportunity," I replied in satisfaction. "You're going to be free of him."

"Thanks to you." He cast a quick glance in my direction. "Tell me something. Are you *really* hundreds of years
old? Because you don't seem like it."

"Does Terence?"

"No," he answered thoughtfully. "I guess not. In fact, sometimes he's really childish, in a scary kind of way."

"It's because we were built with the intellects of adults—very smart adults—and the emotional capacity of infants. For us, 'aging' is our emotional maturity catching up with our mental maturity, and that means learning to process emotions." I spotted another crow and gave it a little wave. "Unfortunately, only one of us was ever very good at it."

"Not Terence, I take it."

"No, not Terence. Someone else—the youngest of us, and the best. The most human. He was the one who taught us how to grow up. Or started to."

"Why did he stop?"

I shouldn't have let myself be drawn into this conversation. "He died."

Jules made a startled exclamation. "From killing someone?"

"No. This was before Dad made it hard for us to kill. It was—something else." And I didn't want to think about that long-ago death, any more than I wanted to contemplate the deaths earlier today. "It's not important how. What's important is, after that, we found it difficult to learn how to process what we felt. We've been a bit unstable ever since."

He frowned. "You seem fine to me, Red."

"That's because you're comparing me to Terence." *And Terence's unstable emotions are directed at other people. Mine are directed at myself.*

"How old *were* you when your brother died?"

"It depends on how you count. I'd . . . existed for a while, or my body had. But I'd only been awake and aware for seventeen years."

He nodded. He wasn't surprised by that answer. *Smarter than he likes to pretend.* Good at reading people, as well. I wondered whether that was itself an aspect of his ability; if he was able to mirror emotions the same way he mirrored appearances. Whatever it was, he'd understood me sufficiently to realize that, in so many ways, I really was seventeen years old. *And not just because that's the age I was when I lost my baby brother.* But I was too tired, now, and too low, to launch into any further explanation of the complicated mess of my long life.

We sat in silence for a while, winding our way along the meandering road. Eventually I did sleep, and felt the better for it. When I woke, the afternoon light was fading to the gray of early evening. I persuaded Jules to let me take the wheel for a while, giving him a chance to get some rest.

He dozed in the seat beside me. I kept stealing glances at his face, thinking about everything that had happened since I met him, and the last time I'd seen him on the train. Finally he said, without opening his eyes, "Stop watching me, sweetheart."

"Sorry. I was wondering what made you change your mind."

"Change my mind about what?" He looked at me.

"Helping me."

He blinked, seeming confused.

"You let the minions take me," I explained, "but then you changed your mind."

"Is that what you think?" He sat up. "Guess I can see why. It took me a while to figure you out, but I wasn't— look, those two caught me by surprise, back on the train, and they were between me and the weapon before I knew it. I only let them take you because I couldn't win, not until I got my hands on something that would give me a fighting chance."

"Such as a very large truck?"

"Yeah. Well. I would've tried something else if I'd known you could be hurt. But I was always coming for you, Red."

If I continued to stare at him, I was going to drive right into the forest. I redirected my attention to the road. "Well, that's . . . I mean—it's good to know that." There was a very silly smile pulling up the corners of my mouth. I forced it away. It was foolish, and I could feel his gaze on me. "Stop watching me, Jules."

He laughed and sank back into the seat.

I drove on, listening to Jules's breathing grow steady and deep. He really was asleep this time.

There was no one to witness my foolishness now, except perhaps for the crows, and crows kept each other's secrets.

I was always coming for you, Red.

I let myself smile.

THE HIDEOUT

"Exactly *where* is this hideout?" I asked.

Jules and I had been wandering the narrow backstreets of Fern City for some time now, and I was tired. I still needed more rest to recover from the aftereffects of killing someone, and I wished we could have driven through the city rather than walked. But the truck wouldn't fit down these streets. Besides, we were trying to blend in and the truck was far too noticeable.

"We're almost there," Jules replied.

"You said that twenty minutes ago."

"Yeah, and it's even truer now." He stopped in front of a lane. "Actually—here we are."

I peered into the alley, which ended in a dark tangle of king-ferns and pepper vines. This was obviously one of the parts of the city that had been abandoned to the Deepwood when the vegetation became too aggressive to tame. "I think you've taken a wrong turn."

"I never take wrong turns. Come on."

He dived into the forest, and I hurried after him. We forced our way through the plants until he stopped in front of a gnarled tree that was growing against a crumbling wall.

"Now we climb," he said, and scrambled upward. I followed, pausing to watch as he uncoiled something from a high branch and sent it dangling down the other side of the wall. *Rope ladder?* My day was not improving. I hauled myself up the tree, along the branch, and—slowly—down the ladder. Then Jules and I pushed through yet more forest until we reached another wall. This one was completely covered with pepper vines, and Jules took hold of a handful, yanking them aside to reveal a door. "Welcome to my Fern City hideout."

I pushed at the door, which swung open onto utter darkness. Jules went in and suddenly there was light. He'd switched on three portable solar lamps, and the soft glow they cast showed a narrow folding bed, two chairs, and a small camp stove in the corner. The rest of the space was taken up with piles of things—clothes, jars of food, cups and plates, blankets, and an array of containers holding who knew what else. I collapsed into one of the chairs and motioned to the other. "Sit down and I'll deal with that toxin."

He shook his head. "You look worn out, Red. Maybe you should get some more sleep first."

"We have to do this now. I don't know how long the antidote Terence gave you will last."

He sat, and I leaned over to take his hand in mine. The truth was, I probably *was* too tired to attempt this, but I wasn't willing to leave Jules at risk for one second longer than I had to.

I called upon the nanomites that lived within my body. They responded, waking from an inert state into a buzzing swarm, eager for instructions. Signals bounced back and forth between us as I explained what they had to do. The mites chattered among themselves, deciding how many of them were required. Most returned to a dormant state, while the chosen few waited, quivering with impatience to begin their task. I sent them forth and they flowed into Jules, charging after the toxin.

"It's done." I let him go and sat back. It was becoming extraordinarily difficult to keep my eyes open.

Jules stood, grasping hold of my shoulders and peering into my face. "Are you all right?"

"I'm fine. Everything is fine." I'd pushed myself beyond my limits and desperately needed sleep, but it had been worth it. *I saved you. I did.* "I do not yield you to Terence," I whispered. "Not body or soul."

I had just enough energy left to smile before sleep carried me away.

Awareness returned by degrees, a slow and pleasant drift into wakefulness. I was lying on a bed, my head cushioned on a pillow. Jules was sitting opposite me, slouched in a chair. He was sleeping; I must have been out for a while.

I yawned and sat up. The bed creaked, the sound loud in the small space, and Jules jerked awake.

"Hi," I said.

He leaped out of his chair. "Are you all right? What can I do? How can I help?"

I eyed him in bemusement. "I don't need any help."

"You've been asleep for five days!"

Five days? I'd underestimated how long it would take me to recover. "I must have needed more rest than I thought."

"I couldn't *wake* you, Red." His voice was shaking. "I thought you were dead. Your version of dead, I mean. I thought . . . helping me, with the toxin . . . had somehow killed you."

I couldn't quite stifle a laugh. He glared at me.

"I'm sorry," I said, "but there's no way removing the toxin could have killed me. I simply needed to rest, and now I don't."

Except I did, a little, which was rather strange. I shouldn't have woken until I was completely recharged. Then I felt it: a faint tugging at the periphery of my senses.

I was being warned.

My gut churned in fear. "Jules, remember how I told you that I can do things my brothers and sisters can't? One of them is being able to tell when a member of my family is nearby. Someone's coming this way."

"*Terence?* Where? How close is he?"

"I don't know! Let me concentrate for a moment."

I swung my legs over the side of the bed, perching on the edge and closing my eyes as I tuned in to the feeling. Whoever was approaching was on the road that led to the city, and still some distance away. It probably was Terence, but I had no way of determining that for certain.

I opened my eyes again. Jules was watching me, tense and poised for flight. "I don't know who it is, but they're half a day from here."

He relaxed, dropping back into the chair. "We've got time to get out. I've got places we can go. Unless you have somewhere in mind?"

He didn't understand. There was no reason why he should, of course, because I hadn't explained yet. I reached into the neck of my shirt, drawing out the river stone that I'd carried all the way from the Firstwood. "I need to talk to you about something."

"This is hardly the time for a chat, darling—"

"It's important. Listen, *please.*" I held out the stone. "I can put memories into things, and I'm going to put some into this. They're for Ash. I mean Ashala Wolf, leader of—"

"I know who she is. You're saying you want to go to the Firstwood?"

"No, I want you to. With the stone that has the memories in it. Because I'm going to Terence."

He spluttered. "You are not!"

"I have to. Terence wouldn't have gone to so much trouble to find me if he didn't want me for something

192

particular, and I need to know what it is. I'm worried about what he's planning."

"So spy on him. From a *distance.*"

I sighed. "Jules, almost the first thing you said to me was that I was a 'runaway, rebel, and Tribe member.' You knew I was with the Tribe, which means Terence knows, and don't try to tell me he doesn't."

"Yeah, he said there was no way a group of kids could survive in a forest without help. So what?"

"So if I go back to the Firstwood, he'll eventually come after me there. I won't put my friends in danger." *And by the way, it isn't me who makes the Tribe possible. It's Ash.* Only I didn't tell him that. It was hard to explain how extraordinary Ash was to someone who hadn't met her, and once they had met her, no explanation was required. "I've left Ash some clues—there's a hidden room, and a poem in my lab. Tell her about them if she hasn't found them yet. And tell her I put the poem in order, from the most trustworthy of us to the least. And—"

"There's another way to do this," he interrupted. "Leave the Tribe."

"What?"

"Leave 'em! Terence'll have no reason to go after your pals then." He grinned his crooked grin. "Run away with me, Red."

"I don't have time for jokes, Jules!"

The smile faded. "Don't think much of me, do you?"

He was serious? *He's been sitting here for five days, thinking I was dead because I helped him.* He felt a sense of obligation. Except he was asking the impossible. "I can't run. I can't take the chance that Terence will hurt the Tribe to draw me out."

He shook his head. "I thought you were a lot of things, but I never thought you were crazy. Going to Terence is *nuts.*"

Perhaps it was. That didn't bother me. There were times when protecting the people you loved, the people you were responsible for, required doing something crazy. Ash understood that. All of the Tribe did.

Jules didn't. He didn't have a family. I tried to make him see it anyway. "You helped someone escape from Terence once, that woman who died of the poison. You wouldn't have known where she ran to if you hadn't helped her. When someone you care about needs help, you take a risk—"

"You think I cared about her?" He let out a bitter laugh. "I wanted to find out if it was possible to escape from Terence. It was an experiment. A test." He leaned closer and added in a low voice, "You know who I am, Red? I'm the person that lives when everyone else dies. I'm the

194

one that's okay when everyone else isn't. And if you were as smart as you like to think, you would be, too."

I have been that person. That's how I know the gain isn't worth the price. "Jules, sometimes there's not a lot of . . . of honor, in the things we do to survive. But survival isn't life. It's just existence."

"I have no idea what you're talking about."

Yes, you do. Only I had no time to argue with him, not when I still had to put memories into the stone. I rose and held out my hands, pulling him to his feet. Then I stood on tiptoes, to brush a kiss against the stubble on his cheek.

"What I'm talking about is that you're better than the person you have been," I whispered. But to the nanomites in his body, I whispered something else: *Sleep.*

He collapsed. I caught him as he fell, maneuvering him onto the bed, and stood motionless, staring down at him. I needed to do things: leave instructions for Jules, and write a note for Ash. I couldn't make myself move yet.

He seemed younger when he was asleep. I could almost glimpse the Jules of long ago, the boy he'd been before he'd met my brother. Or perhaps the person he would have become, if he hadn't been born into a world that feared abilities. *I grieve for all the lost chances, and all the lost people.*

He couldn't hear me. I still spoke as if he could. "I saved you from Terence. Now I'm going to send you to Ash, and she'll save you from yourself." I reached down to clasp his hand, feeling the warmth of his skin for the last time. "Good-bye, Jules. I will always remember."

THE DEPARTURE

I waited at the side of the road that led into Fern City, standing beneath an oversize fan palm. It had a thin trunk that soared to a truly ridiculous height before bursting into long stalks, each one capped with a ruffled circular leaf. Jules and I had passed the palm on the way in, and it was so large that he couldn't fail to remember it. I'd left him a note in the hideout, telling him that I would leave the stone here for him to collect.

The weapon was shoved in my pocket. I would have liked to have sent it to Ash, but Terence would turn the world upside down to find the thing. All I could send to her were my memories, and Jules. *I'm so sorry, Ash, for all the things I never said.* When I'd left the Firstwood I'd thought I might be able to go back and explain in person; I knew now it would be a very long time before I could go home. If I could ever go home.

A crow came flying through the air, landing in the palm above. I looked up, and he examined me out of a single gleaming eye. Then he fluffed out his feathers and lifted his head to direct a challenging gaze at the world. I understood his message. *We are tough, we crows.* We were indeed. The saurs might have been one of the first new species to be born after the Reckoning, but the crows had survived it. *I can cope with Terence. I can cope with anything.* I was a crow now, and Terence didn't know it. My brother would remember me the way I had been before I'd gone to the Firstwood: fragile and sad.

I lifted my head, exactly as the crow had done, and stared down the road. *I'm not who I was.* I was no longer as susceptible to spiraling into despair, and I could defend myself, and others, if I had to. When Terence had last seen me I'd been incapable of violence, so much so that I couldn't have shot the girl-minion regardless of what was at stake. I'd known for almost a year now that I'd changed. When Connor had arrived in the Firstwood and we'd thought he was a government agent come to destroy us, I'd been prepared to kill him if we had to. I'd realized then that there were no limits to what I'd do to protect my Tribe.

I lifted the cord off my neck and clasped the river stone in my hand. It would take me some time to give Ash the memories she needed and edit out the ones she didn't. I concentrated on building a story, sending one memory after another into the rock as the hours ticked past. Finally I was done, except for the very last memory that Ash would need.

The memory of what would happen next.

For a while, nothing happened. Then I heard an engine roaring. I stepped back into the greenery, hiding the hand that held the stone among the ferns. Another few moments, and the car came into sight around a bend. I could tell the precise second the driver caught sight of me. Whoever it was slammed on the brakes, and the car screeched to a halt, twisting sideways in the middle of the road.

The door opened and someone came running out. Not Terence. A tall olive-skinned woman with almond-shaped black eyes, dressed in Cloud City white. *Delta.*

She tore toward me, long hair flying and arms outspread for a hug. I stiffened and stepped back.

Delta stopped, looking hurt. "Aren't you glad to see me?"

Typical Del. "I got shot with a weapon that *you* designed. No, I'm not glad to see you."

"Terence said you wouldn't come otherwise."

"It doesn't matter what he said! Since when do we kidnap one another?"

She shrugged and pouted. You'd never know, when she behaved this way, that my sister was a genius. Or perhaps you would; my father had been a genius, too, and he'd certainly had his quirks.

"You were supposed to come to Cloud City," she said, a petulant note in her voice. "What happened?"

Those minions had been taking me to Del. Things were more complicated than I'd thought, if Terence and Delta were working together so closely. "You mean, why wasn't I delivered to you in a box?"

Her eyes widened. "They put you in a box?"

"Yes, Del! I didn't like it much. And I wasn't as unconscious as they thought." I chose my words with care, avoiding a direct untruth. "There was a crash. Two of Terence's servants died. As for that Impersonator . . ."

I paused, gathering strength for the lie. We'd each been built with a fundamental inability to deceive one another, but I could override the prohibition, provided I was convinced it was necessary to preserve someone's life. I imagined what Terence would do to Jules if he knew that he was alive and free of the toxin, and spoke with confidence. "I haven't seen the mimic for days. I expect he's gone scuttling back to Terence."

Delta nodded, satisfied. I relaxed, and she said, "I need your help, Ember. With Dad."

My heart beat faster. Delta couldn't possibly have discovered the secret I was keeping about Dad. I was almost certain of it. "What kind of help?"

"I don't think he's coming back this time," she said earnestly. "You understand that, don't you? He's been gone five years. He's abandoned you, the same way he did the rest of us."

I looked away, allowing her to think I was flinching from the truth when really I was hiding my relief. Delta still believed that my father was off on yet another one of his adventures. *Probably thinks he's sitting on a mountain somewhere, studying some hitherto undiscovered species of plant.* He wasn't.

Hundreds of years ago, my father had found a way to shift the essence of who he was from his original organic body into an artificial one. He hadn't realized that doing so would cause an instability that grew progressively worse as time passed. None of the others knew how bad that instability had become. In the end, shutting him down completely had been the only way to save his mind. Dad had asked me to keep it secret. He'd worried that some of my siblings would try to revive him at any cost, and he hadn't wanted to live if he couldn't have full use of his immense intellect.

I couldn't allow myself to be drawn into a conversation

with Delta about where Dad was. It would become increasingly difficult to avoid a lie. Instead I snapped, "That was a mean trick to have that Illegal imitate Dad! Was that Terence's idea or yours?"

"Mine," she confessed, staring down at the ground. "I needed to see you, Ember, and I knew you'd come to speak to Dad, if you thought he was back."

Her reasoning was sound, except that I *hadn't* thought he was back, not in the way she meant. For the past five years, my father's inert body had been lying in the tunnels beneath the Firstwood, waiting for me to reactivate him if I ever found a way to fix the instability. Unfortunately, it was possible that there was more than one version of my father in existence.

Del offered me a hopeful smile. "You forgive me for the Impersonator, don't you, Emmy?"

No, I don't. I don't forgive you for a lot of things. I almost said those words out loud, purely to see if I could; if they were a lie, they should stick in my throat and be impossible to speak. I truly wasn't sure how I felt about Del, because while she did dreadful things, she did them without *appreciating* that they were dreadful. We'd each lost something when the best of us died, and Delta had coped by becoming the most childlike of us all.

She seemed to take my silence for agreement, because she continued eagerly, "I have a way to make a new Dad, Ember. That's why I wanted to see you." She stepped closer, her entire face lit up with excitement. "I've unlocked the other consciousness."

Oh, no. This was exactly what I'd been afraid of. Dad had long ago preserved what was effectively a backup copy of himself on a massive computer. He'd locked it away with a complex, ever-changing code. I'd warned him Del might break it one day, but he'd said she was so easily distracted by a new project that she'd never give it enough attention. *Dad, you fool. I told you to destroy it!*

I tried to reason with her. "Del, Dad deliberately locked that consciousness away to *stop* anyone from putting it in a body and making another version of him. You know that."

Delta stomped her foot. "I don't care! Dad left. Again."

He had to, and if you make a new Dad, the same instability will eventually destroy him. Except she didn't know that, and I couldn't talk to her about it. I couldn't tell her how wrenching it had been to watch the greatest mind of his generation collapse in on itself. When Dad had told me to shut him down in one of his increasingly infrequent moments of lucidity, I hadn't hesitated to obey.

202

It had been the last measure of dignity I could give to him. *You don't want to see him like that, Del.*

"Dad always leaves," I pointed out. "Do you really think an alternate Dad is going to be any different from the original?"

She nodded. "Yes. Because the backup was made *before.*"

I should have known she'd think of that. My father's backup consciousness would not contain anything that he'd experienced after the point at which it was created — and it had been created before the end of the Reckoning.

I sighed. "Dad will still be Dad. He'll end up having the same fight with you about the accords. And he did always leave us, to go somewhere or other. He simply had more places to visit after the Reckoning was done."

"He didn't! He won't."

"Come on, Del. Do you really think that of the two of us, it's *me* that doesn't remember him properly?"

Delta stuck out her lower lip stubbornly. She didn't want to listen, even though she must have known I was right. Like the rest of my siblings, she had the flawed memory of organic beings; I was the only one who remembered everything in complete and often unwelcome detail. Clearly, she wasn't going to be convinced that this was a bad idea. "What do you need from me?" I demanded.

Delta brightened. "You were the only one he ever taught to transfer a consciousness into a new body. Also, I don't have a body yet. I thought we could build one together. It'd be faster that way."

"And what does Terence want from me?"

She looked blank. *I'm a colossal idiot.* I'd been proceeding on the basis of an assumption that I should have questioned the moment she arrived. "You're not helping Terence to get to me, are you? *He's* helping *you.*"

"I need you, Ember."

"And exactly what are you doing for Terence in return for having me kidnapped? Other than making him that weapon, I mean."

"Nothing!"

I glared at her until she finally conceded, "Nothing yet. He's worried about this reform movement, and he wants me to help him make sure it doesn't get out of control."

The implications of that were horrifying. My father had designed each of his children to have a particular gift; mine was memory and Delta's was invention. There was simply no end to the devices my sister could design to hurt Illegals.

I thought quickly. *I have to break the alliance between Terence and Delta.* I already had a way to do that, but I wasn't going to try it yet. I needed to use Del to get close to Terence first, and find out what he was planning for the reform movement that my father and I had started.

I smiled at my sister. "I'll help you, Del." *Right up until I don't need to anymore.*

She clapped her hands together in delight, as if I'd really had a choice about it. Then she darted to the car, opening the passenger door for me. I took the weapon from my pocket and tossed it across the road. "Put that away, will you? I can't stand to touch it anymore."

Delta didn't look particularly enthused about picking it up. None of us would ever be comfortable around a weapon that could harm us. *Should have thought of that before you invented it, big sister.* As she bent to retrieve it, my hand clenched on the stone, and I poured these last memories in.

This was truly good-bye: to Ash, to the Tribe and the Firstwood. Good-bye to the person I had been there. I'd have to become someone else now, to safeguard the people I loved. To make sure they survived my family. *Sometimes there's not a lot of honor in the things we do to survive.* I relaxed my grip, ready to drop the stone into the undergrowth.

There are a thousand ways to disappear.

THE LOCATION

I was sitting at the base of a hill, surrounded by cold air and yellow grass.

This was wrong. I had been outside Fern City — no. *Ember* had been outside Fern City.

I am Ashala Wolf. I have never been to Fern City.

My best friend is an aingl.

"Ashala?" Connor's voice. He was sitting beside me. I shifted to face him. Opened my mouth to speak.

No sound came out. I couldn't find words big enough to wrap around what I'd experienced.

I swallowed and tried again. This time the words came. Slow and halting at first. Then so fast they spilled out, tripping one another up and jumbling together. Now and then Connor interrupted, asking a question or getting me to explain something again. It took a long time to tell it all. At the end of it, we were both silent, staring out over the familiar grass and hills. The world looked the same.

The world was different.

"So, Ember is one of the aingls," Connor said, astonishment echoing through his voice. "And *Alexander Hoffman* is lying in the tunnels beneath the Firstwood?"

"Apparently. Except he's all shut down. Oh, and plus there's some other copy of his consciousness out there somewhere!" I put my hands to my head, which was aching from having to absorb so much impossible knowledge.

"He really did write all the *Histories,*" Connor said. "This is . . ."

"Yeah. Nothing makes sense."

"And in a strange way, everything does."

"How do you figure that?"

"The way people revere Hoffman, for a start. He was *here,* after the Reckoning. He and the aingls must have had a tremendous influence on the way society developed, even if no one knew he was still alive."

I supposed so. I wasn't really up to considering the bigger implications of any of this. I was still struggling to fit Ember's real past with what I'd known about her before. Although some of what she'd told me had been true, in a way. Her father had kind-of died on the way to the Firstwood, and he'd been in the reform movement—actually, he'd *started* the reform movement. The fragments of truth she'd given me didn't make it any easier to reconcile the Hoffman I'd always heard about with Ember's thoughts and feelings about him. I'd been told about a visionary, a hero; to Ember he was just . . . her dad.

"He's nothing like the paintings of him, or the sculptures."

"Hoffman?"

I nodded. "He's an ordinary guy. In the paintings he's got that long flowing hair, and he's so tall, you know?" I sighed. "I guess people painted him how they imagined him."

"I wonder if he wrote the angel poem?" Connor mused. "About his children."

Count the angels, one by one. "Seven to remember has got to be Em."

"And six to invent—Delta?"

"Must be." *87543621.* From the most trustworthy

to the least, Ember had said. Why hadn't she begun with herself?

Eight to bring the rest together. "I think the eighth is the one who died. And if Terence is the least trustworthy, that makes him number one. As in, *one to lead*!" I shook my head. "Guess he must've been a big disappointment to his dad." I picked up a handful of rocks and sent them flying into the grass. "She should have told me!"

"I'm fairly certain she was afraid."

"Of Terence?"

"Of what you would think of her. When you knew she was synthetic."

"She *can't* have believed I would care!" Then a horrible thought occurred to me. "Connor, do you care?"

He shook his head. "What I care about is whether people help the Tribe or hurt us. If anything, Ember's knowledge makes her an asset. At least, it would have if she'd told us the truth. To other people, though . . . it might matter."

Jules had called her a collection of circuits without a heart. That had hurt her. It had hurt her a lot. *Em, you idiot. As if I'd ever think you didn't have a heart.* I'd tell her that if she were here. Only she wasn't. Jules was.

The guy who'd kidnapped her.

In her note, Ember had asked me not to judge him until I'd seen him through her eyes. I had now. And I thought he was a smug, self-interested, unscrupulous excuse for a human being.

I lurched to my feet. "Let's go deal with the Impersonator."

Jules, Pepper, and Wanders were waiting where we had left them. Wanders was stalking back and forth, and Pepper and Jules were skipping rocks across the river, competing to see who could make their stone go the farthest.

I called out to Pepper as we drew close. "I need to talk to Jules alone."

Her black eyes lit up with curiosity. "I'm the one who captured him!"

"I know. And thank you. But I need you to go now."

She shrugged, picked up another stone, and sent it flying over the water. Behind her, Wanders rolled onto the ground and lifted his head to the breeze, as if he had nothing better to do than lounge there for the day.

I had no time for this. "I'm serious, Pepper." And in mindspeak, I added. *This is Tribe business, and I'll tell Jaz what the Saur Tribe needs to know about it later.*

Her shoulders sagged. "All right, all right, I'll go."

She and Wanders strolled away, moving at a speed that was slow enough to be annoying but not quite slow enough for me to hurry them up. Pepper kept glancing back, her small face full of woe, while Wanders let his long neck dip to the ground. I ignored their antics, waiting until they were too far to overhear. Then I shifted my attention to Jules.

He spoke before I could. "You seem a bit upset, darling. Shocked by what Ember really is? Didn't you ever notice there was something wrong with her?"

"There's nothing wrong with her!"

"She's a machine."

"She's my best friend. And she saved you."

"Yeah. And I'm grateful. That's why I brought the message." He scratched his jaw. "Would've been useful to have her around, too, in case Terence ever came after me, only she had other plans."

Connor cast a quick glance at my face, and spoke to Jules in a tone that was much calmer than anything I would've been able to manage. "Do you have any idea where she is?"

"'Fraid not. Terence has places everywhere." His gaze drifted to the Firstwood. "So when are you going to ask me to join your Tribe?"

"I'm not!"

"You're going to have to, if you want to find out what I know about Terence."

He wants to trade information for a place in the Tribe? I spluttered, so angry I couldn't even form words. Jules grinned that irritating crooked smile that Ember inexplicably found so attractive. "Come on, wolfgirl. I need a new place to hide out, and it's not as if you're very picky about who you let in. I mean, if *machines* can join—"

My fist seemed to fly out of its own volition, straight into his face. He staggered backward, tripped over his pack, and fell. I shook out my aching hand, enjoying the sight of him sprawled on the grass. That had hurt, but it had been worth it.

"If you really want to beat him up," Connor murmured, "I could do it much more efficiently."

He was joking, sort of. I played along. "True, but it would take a while. Maybe we should get the saurs to bite pieces off him until he starts talking."

"There's no need for that!" Jules said hastily. He climbed to his feet, studying me with an intent expression. "You really don't care, do you? That she's synthetic?"

"Of course I don't—" Then I stopped. He'd said "synthetic," not "machine." And he suddenly looked and sounded different, in a way that was hard to define. Less arrogant, maybe? Definitely less annoying.

Realization dawned.

"You bastard," I breathed. "You were testing me."

He rolled his eyes. "Obviously. Not as quick off the mark as Red, are you? I had to know if you'd want her back, even after you found out about her."

"Of course I want her back!"

"Glad to hear it," he drawled. "Because I know where she is."

"Where?"

"Spinifex City."

I'd never been there, but a vague image of a white-walled city rising up from the desert sands came to mind. *I know where she is. I know where she is.* . . . I was so happy I could have danced.

"Are you absolutely certain?" Connor demanded.

"Yep."

We both eyed him skeptically. He sighed. "Since I last saw Ember, I've worn a dozen bodies, conned my way into and out of a bunch of different places, and talked to a whole lot of people who never knew who they were really talking to. I'm certain."

"I hope you were careful!" I said. "You might have warned them someone was coming for her."

"I'm not a fool."

He wasn't, either, and this was the kind of thing he was good at. He'd spied for—and on—Terence for years. "Do you know exactly where in Spinifex City?"

"Terence has a house, which is probably where she is. I can find out for sure once we arrive. I've got a contact there."

Connor frowned. "It doesn't seem like you need our help, Jules. Why didn't you go after Ember yourself instead of coming here?"

"Because she'd send me away." He nodded at me. "It's you she's trying to protect, darling. You and your Tribe. I can't convince her that staying with Terence is a bad idea. You can, though."

He was right that I was probably the only one who could get Ember to come home. Except . . . Connor and I exchanged glances. To reach Ember, we were going to have to rely on Jules to a worrying degree. I raised my eyebrows in a silent question. He gave me a half-shrug, as if to say, *you're the one who's good with people. What do you think?*

I stared at Jules, trying to put my impressions of him together with Ember's. Trying to see into his heart. "Why should we believe you really want to help her? You don't seem to care about anyone or anything, other than yourself."

"I don't." He laughed at my obvious surprise. "Expected a different answer, huh? I am who I am, wolfgirl. I don't care about you. I don't care about your Tribe, and I certainly don't care about your cause. But Ember helped me, and I owe her."

Not good enough. I stepped closer, fixing him with a challenging stare. "I'm not sure you care about obligations, either. You're going to have to give me a better answer than that, Jules."

He stared back at me for a second. Then his gaze flicked away from mine, and the mocking edge faded from his expression, leaving behind a vulnerability that was weirdly familiar. It took me a moment to realize where I'd seen it before—or rather, where Ember had. *Run away with me, Red.*

Jules answered, in a voice so soft I barely heard it, "She's the only person in the world who ever thought I was any better than I am."

Good answer. And a good reason for him to help Ember, as well. I of all people understood how powerful it was to see a better version of yourself reflected in someone else's gaze. *I don't think he was joking when he asked you to run, Em.* Only she hadn't known it. Deep down, I wasn't sure Ember truly believed anyone could care about her. I was going to have to do something about that when I got her back.

I glanced from Jules to Connor and grinned. "Let's go to Spinifex City."

THE CITY

The next few days were a blur of preparations. I left most of the details of organizing the trip to Connor, while I—well, talked. First to Georgie and Daniel, explaining what I'd discovered and putting them in charge of the Tribe while I was gone. Then to Jaz, explaining it all again. He promised that the saurs would keep up their patrols and make sure no one was caught unawares by anything to do with the Adjustment. After that I tried to contact Grandpa, only he still wouldn't come out. So my last conversation was with the wolves. Pack Leader was unimpressed that I'd stopped off to say good-bye. He obviously thought it was a waste of time when I had a Pack member missing. It was a bittersweet reminder that I was now a girl who was part wolf, rather than the other way around. Wolves weren't sentimental. Humans were.

Spinifex City lay in the desert on the far side of the Firstwood. Connor, Jules, and I hiked part of the way, then took to the skies once we neared the homelands of the sabers who populated the edge of the forest. The big cats were aggressive and insanely territorial; it would have been next to impossible to walk through their lands without being eaten.

I wasn't prepared for what was beyond the western side of the Firstwood. I'd imagined sand, and little else. I was wrong. There *was* sand — bright-red sand — but there was so much more. The desert was a place of contrast and color. Yellow spinifex grass, mostly bleached white by the sun. Taffa vines, trailing their bulging purple pods and lime-green leaves across the earth. Chunky formations of orangey-brown rock. Tall pines and the strange bottle-like shapes of gray boab trees. And everywhere, thin streams of water that pulsed through the landscape like veins. It was beautiful, even though it wasn't my forest.

By the time we finally neared Spinifex City, ten days had passed. There was a high composite wall surrounding it, the same as all the other cities, only the one here was stained red by the desert dust that seemed to get into everything. The closer we got to the wall the more nervous I felt. *We'll be fine. We look as if we belong.* The three of us were wearing clothes of mixed colors and carrying heavy backpacks, befitting our supposed identities as traders. I had a Citizenship tattoo on my wrist as well, inked there by Connor using leftover dye we'd found in Ember's lab.

I rubbed anxiously at my wrist.

"Will you quit fretting?" Jules said. "I told you, no one will check the tattoo properly. Not when you're with me." He waved at the distant wall. "This is my city!"

"You're originally from Gull City," Connor pointed out.

"Spinifex City isn't only a place. It's a way of life."

I rolled my eyes. Then I frowned, staring at Jules. The journey here seemed to have taken a lot out of him.

"Are you sure you're okay?"

"I told you before, I'm fine. Just not used to so much walking." He nodded at the city. "We're getting close. I'd better change."

"Don't do it out here! We're probably still too far away for anyone to spot anything strange, but . . ."

"Worry a lot, don't you?"

I gave him a flat stare, and he threw up his hands. "All right, I'll hide." He disappeared behind a large rock formation at the side of the road. Moments later, a stranger emerged. A round man with a trim dark beard, wearing pants of Gull City blue and a shirt of Cloud City white. He walked up to us with a springing step, managing to bounce along even with the pack strapped to his back. *He really is good at what he does.* It wasn't just that his body changed; all his mannerisms did, too.

"Meet Diego!" Jules announced in a deep musical voice. "The real version lives in Cloud City. Trades in fish and potatoes. I like to think I'm giving him the life he wishes he had."

"He's an actual person?"

"I can only Impersonate actual people."

"And Diego will help to get us past the gate guards?" Connor asked.

"Of course." He began moving along the road again. "When I'm Diego, I am a taffa trader."

Taffa was what Spinifex City was famous for. It was a sweet, spicy drink brewed out of beans harvested from the pods growing on taffa vines.

"I don't see how being a taffa trader particularly helps us," I said.

"Are you kidding? People will do anything for taffa in Spinifex City."

It *was* a popular drink. So much so, in fact, that all the governments of the world included a small supply of beans in everyone's weekly nutrition allocation. "I've never understood why people are so keen on it."

Jules's jaw dropped. "You've never . . ." He shook his head. "Don't say that out loud again. Taffa is important in this city."

I dredged up what I'd learned about Spinifex City in school. "I get that it's their main export—"

"It's got nothing to do with exports. It's the dreams."

"What dreams?"

It was Connor who answered. "Taffa is supposed to occasionally cause very vivid dreams."

"I've never heard that!"

"It only happens in Spinifex City," Jules said. "Anywhere else, taffa is just a drink. People around here take those dreams very seriously. They believe they're connected to the Balance."

"How?" I demanded.

"They have strange things in them, stuff that no

221

one's ever seen before. Things that don't exist. The theory is, there are all these moments in time floating in the greater Balance, and taffa connects you with them."

I frowned. "If that's true, why do the dreams only happen in Spinifex City?"

"That's easy. The Balance is stronger here than anywhere else."

"I think you'll find it's the same everywhere," Connor told him.

I nodded agreement. *And besides, if it's stronger anywhere, it's in the Firstwood.*

Jules shrugged. "You two can think what you want. Just don't go telling people in Spinifex City the Balance is the same everywhere."

We walked on until we neared the half-open gates. I searched for—and found—the enforcer guards, lurking in the shadow of the arch that formed the entrance. One male, one female, and both more than a little overweight, for guards. Plus . . . I squinted, not sure I was seeing right. They were *lounging,* leaning casually back against the archway. Enforcers, at least in my experience, didn't lounge. I glanced questioningly at Connor, who gave a faint frown in response. He didn't understand it, either. *They're not acting like enforcers.* They didn't even straighten up as we approached.

At least not until they spotted Jules.

"Diego! Haven't seen you in a while," the woman called as she waddled over. The man was right behind her, reaching out to shake Jules's hand.

"Have you got any taffa beans for us?" he asked, running a hopeful gaze over our packs.

"Not right now," Jules replied regretfully. "I'll have something for you on my way out. Government allocation no good this week?"

The woman made a face. "We both got blues. We were hoping for reds. Or greens, even."

I had no idea what that meant, but Jules seemed to understand. "I'll see what I can do." He held out his wrist. "Want to check our tatts?"

The man laughed and shook his head. "I think we can trust you, Diego. Go on through."

"And don't forget about the taffa!" the woman shouted after us.

I forced myself not to look back as we left the guards behind, unable to believe it had been so easy. Things were obviously different here. Very different. I was still puzzling over it as we stepped through the gates and into another world.

The three of us were on a wide street lined on either side with white-walled houses stained red by dust. Each house had small, narrow windows covered with shutters. Ember had once described the place where she'd lived here, so I knew the big windows in Spinifex City houses were on the inside, facing onto internal courtyards. Taffa vines were growing up the sides of the houses and over the roofs, smaller than the ones we'd seen in the desert but still big enough to saturate the air with a cinnamon-like scent. There were a bewildering number of people on the street, mostly dressed in loose robes of Spinifex City yellow. And there were an even more bewildering number of cats. The long-legged desert moggies were everywhere, grooming their mottled brown fur, twitching their overly large tufted ears, and generally acting as if they owned the place.

The noise of the crowd, the smell of the taffa, and the sheer strangeness of it all made me feel unsettled, and I'd already been thrown off-balance by the behavior of the guards. I edged closer to Connor as we moved into the city. When we were far enough from the gates, I hissed at Jules, "What was that back there? Do the enforcers here always behave that way?"

"Pretty much."

Connor shook his head in bemusement. "I'd heard

they took something of a relaxed attitude in Spinifex City, but I had no idea how relaxed."

"Well, there's a saying here," Jules replied. "The only trouble is taffa trouble."

"The only trouble is taffa trouble?" I repeated, testing out the strange phrase. "What's that supposed to mean?"

"That the only thing worth fighting over, or worrying about, is taffa. Nothing else really matters. So they enforce the Citizenship Accords, but they don't go *looking* for ways to enforce the accords, if you know what I mean."

"That—insane. And what was all that stuff you were saying to them about the colors?"

"You *really* need to learn something about taffa."

"Why don't you teach us?" Connor asked, pleasantly but with a suggestion of teeth in his voice.

Jules cast a wary glance at him and explained, "The beans change color depending on things like soil and weather conditions, and when the pods are harvested. Different colors have different tastes."

And the gate guards hadn't wanted the ones they'd got in their weekly allocation. *We both got blues. We were hoping for reds. . . .* This city was weird.

I watched the houses as we went by, wondering if Ember was in any of them. *Probably not.* Jules had told us before that Terence's house was near the city center. I would've loved to charge over to it right this minute, but Em might not even be there. Plus the place would be guarded by minions if she was, and none of us wanted to risk alerting anyone that we were here yet. *Hold on, Ember. I'm coming for you.* I tried to sense her the way I could Connor—with everything she and I had shared, it seemed as if I should have been able to get a vague inkling of where she was. I couldn't. All I felt was the city looming over me. It made me want to hunch in on myself and duck my head to avoid prying eyes. *Don't be ridiculous. It isn't alive.*

On that thought, I stopped.

Jules was ahead of me and didn't notice. Connor did, of course. "Ashala? Are you all right?"

"Um. Yeah. Sorry." I started walking again. "Can you feel that?" I asked him in a low voice. "The air. The . . . atmosphere. It's as if the city is, I don't know, conscious or something."

He was silent for a long moment, then nodded. "You're right. It's like the Firstwood. Only—not like the Firstwood."

"Do you think it means there's something here? Something the same as Grandpa?"

He grinned. "You think there's a giant snake living in one of these houses?"

I imagined that and stifled a laugh. "Maybe not."

We turned onto another street, not as crowded as the one we'd been on, and detoured past some more cats. They seemed to lounge wherever they wanted and expect people to walk around them. Everybody did.

"Doesn't anyone here own a dog?" I muttered.

Jules caught the comment. "This place only exists because a desert cat led a bunch of Reckoning survivors to a Hoffman cache hundreds of years ago. They say cats helped to found the city, and the city has never forgotten."

"Seems to me that the *cats* have never forgotten," I observed, eyeing three fat, glossy moggies lying in the center of the road ahead. "Are we going to see your, um, contact?"

"Yep. He'll help us get into Terence's house. For a price. I've got to make a quick stop first to get something to bargain with."

"Let me guess," Connor said dryly. "Taffa beans?"

"Now you two are getting the idea of how things are done."

Jules turned again, onto a short street that ended in a large building with a single door and no windows. *A warehouse?* There were a bunch of people outside, kids and adults both, dressed in Spinifex City yellow and kicking a ball back and forth.

A freckled girl called out to Jules as we approached. "Hey, Diego! Come to do business?"

"Of course." Jules waved at Connor and me. "I've taken on a little help. Got a lot of trades to make."

"You know what they say, my friend." She tossed the ball to Jules, who caught it easily. "The only trouble is taffa trouble."

He threw it back. "We're all followers of the bean."

I leaned closer to Connor as we passed the ball-players. "Am I imagining things, or was that a coded message?"

"Password, I think. Question and answer. They're guards of some kind."

Jules pushed open the door of the building, revealing a corridor that branched off into other corridors. *Not a warehouse.* At least, not of a type that I'd seen before. There were doors along the hallways, spaced at regular intervals, and we followed Jules until he stopped in front of one of them.

He dug in his pack, producing a key, and unlocked the door to reveal a large rectangular space. There was a tiny bathroom down one end and a bed against a wall. The rest of the room was filled with crates and a familiar cinnamony scent.

Jules dumped his pack, shimmered into himself, and strode to the back of the room. He started opening one crate after another, checking inside and muttering, "Not this one . . . no, not this one, either . . ."

It seemed like he was going to be a while. Connor and I dropped our packs as well and looked around.

"Where did you get all this taffa?" I asked.

"I traded for it," Jules answered absently. "It's useful stuff, and besides, I needed it to maintain Diego's identity. These are my trader's quarters. They call them pods. Excellent hideouts."

Connor surveyed the crates and shook his head. "Want to tell us exactly how many taffa growers are underreporting their crops?"

Jules didn't respond. I cast a suspicious glance at the crates. "What do you mean, underreporting?"

"Taffa growers are supposed to hand over most of

their taffa to the government, the same as the fishers in Gull City hand over their fish," Connor replied. "But Jules seems to have far more taffa than he should have been able to acquire, and if the rest of the 'pods' in this place belong to other traders . . ."

I calculated how much taffa must be contained within this building. "There shouldn't be so much to trade!" Unless, of course, the growers were lying about the size of their crops. I glared at Jules. "Taffa growers are *breaking* the Food Distribution Accords?"

He laughed. "You're one to be indignant, darling! Your entire Tribe is breaking the Citizenship Accords."

"That's totally different," I snapped. "The Citizenship Accords are wrong. The Food Distribution Accords are there to make sure everyone always has enough to eat, not like the old world, where more than half the planet went hungry and the rest ate to excess."

"Well, no one's going to go hungry from lack of taffa. Anyway, growers don't break the accords. They're only required to report the crops they grow in the registered taffa fields. People can harvest wild taffa without reporting it at all."

"In other words, people have planted unregistered taffa fields," Connor said.

"Desert's full of 'em."

I looked helplessly at Connor. "This entire place is so . . ."

"I know. I can't believe the Prime lets it go on."

"That would be Prime Lopez," Jules put in, "owner of the largest collection of rare taffa beans in Spinifex City." He pulled something out of a crate. "Aha!"

I eyed the small brown bag in his hand. "There can't be many beans in there."

"There doesn't have to be. These beans were harvested during a solar eclipse. Won't be another one for hundreds of years. They're rare, and that makes them valuable." He tucked the bag into his shirt, shifting back into Diego.

"Where to now?" Connor asked.

"Now we go to the taffa market," Jules answered cheerfully. "Because we need to see the Lion."

THE LION

"So," I said, as the three of us strolled through the city, "why does this guy call himself the Lion? Weren't they giant lizards, sort of the same as saurs?" I'd never seen a lion, nor had anyone else; they were one of the species that hadn't survived the Reckoning.

"Lions were cats," Jules replied. "Big cats. Like sabers. Only I think they had spots."

"And you're certain that this man can be trusted?" Connor asked.

"He can be trusted to stick to a deal, and he has no love for Terence. There's some old taffa dispute between them."

I snorted. "Seems as if everything in this place comes back to taffa."

"It does with the Lion. He runs the taffa trade."

"Runs how, exactly?"

"Makes sure deals are honored, and keeps the government out of things that don't concern them. He manages the ecosystem, too. Stops people from messing it up by planting too many vines."

Connor frowned. "What you're saying is the Lion is one of the most powerful people in Spinifex City."

I didn't like the sound of that. "Shouldn't we be going to see someone less important? We don't want to be noticed."

"We need the Lion. There's nothing that happens in this city that he doesn't know about. Besides, he always keeps a close watch on Terence."

"Because of some old taffa dispute?"

"Because he's not an idiot. He knows Terence is more than the ordinary Citizen he pretends to be."

We were nearing the market; I could tell by the sudden hubbub of voices and the way the taffa scent in the air increased. The three of us emerged from an alley, and there it was—a vast open square filled with a sea of colorful canvas tents and a cacophony of shouts: "Midnight Rains here! Marble Ridge Mornings! Smoky

233

Dawns!" It took me a second to realize the traders were calling out the names of taffa varieties, advertising what kinds of beans they had.

We pushed through the crowd, stepping over cats as we moved deep into the maze of tents. A few food stalls were interspersed between the traders, but other than that, this place was all about the taffa. Everywhere, people were swapping beans — for other beans of a different color and for almost anything else, as well. *Books, jewelry, paintings* . . . Some enterprising soul had lugged in a Hoffman sculpture and was trying to argue it was worth its weight in taffa. Before the Reckoning, I supposed, people would've exchanged money for the things they wanted. Not any longer. Currency had been on Hoffman's list of the evils of the old world.

Jules threaded his way to the far edge of the market and stopped in front of an enormous blue tent that was positioned against the side of a building. The tent was surrounded by pots of taffa vines, and by people. They were sitting on upturned crates, gathered in loose circles around camp ovens upon which they were — of course — brewing taffa.

No one looked up as we approached, but there was a quiet vigilance about them that was instantly

recognizable. *More guards who don't appear to be guards.*
Jules gave a merry wave and strode up to the tent;
we followed behind. I stepped away from Connor
to make room to fight if we needed to defend ourselves, but nobody bothered us. Obviously, Diego was
known here.

Inside was dimmer and cooler. The floor was lined
with thin composite tiles, atop which sat piles of cushions and yet more pots of taffa vines. People sat on
the cushions in groups of two, one person speaking
and the other writing notes in books with red covers.
Curious, I edged closer to one of the pairs so I could
hear what they were talking about.

"I was on a street," a woman was saying. "The build-
ings reached the sky, but there were no trees or plants.
And the sky was brown. Can you imagine? A *brown* sky.
It was horrible."

The man sitting beside her scribbled down her
words. "How long do you think the dream lasted?"

People were recording their taffa dreams? I guessed
they really did take them seriously.

Jules jerked his head in the direction of a patchwork
curtain on the far wall. "This way."

We'd almost reached it when we were intercepted by
a tiny woman with a shaved head. I tried not to stare

235

at the intricate designs of taffa vines that were inked onto her skull. "Hello, Diego."

Diego swept a bow. "Elle. Can you tell him I've come to trade?"

She nodded and vanished behind the curtain, reappearing a few moments later. "Two can go in," she announced. "Diego and one other."

I pulled Connor away for a quick conference.

"I'll do it," I whispered.

"I'm not happy about you going in without me. You can't use your ability on cue, and you're not armed. We should have brought the stunner."

The stunner was back in my pack, left behind in Jules's pod. I'd carried it all the way from the Firstwood, but Jules had said not to bring weapons to the Lion.

"It'll be fine," I said. "Anyway, Jules will be with me."

"That's not very reassuring."

"Would you really rather I waited out here?"

He examined the tent through narrowed eyes, and I knew he was picking up on the same thing I had. Not everybody in this room was absorbed in talking about their dreams. One way or another, we were surrounded by the Lion's crew.

Connor sighed. "Be careful."

I walked back over to Jules. Elle stood aside, letting

us past to the curtain. Jules issued a set of low-voiced instructions. "I'll give him a false name for you, because he's probably heard about Ashala Wolf. He'll offer us taffa. Don't refuse it. He won't do any trading until we've drunk it. It's kind of a ritual with him."

"Got it."

We ducked through, and I blinked in surprise at the sight of walls made of composite, not canvas. The opening we'd come through must have cut into the side of the building that adjoined the tent. Two things struck me immediately. The first was the familiar red books on the shelves that lined the walls. *The dream journals.* The Lion was the one keeping records of the taffa dreams, and judging by the number of books he had, it was something of an obsession.

The second was the Lion himself.

He was dressed in a yellow robe and reclining on one of the two couches that were positioned on either side of a small table. I studied him, taking in as many details as I could. The Lion was a big guy—tall, broad shouldered, and a little overweight. He had a flat nose and caramel-colored skin that contrasted startlingly with his shaggy platinum-blond hair. His eyes were half closed, as if he were almost asleep. I didn't make the mistake of thinking that he was.

A mottled desert cat emerged from behind the couch to wind around Jules's legs. "Hello, Misty," Jules said, bending to pet her. He nodded at the Lion. "Hello, Leo. This is my — ah, associate, Rachel."

Leo opened his eyes a fraction wider. "Pleased to meet you." He waved at the couch opposite. "Sit."

We sat. The Lion rose and strolled with lazy, easy grace to a sideboard at the end of the room. He returned with a tray containing a flask and three cups, which he set down on the table before sinking back into the couch. The cat leaped up to sit beside him.

Leo shook his head at Jules. "Diego, is it? That face is giving me a headache."

Jules shimmered, changing back into himself. *He's using his ability in front of a Citizen?* I tensed, ready to fight or run. Jules finished his transformation and grinned when he caught sight of my expression. "Leo doesn't care, darling."

I cast a wary glance at Leo, who — well, didn't seem to care. He poured taffa into the cups, setting one before me and one before Jules. We picked them up.

"New blend, Leo?" Jules asked, taking a deep appreciative sniff of the taffa.

"A mixture of Dawn Scarlets, Moonlight Mists, and Summer Storms."

I took a cautious sip. It tasted . . . good. Really good, much better than the taffa I'd had in Gull City when I was kid. It was rich and sweet, without being too sugary. I gulped down another mouthful.

"What do you think?" Leo asked.

"Excellent," Jules replied.

I opened my mouth to agree, only before I could speak, there was a whisper at the edge of my mind. **Greetings.**

I froze, my fingers tightening on the cup. Except the whisper faded so fast I wasn't sure it had been there at all.

Jules nudged me. "Rachel?"

Who's Rachel? Oh yeah, that was the alias he'd given me. I pasted a bright smile on my face. "The taffa's really good."

"A well-balanced blend, if I do say so myself," Leo said in satisfaction. "You must pay close attention to your dreams tonight." He paused and then added, "I study taffa dreams, you know."

As if I hadn't noticed. But I knew the signs of someone who wanted to talk about their particular obsession. It was exactly how Trix acted about her giant hoard of quandong seeds. "Do *all* those books have dreams in them? That's amazing!"

239

Leo shrugged offhandedly, but I could tell he was pleased.

"Rachel's never had a taffa dream," Jules said, in a tone that indicated this was a terrible tragedy. "She's from Gull City."

Leo's eyes sparked with interest. *Because the only thing obsessive types enjoy more than showing off the collection is educating people about the collection. . . .* He could educate me all he wanted if it encouraged him to help us.

"You must know a lot about taffa dreams. What do you think they mean?" I asked.

"Some say that the dreams show us the past," Leo answered. "Others say it's the future. I believe both those things are true." He leaned closer. "Except I also believe the dreams can show us the Balance itself. A glimpse of a single moment from what lies beyond." His expression grew introspective, dark eyes staring at something I couldn't see. "I have spent my life in search of the perfect moment."

He looked sad—no, more than sad. *Bleak.* Had I done something wrong? I cast an alarmed glance at Jules. He didn't seem concerned, just drank his taffa and motioned to me to do the same. I wasn't enthusiastic about consuming any more of the stuff, not after that weird whisper, but I knew I had to. Leo wasn't going to trade until the taffa was gone.

I took another sip and waited. There was no whisper. I was starting to relax when a voice rolled across my mind.

I am She-Who-Stalks-by-the-Light-of-Stars-and-Is-Adored-by-All-Who-Gaze-Upon-Her. You may call me Starbeauty.

It took all the self-control I had not to jump off the couch. Was I the only one hearing that? I certainly seemed to be. Jules was chugging taffa, and Leo was staring broodily into his cup. *Where is the voice coming from?* There was only me and Leo and Jules in here. Then my gaze fell on the cat. What had Jules called her? *Misty.*

It was the sort of name that a human would give a cat. Only I'd bet it wasn't at all the kind of name a cat would give herself. I stared at her. She stared back out of smug green eyes, twitching tufted ears in my direction. She seemed to be a totally ordinary desert cat.

I am the First.

Or maybe not.

I tried answering in my head. *The First?*

For all things, there must be a first. I am the First Cat. I thought I was the oldest of those that survived the great chaos. But your grandfather is older even than I. There was a reluctant note of admiration in her voice. A most ancient and powerful being.

I have been traveling, Grandpa had said, *and met others like me.* When I got back to the Firstwood I was going to have to ask him exactly where he'd gone. Apart, obviously, from here. These were so *not* the best circumstances to be encountering an old earth spirit— and Leo and Jules were staring at me again. They'd finished their taffa, and I hadn't.

I began to gulp it down, and called out to Starbeauty, *Does Leo know what you are?*

No. I am not certain he knows how to know.

That actually made sense to me; it wasn't an easy thing to absorb the presence of ancient spirits in this world.

I do not wish to worry him. He is my pet.

I choked on taffa.

Jules slapped me on the back as I coughed and spluttered. After a few moments I got control of myself and managed to swallow the last of my drink. The second I set down my empty cup, Jules reached into his pocket and drew out the little bag. He put it on the table, loosening the top to allow a single bean to spill out.

Leo straightened. "Are those . . ."

Jules nodded. "Blackout Grays."

The Lion reached down to pick up the bean between thumb and forefinger, studying it. He was impressed; it was a good start.

I'm here to rescue my friend, I said to Starbeauty. *She's in a lot of trouble. If you've got any advice on how we can persuade Leo to help us . . .*

If I help you, you will be indebted to me.

I'll pay you back, I promise. I knew it was reckless to say that to an ancient spirit, but I didn't care. I'd do anything to save Em.

She leaped down and padded across the floor to jump onto my lap. *Is this supposed to be the help?* I asked, stroking her silky fur.

Starbeauty didn't answer, just purred.

Leo put the bean carefully on the table. "What is it that you want for these?"

"Information," Jules answered. "On our old friend Terence."

"Something you don't feel able to ask him yourself?"

Jules spread out his hands. "He and I have had—a falling out."

"Indeed?" Leo eyed him up and down. "May I compliment you on being surprisingly healthy. People who have a falling out with Terence generally begin to feel rather ill."

Jules grinned. "I've found a way to solve that problem. Leo, we think Terence is holding someone here in the city."

"A red-haired girl?"

"Yes!" I exclaimed. Leo and Jules both looked at me—Leo with interest and Jules with a frown.

"Um, I mean," I stammered, "yes, that's who we're trying to find." Then, because I couldn't help myself, I asked, "Do you know if she's okay?"

"From what I understand, she is well enough," Leo replied. "And I do not think she is being 'held.' She appears to be with Terence of her own accord."

"The situation is complicated," Jules said, shooting me a glare that I had no difficulty in interpreting as S*hut up*. "Is Terence staying in his usual place?"

"He is."

I heaved a silent sigh of relief. Even if Leo wouldn't help us, we had a location, and Jules knew the layout of that house. *We can save her.*

"I won't attack Terence, Jules," Leo warned. "Not even for Blackout Grays. It would invite retaliation, and I have no intention of starting a war with him. At least, not over some scheme of yours."

244

"I'm not asking you to attack him. I just need to know exactly where the girl is in that house. And I want a way in. A quiet way."

The Lion sat back, subjecting Jules and me to a contemplative stare. He wasn't sure about helping us. I called out to Starbeauty, *What should I do?*

Wait. He has not yet asked you the question he must ask.

What question?

She didn't answer. Leo's gaze dropped to Starbeauty, then lifted to my face. "She does not usually take to strangers, although I suppose I shouldn't be surprised that you are good with animals, Ashala Wolf."

I froze, clutching Starbeauty's fur. She hissed, and I relaxed my grip as I stared at Leo. *He knows who I am!*

He is a very clever pet.

"Ah, Leo," Jules began, "it's —"

The Lion held up a hand. "Spare me the denials. Did you really think the leader of the Tribe could come into Spinifex City and I wouldn't know?"

"Does anyone else know?" I demanded. "The government — or Terence . . ."

"Of course not," Leo replied in an offended tone. "This is *my* city. And I have no interest in anyone discovering you here. In fact, quite the reverse. I do not

245

want other governments in the world to begin paying attention to what is happening in Spinifex City. But," he added, fixing me with a cold stare, "for exactly the same reason, I will not have a revolution here, Ashala Wolf. It will cause a disruption that could affect the taffa supply."

"Believe me, I'm not here to cause a revolution."

"Then why are you here? For this girl who does not appear to be in trouble, and who is involved with Terence in some way? A man who is known to loathe Illegals?"

Jules opened his mouth to speak. Leo shook his head at him. "No. I want to hear from her."

The question he must ask . . . He'd always known who I was, and he suspected my motives because of it. I thought reproachfully at Starbeauty, *You might have told me that he knows who I am.*

You are not my pet. And you should tell him the truth. About why you wish to rescue her.

It wasn't as if I had another plan. "I don't have a scheme, and I'm not here to disrupt the taffa, or anything! All I want to do is save my friend. The red-haired girl. Her name is Ember, and whatever you think, she's in terrible trouble."

Jules chimed in. "It's Terence you should be worried about, Leo. Ember is a Tribe member, and Terence brought her here. He's the one who's delivering problems to your door."

Leo ignored him. "She is your friend?"

"My *best* friend." I suddenly remembered the bleakness I'd seen in him before. I'd experienced enough loss in my life to know grief when I saw it. *I have spent my life in search of the perfect moment. . . .* A glimpse into the beyond. The Lion knew what it was to lose somebody, and to be desperate to see them again.

I'd been keeping a tight control on my emotions ever since we'd arrived in the city. I stopped, allowing my own desperation to rise up and show in my face. "She's in danger. She's alone. And I won't abandon her. So if you want me out of this city, help us. Because I'm *not* leaving without her."

For an endless moment the Lion and I stared into each other's eyes. Then he gave a slow nod. I leaned back, feeling at once shaky and triumphant.

I have given you wise and sage advice.

And I'd thought Grandpa could be annoying.

Leo switched his attention to Jules. "I have someone in the house. I will arrange for them to let you in, and you can wear their face. It will allow you to move around undetected." His hand hovered over the Blackout Grays. "Do we have a deal?"

"We'll need to know exactly where she is," Jules said.

"My agent will tell you that. But, Jules—I will only get you in. You must get yourself out."

Jules nodded. "We have a deal."

Leo swept up the bag.

"How long will it take you to organize this?" Jules asked.

"Not that long. Are you staying in your pod?"

"Yeah."

"I'll get word to you there. You should expect to hear from me this afternoon, or tomorrow."

"We'll be waiting."

Jules rose to his feet, shimmering back into Diego. Starbeauty jumped down from my lap to curl up at Leo's feet. I stood as well, dusting cat hairs off myself as I followed Jules out.

I will not forget that you owe me a debt.

I paused, hand on the curtain. *I figured you wouldn't.* Then I hesitated, watching Leo. He wasn't paying attention to me; he'd tipped the beans onto the table and was examining them one by one. He seemed so . . . isolated in his obsession. So sad. Would I have become like this, if I hadn't had Georgie to help me after my little sister died? Probably. Even *with* Georgie and the Tribe, I'd only recently been able to remember the joy of Cassie's life without being overwhelmed by the horror of her death.

On impulse, I said, "You know, I saw the sunrise over the desert this morning."

Leo glanced up, blinking as if he was surprised to find me there.

"I've never seen a sunrise like that," I continued. "The colors are softer where I'm from. Here it's all reds and oranges, the same as the sand and the rocks. For a while, it seemed as if the land was in the sky, and the sky was in the land."

He frowned. "Is there a point to this?"

"Yeah. I think there're a lot of perfect moments in this world."

He stared at me for a moment longer. Then, for the first time since I'd met him, Leo smiled. It was a surprisingly sweet smile, with something open and innocent and joyous about it.

"Go save your friend, Ashala Wolf."

THE REVELATION

We had some time, so the three of us wandered through the market. A few hours and a good meal later, and we were all back in the pod, sitting on the floor among the crates of taffa.

"We should talk about who goes in to get Ember," Jules said. He'd changed into himself again and was leaning over a piece of paper, sketching out a map of the house.

"All of us!" I replied.

"We're trying to be sneaky, darling. I'm the one who'll be masquerading as someone who belongs there. It's better if it's only me."

"You won't be able to convince Ember to go," Connor pointed out.

Jules stopped sketching and nodded in my direction. "You could tell me something to say to her, something that only you would know. She'll come if she knows you're here."

She would, too, because she'd realize I wouldn't leave this city without her. It was still a bad idea. "You're not going in alone!"

"No," Connor agreed. "I'm coming with you, Jules. Ashala—I do think you should stay here."

"What?"

"Ember will know you're here the second she sees me, so we don't need you with us to persuade her, and two people are better than three for getting in and out quietly. If there's trouble, you can't defend yourself with your ability."

"I can use the stunner!" But the second I spoke, I saw the problem with that idea. If I had the stunner, Jules didn't, and he couldn't use his ability to defend himself, either. Which meant if we got into a fight with the minions, Connor would have to protect whoever wasn't armed.

It would put him in danger, and I wasn't going to do that.

"All right," I agreed reluctantly. "I'll stay behind."

Jules still didn't seem very happy. "Why don't you both come out and say it? Neither of you completely trust me."

"No," I told him cheerfully, "we don't. Now, how about finishing that map?"

He sighed and went back to drawing. When he'd finished we all stared down at what was, I had to admit, a pretty good blueprint.

"How many of the minions are likely to be in the house?" Connor asked.

"Probably three," Jules answered. "He generally keeps three with him."

Connor ran a thoughtful gaze over the map. "It's a big house. If we're careful, if we're lucky, we should be able to avoid all three."

He and Jules got into a discussion about escape routes, while I kept staring at the drawing. There was something about the arrangement of the space that was bothering me. *The long room that fronts onto the internal courtyard . . . the upstairs room right above it, the one with the balcony . . . It couldn't be.* She'd told me her house had been reassigned to another family after they'd left.

"Is there a fountain in that courtyard?" I demanded.

"One with Hoffman quotes etched into it? And a tree right beside it that has pink flowers in the spring?"

"Yeah," Jules said. "How did you know?"

"It's *Ember's* house!"

Connor frowned. "This is where she lived before she came to the Firstwood?" He eyed Jules suspiciously. "And you didn't know?"

"Hey, that house was empty the first time I saw it. I figured Terence picked it at random."

"When did he start using it?" I asked.

"'Bout three and a half years ago. Before that . . . he never used to come to this city. Sent me a few times when there was something he wanted here."

"Ember and her dad left over four years ago." So it made sense that Jules didn't know about the house. "He must have taken it over after they went."

Jules grinned. "She's done this."

"What?"

"Think about it, darling. Out of all the places in the world Terence could have taken her, she's here. Somewhere she knows. Somewhere she understands."

Somewhere she has friends. All those reformer types her dad had been involved with, for a start . . . I grinned back at Jules. He was right, Ember had to be responsible for

Terence being here. It made me feel better that she was acting like her usual tricky self.

The three of us talked for a while longer, making plans until we ran out of things to discuss. Then we settled in to wait. Jules lounged on the bed. Connor sat with his back against a taffa crate, and I cuddled up against him with my head pressed to his chest. The afternoon wound slowly on, creeping toward evening. I measured the passage of time by the sound of Connor's heart beating against my ear and didn't mind the wait at all.

I was starting to wonder if we'd hear from Leo today when there was a knock at the door.

Jules shimmered into Diego and bounced over to open it. He spoke to someone outside—Elle, from the tent—and closed the door again, rippling into himself.

"Well?" I demanded.

"We're on. We need to be at the back entrance of the house at seven tonight."

Yes! We had our way in.

"We should leave pretty soon, actually," Jules said. "It'll take the best part of an hour to get there."

He bit his lip, seeming—nervous? It was hard to tell; I'd never seen him nervous.

"Jules? Is everything okay?"

"Yeah. 'Course! It's only . . . I mean, I'll be seeing her again. . . . I wonder what she's . . ." He shoved his hands in his pockets. "Can I talk to you? About Ember?"

"Go ahead."

"It's, um, kind of personal. . . ."

I couldn't be sure from this far away, but I thought he was actually blushing. I exchanged an amused glance with Connor.

He pressed a kiss to the top of my head and got to his feet. "I'll wait outside for a few moments."

Jules looked relieved. "Thanks." He came over to drop to the ground in front of me as Connor left the pod, and leaned in to whisper, "You need to speak quiet, okay? He shouldn't be able to overhear through the door, but I don't want to take any chances."

"Okaaaay." I was starting to get a little worried about exactly how personal this conversation was going to be.

"I've got to tell you something. Something Ember left out of the memories."

"Wait, what? I thought you were going to talk about—"

He grinned. "I know."

I threw him an exasperated look. "You realize I'm

one of the people who doesn't find you at all charming, right?"

"Really?" He assumed an exaggerated expression of hurt. "Not even a little?"

"Jules," I growled.

"Okay, okay. Now, when I tell you this, I need you to stay calm. Because . . ." He jerked his head at the door. ". . . I know he can feel what you're feeling when you get real upset."

"Who told you that?"

"Ember. And you're going to want to think about what I've got to say before you tell him anything."

This didn't sound good. "What's this about?"

"You remember how I told you Terence goes by different identities, in different cities?"

"Yeah. I remember." It was one of the things we'd talked about on the way to Spinifex City. "So what?"

"I gave you the impression he moved around a lot, which he does now. Only he didn't used to. In fact, for as long as I've known him, he's mostly stuck with one city. Gull City."

"Terence is from Gull City? What does that have to do with Connor?"

"You're concentrating on staying all serene and relaxed, right?"

I glared at him. "Would you just tell me what you're trying to say?"

"He isn't only 'from' Gull City. Until a bit over a year ago, Terence *ran* Gull City."

I choked. "You can't mean . . . Terence *Talbot*? Ember's brother was the Gull City Prime?"

"Remember to stay calm!"

He was right, I had to control my reaction before Connor sensed it and came back in. I couldn't tell Connor this, not until I'd had a chance to process it. I drew my knees up to my chest and rested my head against them. Then I focused on breathing, slow and deep and steady. *Don't feel. Think.*

Terence Talbot. The Prime responsible for the harshest enforcement of the Citizenship Accords in decades throughout Gull City and its associated towns.

The Assessor who'd scared a Rumbler into causing the quake that had killed Connor's mother.

He was supposed to be dead. In fact, it was his unexpected demise that had changed the entire trajectory of Connor's life, putting him on the path that had led him to the Firstwood, and me. Talbot had died of a stroke.

Aingls couldn't die of a stroke.

I lifted my head. "Why did Terence fake his death?"

Jules shrugged. "Your guess is as good as mine. All I could think of was that he'd got tired of having the responsibility of running a government. He didn't exactly share his reasons with me."

And my best friend had always known that Prime Talbot couldn't possibly be dead. I choked back a bitter laugh. *More secrets, Em?* "When did she talk to you about this?"

"She didn't, exactly. She left me a memory. Contained in a can of soup, of all things."

Of course she did. There had been a gap in the memories, between her leaving Jules in Fern City and meeting Delta. Even when Ember was telling me things, she wasn't telling me everything. "I don't understand why she'd leave out something so important!"

"She didn't want you blurting it out to Connor without thinking about it. I was supposed to find a moment alone to tell you."

"And you couldn't have picked any *other* moment?" I asked through gritted teeth.

"Hey, it hasn't been easy to get you alone. Besides, I wasn't going to tell you at all."

"Why not?"

His expression was uncharacteristically serious. "Because I'm here to save Ember. And I didn't want to take the chance that you and Connor would be here for something else."

"You think I'd put her at risk for revenge?"

"I couldn't be sure you wouldn't. Not when it involved him." He shook his head. "You don't even see the way you two are with each other. All tangled up together. Why do you think I was trying to get you to let me go into the house alone?"

"I would *never* put Ember at risk, nor would he."

"I'm not so sure about him, darling. You, though . . . When you said to the Lion that you weren't leaving without her, you really meant that." He sighed and added, "You know, if we do this right, we'll get Red out without running into Terence. Except things might not go right."

I would've liked to smack Jules's head against the floor. And Ember should have told me this a very long time ago. But I didn't have time to be mad at either of them, so I shoved my anger away and tried to think.

I'd told Jules that Connor wouldn't put Ember at risk, but I actually wasn't sure what he'd do if he had a shot at Terence. Because in a lot of ways he and I were alike, and I wasn't sure what *I'd* do if I were confronted by any of the people involved in my sister's death. *He could get himself killed.*

And I'd already watched him die once.

There was only one thing to be done. I didn't know if it was the right thing. I was afraid it wasn't. But it was the only thing. Because I could not lose him. Not ever again.

I stood up. "Go tell Connor to come back in here. And stay outside. I want to speak to him alone."

Jules rose as well. "What are you—"

I snarled. "Get out and let me handle this, Jules!"

He hurried to the door. I darted over to where my pack lay on the ground and rifled through the contents until my fingers closed over a cold metallic object. I'd barely gotten it into my pocket when Connor came back in.

At the sight of him, feelings rushed over me like a wave; I concentrated on rising above them. I obviously wasn't successful, because he took one look at my face and demanded, "What did he—"

"It isn't Jules. It's you."

"Me?"

I'd learned, from the way Ember had talked to her sister, that it was possible to say things that were true without being quite the truth. "Connor, I . . . Hearing Jules talk about how he feels about Ember made me think about how I feel about you. Going into that house will be dangerous."

"Ashala. I'll be fine. Anyway, Jules will be with me."

He was teasing me, throwing back the same words I'd said to him in the Lion's tent. I discovered it was possible to smile even when you wanted to cry. He smiled back.

I let myself drink in his expression, just for a second, the curve of his lips and sparkle in his eyes. Then I stepped closer, bowing my head to rest it against his chest and reaching my hand into my pocket. He put his arms around me and whispered, "You won't lose me."

I answered miserably, "I know." And fired the stunner.

He let out an odd, shocked gasp, then was silent. I grabbed his body as he slumped, lowering him to the floor as gently as I could.

Jules stuck his head around the door. "Hey, don't mean to interrupt, but I thought I heard . . ." His eyes widened and he came in, slamming the door behind him. "What happened?"

There was a wolf howling in my head, only this time the wolf was me. "I shot him."

"You did *what?*"

I ignored Jules, grabbing one of the packs and using it to cushion Connor's head. Then I retrieved a blanket and laid it over him. It would get cold later. After that I couldn't think of anything else to do, so I sat on a crate and shook.

Jules took a step toward me, eyeing the stunner in my hand. "Ah, why don't you give me that?"

I pointed it at him. "Why don't you try to take it?"

He backed off. "Just a suggestion, darling."

I lowered the weapon. Jules looked from me to Connor and shook his head. "I can't believe you shot him."

"That is because you don't know me at all," I hissed. "You think spending a few days with Ember means you understand her, or me, or the Tribe? You don't."

"Yeah. Listen, I can see you're upset—"

"Shut *up*, Jules." I lurched to my feet. "You should have told me about Terence the moment you came to the Firstwood. If you had, we could've found another way to handle this. You didn't, and now . . ." I paused, took in a painful breath, and gestured at Connor. "Now it's come to this. So. Is there anything else you haven't told me?"

"No."

I waved the weapon in his direction. "Don't lie to me!"

He held up his hands. "I swear to you, there's nothing."

He seemed to be telling the truth. I sat back down. Jules did, too — cautiously, and about as far away from me as he could get.

The shaking in my limbs got slowly better. The churning in my stomach didn't, nor did the tightness in my chest. After a while Jules cleared his throat and said, "Ah — we need to leave now."

I nodded and rose. Spent a moment gazing down at Connor, before bending to tuck the blanket more securely around his body. *He's never going to forgive me. Not for this.* Then I took everything I was feeling and locked it away.

I was Leader of the Tribe, and I had one of my own to save.

THE RESCUE

Forty-five minutes later, Jules and I were lurking in an alleyway. He'd been Diego for most of the journey here, but had shimmered back into himself now that we were hidden in the gloom of the alley. The two of us peered out in the rapidly fading daylight, watching a square two-story house. It looked the same as all the others in the row: made of white composite stained red with dust, with a thin strip of land running along the outside, enclosed by a high wall.

What distinguished it were the two guards standing on either side of the back gate.

The first was a mousy, thin boy; the second a

heavyset older woman. Both were dressed in yellow robes; both were watchful. I couldn't see any weapons. That didn't mean they didn't have some concealed, or that they weren't armed in other ways.

I whispered to Jules, "Minions?"

"The boy is," he whispered back. "The other one . . . don't think so. All the minions are young, at least the ones I've seen."

"What's his ability?"

"Dunno, I only met him once. Whatever it is, I guarantee he'll be able to do a lot of damage with it."

I remembered how the Waterbaby had taken the water from Jules's body on the road through the Deep-wood, so I pressed a little farther into the alley. It occurred to me that the guards and us were the only people on the streets in what was evidently a quiet neighorhood. "Don't the two of them seem kind of obvious?"

Jules stifled a laugh. "Yeah. Terence'd be better off keeping his people inside and blending in with everyone else. He doesn't do real well at understanding things like that. He thinks in straight lines, and in this city . . ."

He didn't finish the sentence, but he didn't have to. *You need to think around corners.* Jules could do that. Ember, too.

The gate between the guards creaked and swung open. I edged forward to get a better view as a dark-skinned old woman shuffled out, holding a tray containing two cups.

Jules whispered in satisfaction, "Marta."

"You know her?"

"I've worked with her a couple of times before, when I've done jobs for Leo."

"*She's* the Lion's agent? She's ancient! What is she even doing in that house?"

"Probably the cook. And don't worry about Marta, she's a tough old bird."

I watched as Marta offered the drinks to the guards. The woman took one of the cups—*bet it's filled with taffa*—and sipped at it. The boy shook his head. Marta held the tray out to him and said something in a quavering voice. She was a round lady, but her wrists and ankles were tiny, and the tray trembled in her grasp.

The boy took the cup, probably for no other reason than to please a sweet old woman. *Guess at least one of the minions isn't completely devoid of human emotion.* Marta rested the tray against the wall and chattered brightly as the guards sipped their drinks.

Then the woman collapsed, the cup falling from

her hand. Marta clung to the boy, babbling in alarm. He was shaking free of her grip when he, too, slid downward to the ground.

Jules strode across the street to catch Marta up in a bear hug. "Hello, darling! How's the best-looking girl in Spinifex City?"

"Don't you try to flatter an old lady," she said, with a laugh in her voice. "And do get moving, dear. We need to get these two hidden away."

Jules and I pulled the unconscious guards through the gate, dragging them behind the trash cans.

"That girl you're after is in one of the upstairs rooms," Marta whispered. "Go up the back stairs, turn left at the end of the corridor, and it's the fifth door on the right."

"What about the minions?" Jules asked.

"There's one on the front door, and one asleep in the little bedroom near the kitchen — she's got the next guard shift, only they won't change over for another hour. You want to watch out for all the other guards as well."

"How many?"

"Five of them, always prowling around and sticking their noses into my kitchen. Be careful."

"I'm always careful."

She didn't seem reassured. *Guess she knows him pretty well.*

"Um, are you going to be okay?" I asked her. I didn't care what Jules said; I felt bad for involving an old lady in this. "I mean, they'll know what you've done. . . ."

"No, they won't, my love," she replied. "I put a Mender's drug in the taffa, something that confuses the mind. They won't remember most of today, and I'm due to go off shift soon." She cast a fond smile at Jules. "As long as he doesn't wear my face for too long, no one will connect me with this. It's sweet of you to worry about me, though." She elbowed Jules. "Don't tell me you've finally met a nice girl?"

"No!" I choked.

Jules shook his head. "She's got a boyfriend. Scary guy. Although," he added under his breath, "maybe not as scary as she is."

It was too dark to make out Marta's exact expression, but I could sense a disappointed gaze aimed in my direction. She reached up to kiss Jules's cheek and trotted off out the gate, moving much faster than I would've thought possible when I'd seen her shuffle out the first time.

Jules transformed himself into Marta, and the two of us sneaked inside.

We crept through the corridors until we reached a hall cupboard that wasn't far from the stairs. The plan had been for Connor to hide in here until Jules returned with Ember; now I would.

"Tell Em that she's not alone," I said to him. "She's got us."

That should be enough to convince her I was here. Jules bobbed Marta's head at me and hobbled onward with the slow walk I suspected was as fake for Marta as it was for him.

I waited in the dark, the stunner clutched in my hand. *He's been gone for an eternity*—no, it had only been a few minutes. *Wait, is that voices?*

I strained to hear. Someone was talking. I couldn't make out who. They were speaking in normal tones, without any shouting or urgency, which meant there probably wasn't any need to be worried.

The voices faded and everything was silent again.

It was horrible being trapped in this cupboard. I began to count, to keep track of time and to give myself something to focus on. *One, two, three* . . . When I reached five hundred, I was worried. Nearly ten minutes had passed, and that was too long. Jules should have been back.

I eased open the door. There was no one around, so I tiptoed up the stairs, one cautious step at a time. *Along the corridor, turn left*—and there was Jules. He was standing in the middle of the hallway, still disguised as Marta and looking frantic.

"What happened?" I demanded.

He waved an arm at one of the rooms that came off the hall. "She's not here."

It was stupid not to believe him. I checked the room anyway. Bed, closet, bookshelves . . . no Ember. "I don't understand! Where did she go?"

"I got delayed on the way up by one of the guards wanting to thank me for dinner. Marta's too good a cook! By the time I got up here . . ."

"She can't have gone far."

The two of us ran along the hallway, pressing our ears to doors to see if we could hear anything, and then opening them up. Every room was empty.

There was a shout from downstairs. Someone had realized the guards weren't at their post.

I stopped still. Breathed. Thought. And shoved the stunner at Jules. "Take this. You probably won't even need to use it. In the confusion, you should be able to slip right by everyone."

"What about you?"

"I'm staying. They'll increase security after this; we'll never get back inside."

"They'll catch you!"

"Em will fight for me in a way she won't fight for herself. She'll get me out. Or you and Connor can come back and save both of us."

He stared at me, hesitating.

We've got no time for this! "You want to save her?" I growled. "This is how we do it. Go hide, Jules. I'll lead them away."

He stepped closer. "You tell Red . . . tell her I don't yield her. Not to Terence, not body or soul. And," he added fervently, "you'd *better* stay alive, because if you die, Connor's going to kill me."

He ducked into one of the rooms, and I ran in the opposite direction of the stairs that were his escape route, crashing into things to make as much noise as possible. It wasn't long before there were pounding steps behind me. I began to scream Ember's name, and the footsteps of my pursuers sped up.

I rounded a corner, skidded, and kept going. A

door ahead of me opened — and there she was. She looked exactly the same as when I'd last seen her, except for the yellow robe.

My Em.

All the color drained from her face. "Ash?"

I stopped, putting my hands in the air for the benefit of the guards. "I surrender! I surrender!"

Ember's odd-colored eyes widened in alarm, focusing on whatever was behind me.

"No!" she yelled.

Something hit the back of my head, and everything went black.

THE AINGLS

I was standing on a hill. I had a vague idea that I should be somewhere else, except I couldn't remember where. Anyway, there was only the hill; everything else was a blurry nothingness.

A man was waiting at the very top. I couldn't see his face from this distance, and I knew it was important that I did. So I started to climb. Up, and up, and up. When I got close, he swung around.

White hair. Long nose. Pleasant brown eyes. And a mouth that turned up at the corners, as if he smiled a lot.

It was my old enemy Neville Rose.

I took a step back. He flung out his arms and shouted, "Look what I have done!"

I looked but couldn't see anything. Until I shifted my gaze downward and realized what I had been walking on.

The hill was made up of bodies. Thousands of them, all piled up together. Not only humans, either — animals. Plants. Trees.

This was the death of the world.

I lunged for Rose . . .

. . . and found myself sitting upright in a bed.

A dream. It was only a dream. I hugged my knees to my chest. *It's okay. Neville isn't here. The world isn't dead.* The whole thing had just been a horrible, scary, unusually vivid dream.

Wait — vivid dreams? I'd drunk taffa with Leo. *Was that a taffa dream?*

If that was what one was like, I never wanted to have another. And what did it mean? Not anything good, if taffa showed you the future. *Please don't be the future.* Surely it *couldn't* be. Neville was a prisoner. There was no way he could cause the death of the world.

I still feared the possibility.

The Adjustment was less than three weeks away,

and Neville might already be at the center. I needed to be home.

I just had to get Ember first.

I stood up and was immediately so dizzy I had to sit back down. *Oh, yeah. I got hit over the head.* I fingered the lump at the back of my head and looked around, assessing my surroundings. I was in a small bedroom. There were tables on either side of the bed with books sitting on top, a wardrobe against the far wall, and low bookcases running under the window crammed with even more books.

I was about to try standing for the second time when there was movement in the corridor outside. I flopped down, pulling the covers over me and pretending unconsciousness. I heard a key turning in the lock. The rasp of the door opening. Measured steps approaching the bed. Then no sound at all, which was much worse.

Someone was in here, and they were watching me. I struggled to keep my breathing even and my body still.

There was a rush of air as someone bent down, and a voice whispered in my ear, "I know you're awake, Ashala Wolf."

I shot up and scooted over to the other side of the bed, away from the voice. The quick movement made my head pound and my stomach lurch, but I had to get away from the man standing over me.

It was Terence Talbot.

He smiled at my reaction. I had no difficulty interpreting that smile.

This wasn't the first time I'd been captured by someone who enjoyed seeing me afraid.

He sat on the side of the bed, and I edged as far away as I could. He looked much younger than he had when he'd ruled Gull City; if I hadn't known he was an aingl, I would've taken him for a relative of the former Prime. Otherwise, he was the same. Pale skin, light-blue eyes, hair somewhere between blond and brown. The color of his yellow robe seemed to be the only vivid thing about him. Everything else was washed out.

Terence crossed his legs and clasped his hands together over his knee. "I am Ember's brother Terence. You will tell me, please, how you knew my sister was here."

He obviously wasn't going to waste any time on chatting. I scrambled for a good answer, one that wouldn't reveal that Jules was still alive. Terence waited. He seemed relaxed, but his knuckles were white where his hands were gripped together. He wanted to know. Ember had called him paranoid in the memories she'd sent me. It would bother Terence that I'd been able to track him down. It would bother him a *lot*.

I couldn't think of anything to tell him, at least nothing plausible. I tried to buy some time. "You weren't that hard to find."

He blinked once, a slow closing of his eyelids. "You will discover that it is not wise to play games with me."

In the space of an instant, the air had grown thick with menace. I grasped hold of an answer and blurted it out. "Ember told me about the house she lived in when she was in Spinifex City, and I thought she might be here. So I came."

For a long moment, he was quiet, watching me out of those faded eyes. Then he nodded. The tension in the room eased, and I gulped in a breath.

"And how did you get in?" he asked.

"Your guards were no match for a Sleepwalker," I lied.

His face tightened in anger, and I could feel the danger again, building up like the beginnings of a rogue wave. "I just need to see her," I said hastily. "To . . . talk to her."

"You will see her."

He said that as if it were a threat rather than a promise. I stared at him, trying to work out what was going on. He stared back, nostrils pinching like he'd smelled something bad. I knew that mixture of revulsion and fear. I'd seen it in Gull City while growing up — it was the way some Citizens looked at Exempts. *He hates people with abilities.* I'd known that about him, of course, but understanding it from a distance wasn't the same as experiencing it up close in this little room.

"I think you know things about me," he said.

My heart slammed against my ribs. "I don't know anything. I only came here for Em."

"She has told you things she should not have. The location of this house, for example. Which is why she is going to make you forget."

"Forget?"

He nodded. "You will lose any information you hold about my family. This house. And much of what you know about Ember."

Ember wouldn't change my memories like that. But she might have lied and promised him she would as part of some plan I didn't understand right now.

Unless she really *would* do it to save me . . .

No, she couldn't. Hiding memories people didn't

278

want to forget made them crazy. Ember was up to something.

I licked dry lips. "What about after she makes me forget?"

"I will let you go." He smiled at my expression of surprise. "You are fortunate that my sister is attached to you. She has insisted that you be allowed to leave."

My mind raced. *Terence needs Delta, and Delta needs Em, and she's convinced him that she'll make me forget, even though she won't. Then how will she escape?*

Maybe she wouldn't. Maybe she was still planning on staying with him. Which meant I had to convince her to come home.

"Let me share a story with you, Ashala," Terence said in his soft, precise voice. "About how memory works."

I eyed him warily, wondering where he was going with this, and knowing it could be nowhere good.

"Some time ago, I lived near a girl who survived a fall from a cliff when she was very young. She had no recollection of the accident. But for the rest of her life, she was utterly, mindlessly terrified of heights." He blinked his slow blink. "Her body remembered, you see."

Creepy story. And I didn't like the cold calculation in his gaze. My hand crept out toward the table beside the bed. A couple of the books on it were thick and heavy, I could do some damage with one of them if I had to.

"I know Ember is the reason you can survive in that forest, and survival is a powerful motivator," Terence continued. "Potentially powerful enough for you to seek her out even after you have lost your memories." His face twisted, slipping into madness. "And I really cannot have you finding her again."

He exploded across the bed and wrapped his hands around my throat. I kicked out uselessly as his grasp tightened. Spots appeared in front of my eyes, and my hand jerked, clutching at the books. I managed to get hold of one of the big ones and swung, smashing it into the side of his head.

He snarled and squeezed harder. I hit him again; it had no effect. *He's willing to endure pain to get what he wants.* . . . The book slipped out of my grasp as I struggled to drag precious oxygen into my lungs. I couldn't get enough. My vision was going black, and my chest was burning, and I was never going to be able to get enough air to survive.

A furious voice shouted, "Terence!"

The hands around my throat were abruptly with-drawn. I rolled off the bed and staggered away. It hurt to breathe. I didn't care; it meant I was still alive. Ember was standing in the doorway. With the light from the hallway beyond making a fiery halo of her hair and her eyes flashing with rage, she looked like . . . an angel. The kind from the old-world stories, the ones that had wings and rescued you from bad sit-uations.

She cast a worried glance in my direction. I couldn't speak. I couldn't do anything but lean against the wall and draw in as much air as possible. But I gave her a small nod, to let her know I was okay. Mostly.

Em shifted her attention to Terence. He'd risen to his feet and had one hand clapped to the back of his head. I *had* hurt him.

It just hadn't mattered.

"We had a deal, Terence," Ember snapped.

"I am aware of that." He seemed a little woozy, but his voice was eerily serene. "I was merely making sure your friend understood something." He looked me up and down, his gaze lingering on my damaged throat in a horribly satisfied way. "Your body will remember, Ashala Wolf."

I managed to stay upright as he walked out,

listening to his footsteps disappear down the hallway. Then I stumbled over to collapse onto the bed.

"Em," I said hoarsely, "there is something very wrong with your brother."

She shut the door, her eyes huge in her pale face. "I know."

THE DEAL

She ran over. "Ash, I can help, but I'll have to use nanomites. I'm not sure how you feel about . . ."

"If you have a way to fix this, do it!" At this point, Ember's nanomites weren't even close to being on the list of things that scared me.

Em sat, leaning across the bed to put her hand on mine. I expected to be able to sense the tiny machines flowing into my body. I couldn't, but after a few moments the fire in my lungs and pain in my throat vanished, along with the lingering throbbing in my head.

I was okay. *And Terence is gone, and Ember is here.*

Em let me go, and spoke in a rush. "I'm so sorry, Ash, I didn't know he was with you. He went crazy when you came, raving that you must know things. I convinced him I could make you forget—he was supposed to leave you alone!"

Yeah, well, he's got this nutty theory about memories. . . . That wasn't important now. "We have to get out of this place, Em. Jules and Connor are in the city."

"I can't come w—*Jules* is here?"

"He's the one who figured out where you were."

"That's . . . I wasn't even sure he'd . . ."

She was getting all mixed up. Ember, who never lost her way with words. *She really likes this guy.*

I wasn't above using that.

"He gave me a message for you. He said to tell you—he doesn't yield you to Terence. Not body or soul."

She stared down at the bed, looking miserable. "I have to stay. If you've seen the memories I sent, you know the reason why."

"It's *because* I've seen the memories that I know you *don't* need to be here. You've got a way to break up Delta and Terence, Em. You thought so yourself, outside Fern City."

"It's not that simple."

"It is, too. Terence only came after you because of Delta. So break 'em up, and let's get out of here."

"Will you listen to me? You know how I tell you that you can't achieve positive change with violence, only with ideas?"

"Yeah, you've said that to me about a zillion times. And I don't see how it matters right now."

"What I never told you was that *ideas* can be violent. That they can shape violence, and justify it and per-petuate it. I once did something very bad, Ash. And as if that wasn't enough, I had a bad idea."

I frowned. "What does this —"

"Listen!" She raised her gaze to mine. "The bad stuff I did, I'm going to tell you what it is, and I'm going to do it in front of Terence and Delta. Because it's something so terrible that you aren't going to want to remember it."

My jaw dropped. "Terence said you'd make me forget — Em, you're not *really* going to mess with my mind?"

"It'll only be temporary, Ash. The bad thing is all tangled together with my family, and I can use it to submerge your memories of us. I'll make Terence and Delta think it's permanent, but I'll do it so everything resurfaces in a few weeks, I promise."

Oh. This was better; she actually did have a plan. Except it was for my escape, not for hers. "I'm not leaving here without you."

"You aren't going to want me to come."

I rolled my eyes. "Em, you can't possibly believe that I care that you aren't, um, organic."

"I wasn't sure how you'd feel about it."

"Well, just to be clear: I. Do. Not. Care! And you should have known that, Ember Crow." I couldn't understand how she'd been so stupid. Or, no, I could, because I'd seen the reason, in her memories. It was hard for her to believe that anyone could value her when she placed so little value on herself.

"I'm glad that you don't care," she said quietly. "That's not why you won't want me with you, though. Once you find out what I did . . . Ash, there're some things even you can't forgive."

"There're really not. At least, not when it comes to you. Tell me what you did and I'll prove it!"

She shook her head. "Please don't ask me. Not yet. I've got to take you to Terence and Delta, and before I do I want to explain something. I want you to understand what you've meant to me."

"I know already."

"You don't." She smiled at me. It wavered at the edges. "You see, the bad thing I did was something I couldn't live with. It made me sad. So sad that Dad had to reset me. He made *me* forget."

"Forget what?"

"Everything, including that I'm synthetic. He made me think I really was a seventeen-year-old Illegal. The knowledge of everything else — everything I'd done, everything I was — came back a bit at a time. Dad thought if I learned about it slowly, I'd figure out how to live with it."

"And that made you better?" I asked doubtfully. It sounded awful, to have everything you believed to be true turn out to be false.

"Only for a while. Dad ended up having to reset me a *lot*. The last time was about five years before I met you. And I was doing okay. The reform movement was finally gathering strength, and it helped to be doing good. Only I lost Dad, and I was sad. Really sad. I was going to shut myself down. Then you found me. And you said . . . you said . . ."

"You're not alone. You've got us."

She nodded. "You see, I couldn't function in the world, not as my whole self. I couldn't overcome the limitations of my nature. I wasn't real. You made me real, Ash."

Oh, Ember. I reached over to squeeze her hand. "I know you think you're like that puppet made of wood in the old-world story. You aren't. You were *always* real. You were always human. I didn't change that. I just helped you to see it."

Her lower lip trembled, and for a second I thought she was about to burst into tears. Ember, who never cried. Then she pulled her hand away and strode to the door. "We have to go, Ash."

Her eyes were dry and her voice was steady. *I'm not going to be able to convince her to run. Not yet.* All I could do now was wait to hear whatever it was she thought was unforgivable, and show her it wasn't. After that point, we'd have to improvise.

I followed Ember out of the room and along the hall. She led me through a door and into a big, airy lounge that was dominated by two puffy couches. Delta was reclining elegantly on one of them. Terence was sitting on an armchair in the far corner, watching me through washed-out, hostile eyes.

Ember nodded at her brother. "I've brought her here, like we agreed."

"Then let us begin," he replied coldly. "This business has already taken up too much of our time."

The two of us sat down on the couch opposite Delta. I perched on the very edge of the seat in case I had to move fast; I had no faith in Terence's self-control. As for Delta—Ember's sister was examining me with the bright-eyed interest of a child being given a new toy. I split my attention between her and Terence, trying to keep watch on them both.

Ember spoke. "Ash, to understand what happened, you need to know how things were hundreds of years ago. Right after the Reckoning, when there were only a few people with abilities, and everyone was starting over. Back then, my family was trying to create a perfect society."

"Each of us took responsibility for a city," Delta chimed in. "It was so much fun! Only . . ." Her voice trailed off, and she directed an angry glare at me. "Human beings messed it up. We needed them to unite so everyone could survive, and they wouldn't. They fought over *everything*."

Terence shifted, drawing my attention, and I tensed at the sight of the anticipatory gleam in his face. We were getting near to whatever it was Ember had done, and it was going to cause me pain. "Then one of us had an idea. A perfect idea for an imperfect species." He looked at Ember. "Will you tell her, or shall I?"

My best friend seemed to have hunched in on herself, becoming very small.

"Em?"

She lifted her head. I'd never seen her look more sad, or more determined. "Ash. I invented the Citizenship Accords."

I stuttered out an instinctive denial. "You—you couldn't have!"

"I did. I came up with the idea that Illegals were unnatural, that they weren't part of the Balance. People needed something to bind them together, or humanity wasn't going to make it. So I gave them an enemy."

I shook my head. "No. *No.* I don't believe it. I won't believe it." I sorted through history in my mind. "Besides . . . besides, you couldn't possibly have been solely responsible! The accords were made after that Skychanger flooded Vale City."

Ember's face was a mask of misery. Delta was watching me with creepy fascination. And Terence was smiling. It was the only warning I had that something even worse was coming.

"I'm afraid you still haven't understood, Ashala," he said, shaking his head in mock sympathy. *"There was no Skychanger."*

I opened my mouth. Words wouldn't come out. All I could do was stare at Terence as he continued, *"We diverted a river to flood the valley, and when it was done, we told everyone that it was the work of a Skychanger. We gave humanity an enemy."*

I turned to Em. I almost expected her to have changed, to look different. She didn't. She was still my Em.

Only not. "Ember? Weren't . . . weren't there people in that city?"

"It wasn't the same as cities are now," she said defensively. "It was only a little collection of houses."

"But you *drowned* it?"

She met my gaze squarely. "Yes."

My head was pounding again, so hard that I could barely see. It was too much. It was all too much. I clutched at the arm of the couch, clinging on to something solid in a world tipped upside down.

Ember's eyes went wide. "Ash? Are you okay?"

No, I'm not okay! How could I be okay after what I'd just heard? Everything was coming apart, and the room was growing dim, and there was a roaring in my ears. No, not a roaring. Barking. I was hearing a dog barking.

How strange. Something was obviously very wrong. Maybe Ember's nanomites hadn't fixed my head after all. Or maybe this knowledge was too great a burden for my mind to bear.

I fell, slipping from the couch onto the floor. Ember shouted out my name. Delta said, "She seems to be having some kind of seizure."

And then I was somewhere else.

I was standing amid yellow grasses, beneath a clear blue sky. *I'm on the grasslands? I can't be!* I waited for what had to be a hallucination to dissolve. It didn't. Instead there was movement in the distance, and a Labrador came tearing toward me.

I was so happy to see Nicky, to see any friend at all, that I didn't care that he wasn't real. I crouched down as he came close, hugging his neck and pressing my face to his soft fur. He let me hold him for a moment before wriggling free. I straightened, watching as he dug for something in the grass.

He returned to drop a bone at my feet.

This was . . . familiar. I'd seen something very like this scene before, when I'd been hooked up to the black box in Detention Center 3. The machine had made me think I was on the grasslands when I'd really been inside my own mind. There'd been a dog there, too, a half-metallic hound that was actually the machine itself, trying to get at my secrets. And bones . . . bones had represented memories.

So why was I seeing all this again now?

Nicky nosed the bone toward me. I stared down at it, noticing that there was something wrapped around one end. A lock of hair.

A lock of red hair.

I sat on the grass and thought furiously. Before I went into the center, Ember had buried one of her memories in my head. A moment that defined her, although I'd never known which one. It hadn't mattered then. What had been important was that having the memory meant I'd carried a fragment of Ember with me into that terrible place.

Was that fragment somehow reaching out to me, trying to show itself? And if it was, did I want to experience it? Nicky obviously thought it was a good idea, but I didn't know what he represented, here in my head. *It doesn't matter.* Because if there was any chance this was the memory that defined Ember, I *had* to see it.

To know, for once and for all, who my best friend was.

I picked up the bone. There was a familiar shifting sensation as the memory took hold of me, and I became someone else.

I became Ember as she had been, hundreds of years ago.

THE MEMORY

Rain sprinkled down, pattering over the lake and misting the air above the wildflowers carpeting the surrounding hills in pink and white. *Everlastings.* That's what those flowers were called. An appropriate memorial for Dominic. He had loved flowers, along with every other tiny thing about this world and all of the people in it.

I stepped toward the man standing at the water's edge. "Dad?"

"Ember."

I winced at the coldness in his tone and did not speak again. Instead I stared out over Lake Remembrance, thinking, as I knew he must be, of the bodies submerged in the depths. Twenty-six people, drowned fifty-four years ago.

"Are you sorry, Ember?"

The asking of that question had become a ritual between us. For as long as I had been meeting my father in this place on this day, I had always given the same answer. *They deserved to die.*

I didn't know what my answer would be today, so I didn't give him one, not yet. "Terence isn't very happy about the virus you introduced into our systems. The one that stops us from doing violence."

"Yes, I imagine it will rather cramp his style. What do you think of it?"

"I don't know, Dad. I'm not sure I know about anything anymore."

He studied my face with fiercely intelligent hazel eyes that had always seen too much, and too little. "Ah."

I delivered my defense. "We didn't hurt the animals or children. Only the adults, the ones who participated in Dominic's death. They deserved to die."

But my voice lacked conviction, and he heard it. "Tell me why, Ember."

I recited all the reasons I'd told him, and myself, a thousand times before. Reasons founded in the awful, wrenching details that Terence had extracted from Dominic's killers. "It wasn't just that they murdered him when he'd done nothing but care for them. It was the way they did it. They *voted,* Dad. The heads of all the families in Vale City held a meeting and voted."

"It was a conspiracy."

"Yes! And it makes me crazy that Dominic saw them after that meeting, and they smiled at him. As if nothing was wrong. When they knew that in a few hours, they were going to take him apart with the tools *he'd* made! Tools that were supposed to build, not destroy."

"It was an evil thing, Ember. Done simply because he was different, and they were afraid of that difference. I am not denying it."

"And he suffered, Dad. What the Nullifier did, the way she suspended the connections in his brain, it would have made him helpless, not numb. He would have felt every cut they made in his body." I stared grimly at the water. "Drowning was a far kinder death for them than what they did to Dominic."

"And what of the girl? The girl your brother loved so much that he told her what he was?"

"She *hated* what he was. She couldn't stand to be loved by a machine. She used her ability to paralyze him. And besides," I snapped, "we didn't kill her."

"No. You dealt her a crueler fate. Forcing her to watch

as you drowned the city. Telling the world that she was the Skychanger who'd caused the flood. And changing her memories so she thought it herself."

"I didn't know I couldn't permanently hide a memory someone wanted to hold on to. I didn't realize it would drive her mad."

"But it did. It was no surprise that she took her own life."

"She *still* died more quickly than Dominic!"

My father rounded on me. "Do you truly think that I did not love my son as much as any of you?"

"No," I answered in a subdued voice. "I know you did. You loved him best. We all loved him best."

"Then *why* am I standing here telling you that you should not have done what you did?"

I sighed. "You'd say it was vengeance, not justice. You'd tell me that you can't defeat evil by doing evil. That . . . that all life matters, or none does. Even if that life belongs to those who have harmed us."

"Yes."

"You could have told us all those things at the time," I pointed out rebelliously. "If you'd been here."

"I may have miscalculated in leaving you all alone," he conceded. "I didn't expect that one of these 'abilities' could be used to destroy you."

"You always think you know everything, Dad, but you don't. We had to do the best we could to protect ourselves."

"And what, precisely, do the Citizenship Accords protect you from, Ember?"

I hunched my shoulders, saying nothing, and he added, "The Nullifier ability appears to be the only one that could ever be used to permanently harm you. And it's apparently an extremely rare talent."

"It isn't only about abilities. They said Dominic was an offense against nature. So I gave them something else unnatural to persecute instead." I swallowed. "We were terrified that they'd come for all of us, and we don't know what happens when we die. We don't know if we go to the Balance, because we're not . . . not . . ."

He shook his head. "Ah, Ember. You are as human as any organic being, though you are made from different materials. Think of your brother. Do you really doubt Dominic had all the best qualities of humanity?"

I thought of my little brother and smiled a painful smile. "No."

"And those who killed him embodied the worst. Don't you see? Whether we are organic or synthetic, whether we walk on two legs or four, whether we are creatures of claw or hoof or wing or feet—it matters not. Composition does not determine character. Or greatness of soul." He was quiet for a moment, then added, "The governments of the world are building more detention centers. Increasing the scope of the accords. Locking up children now."

"I know."

"Are you sorry, Ember?"

No. I'm not sorry. I don't want to be sorry. "Yes."

"Tell me why."

"For all the reasons you would tell me to be," I answered quietly. "But most of all because, if Dominic were still here, or if he's out there somewhere in the Balance, he'd be so . . . disappointed in me."

"Yes. He would."

I bowed my head. "Dad? I'm sad."

My father put his arm around me for the first time in over fifty years, and said in a satisfied tone of voice, "Good. That is a beginning."

THE BREAK

The memory dissolved into mist, and the world returned. I was lying on the floor with Ember crouched at my side. Delta was standing behind her. I couldn't see Terence. *Probably still sitting in his chair, hoping I'll quietly die.*

"Ash?" Ember asked. "Are you all right?"

I croaked, "My head hurts." And closed my eyes.

The truth was, my head wasn't hurting anymore. But I needed some time to absorb what I'd seen and to control my heaving stomach. I felt sick over Dominic's death, and over what Ember had done afterward. Except I understood the reason she'd done it, a reason that my foolish, wounded best friend obviously hadn't been going to share with me. *I know what it is to feel what you felt, Em.* I'd wanted to do something terrible to everyone I blamed for my little sister's death. Only I'd had someone to stand in my way. The one person who could have stood in Ember's way hadn't been there when she needed him. Alexander Hoffman really wasn't the guy I'd thought he was.

Lucky she had me.

I opened my eyes again. I needed to get Em to break Terence and Delta apart, and I didn't want to give either of them a chance to stop her. We had to take them by surprise. Which meant I needed to let Ember know I wouldn't abandon her, *without* letting Delta and Terence know it as well.

Reaching up, I clutched at her arm and hissed, "You're a machine."

She flinched, and I continued, "I can't believe I tried to save you! You really are just a collection of circuits. No one who truly understands what you are would ever try to save you!" *Jules called you a collection of circuits, and he came here for you. Listen to what I'm saying, Em.*

I hauled myself to my feet, dragging Ember up with me. "I understand what you are, Ember Crow,

302

and there will *never* be a place in the Firstwood for a machine. I will never give a home to a machine."

Realization dawned in her odd-colored eyes. Because I had brought a machine into the Firstwood. I'd brought Ember the black box when I'd fled Detention Center 3, and asked her to build a body for the dog-spirit I'd seen at its core.

"You really mean that," she whispered.

"Yes," I answered steadily. "I do."

The corners of her mouth crept up. She nodded, and I let her go.

Ember swung around, pushing me behind her. Terence rose to his feet, looking supremely satisfied. "Are you ready to begin altering her memories?"

"No," Ember replied. "I'd like to ask you something, Terence. About Dominic, and what you did with his remains."

The triumph in Terence's face shifted into alarm. Delta directed a curious glance at him. "Terence? What does she mean?"

"The circuits, Del," Ember said. "The last pieces of Dominic. He gave them to a *human*."

Terence came striding hastily toward us. "Don't listen to her! She's trying to —"

Ember shouted over the top of him. "Ask him, Del. Ask him about how he handed Dominic over to Neville Rose, the former head of Detent—"

Terence lunged. I grabbed hold of Ember's shoulder, spinning her out of the way just as Delta sprang into the space between them. He stopped still, shooting a hate-filled gaze at Em but obviously unwilling to provoke Del further. *Ha! Gotcha!*

"Terence?" Delta sounded very young. "You didn't do that, did you? You wouldn't."

"He did," Ember snapped. "And Rose used the circuits to build an interrogation device."

The machine? I blinked, reeling, as connections cascaded through my brain. A black box. A black dog.

She'd built the body after all.

I'd *met* Ember's baby brother. I'd gazed into his eyes and seen his bright spirit. *I should have recognized him.* How could I have failed to notice the similarities between the goofy, graceless hound who'd once bounded through my head in Detention Center 3 and the dog I'd met in real life? The one who'd remembered me, even when I hadn't remembered him. And, somehow, he could still connect to my mind, just as he'd done when he'd been the machine. Dominic.

Nicky.

"That device was in the center when the fire started," Ember continued. "All that was left of Dominic—" She broke off, shaking her head. Not actually telling a lie but allowing her sister to jump to the wrong conclusion.

Delta turned an accusing gaze on Terence. He held out a placating hand. "Let us be clear what we are talking about. Those circuits weren't really Dominic, any more than a few skin cells constitute an organic being. It—"

She leaped, clawing at him, and the two of them went staggering across the room. He fended her off and she grabbed a vase from a table, smashing it onto the top of his head. Terence backhanded her across the face, knocking her to the ground. It didn't slow Delta down. She flung herself into his legs, sending him sprawling. Then she sank her teeth into his calf.

Terence yelped. I caught Ember's arm. "Let's go!"

The two of us ran out into the long hall. We were about halfway down it when Ember stopped abruptly. "We're going to need something to get past the guards outside. Come on."

She dragged me through a doorway and into a bedroom. Every available surface was covered with bits of electronic equipment. "Del's room, huh?"

305

"Yep." Ember hurried around, gathering bits of machinery. Then she sat down on the bed and began connecting things together. When she was done she had a small, messy tangle of wires and circuits.

"What does that do?" I asked.

"If it works right, it'll help us get through the back gate. But we need to avoid getting caught on the way there."

The two of us raced through the house, moving as fast and as quietly as we could. When we reached the door, I eased it open and peered out into the darkness. No one there, at least not on this side of the back wall. Ember bent over her little device, fiddling with it. Then she dashed outside and lobbed it over the top of the gate.

"Shut your eyes, Ash. Now!"

I did. There were shouts. A popping sound. And the night was lit up with a flash so bright I caught the edge of it even with my eyes closed.

Ember seized hold of me. "Come on!"

We charged past the guards, who were tottering around blindly, and pelted into the night.

"Where are we going?" Ember panted.

Good question. "Jules has this trader pod, only I'm

not sure I can find the way there. It's near the taffa market, though. Do you know where that is?"

"Yes. Follow me."

We sprinted along the well-lit streets. It wouldn't be hard for any pursuers to locate us. I cast a worried glance over my shoulder.

"Those guards won't be able to see again for another hour," Ember puffed, "and everyone . . . will be waiting for Terence . . . to give them orders. He won't be doing that for a while. I think we're okay."

"What about Delta? Do we have to worry about her chasing after us?"

Ember shook her head. "I've been working on her . . . reminding her . . . of all the things she didn't like about Dad. She was already . . . losing enthusiasm . . . for bringing him back. Besides, she's going to be . . . too busy making Terence suffer . . . to think about anything else . . . for quite some time."

I nodded. Another few blocks and the two of us slowed to a jog; we had to make it all the way across the city and we couldn't run flat-out for the entire distance. We went on, saying nothing as we both concentrated on getting far away from the house.

It wasn't difficult to tell when we were approaching

the market. The smell of taffa grew stronger, and the streets more crowded. Eventually there were so many people around that we dropped to a walk so we could merge with the masses. Jogging was beginning to make us conspicuous; strolling, we were indistinguishable from the rest.

"Ash?" Ember leaned closer to me. "Are you sure you want me to come back? I could still—"

"I know how Dominic died, Em."

She stopped dead. I yanked her along. "Keep moving."

"How do you know?" she breathed.

"Nicky told me himself. Sort of. I can see him in my head, same as when he was the machine."

"You can see him in your head? I don't even know how he's doing that!"

"Well, I'm glad he is. How could you not tell me? You know I get what it's like to do something crazy when someone you love is murdered!"

"It was more than crazy. It was unforgivable, and *why* I did it makes no difference."

"It makes a difference to me. And you're not the only Tribe member with a past. Yours is just a little more . . . epic." A lot of the Tribe hadn't had the best of times in the cities and towns, and they hadn't been

308

the best of people, either. "You know how it goes, Em. Before is nothing. All that matters is what Tribe members do with their lives once they've been given a chance to *have* a life. And you—you made a bad choice once. But," I concluded firmly, "you've been making good choices for as long as I've known you."

She was quiet. Then: "Ashala Wolf." I could hear the affection in her voice, and the awe. "Everyone's second chance. Even Nicky's."

"You're the one who built him a body," I pointed out.

"A body is nothing without a consciousness, and he didn't have one. I think you brought him back, Ash."

"Pretty sure I can't do that, Em."

"You brought Connor back."

"*Grandpa* brought Connor back."

"He still worked through you. And they hooked your brain up to the box in the center, the same brain that lets you transform reality when you Sleepwalk. You saw the machine as a dog, and that's what he became. When I opened up that box, my brother was there. Only not quite as I'd known him."

"Did you *know* the machine was Nicky, before I went into—"

"I had no idea! Terence must have been funneling

309

Neville advanced tech to use on Illegals. Neville was always a big supporter of his, when Terence was . . . um, I guess you know he was the Prime."

"Yeah. And that's number one on the list of things you should have told me, by the way."

"I'm sorry," she whispered.

I nodded and let it go. I didn't have the time to pursue it, and I didn't want to; not when I had so many other things to think about. *Did I really bring Nicky back?* I wasn't sure, but I hoped I had. Because I understood, now, that he'd brought me back — not from the dead, but to myself, when I'd wandered too far from who I was. *Those Sleepwalking dreams, back in the Firstwood.* The nightmare where people who didn't love me had been tearing me apart . . . Nicky had been showing me his death, and the importance of holding on to love when you found it. And the later dream, the one about being a monster who was forced to hunt — that was what had happened to him when he'd been the machine. In the center, when I'd freed him from Miriam Grey's control, I'd told him he was a good dog. In my dream, he'd given that same reassurance to me. *You are good.*

I'd thought the forest had been reaching out to help me heal my ability. It had been Nicky all along.

I had to get home to him. I had to get home to everyone.

"Em, did you know Neville and Grey are coming to the center? They're holding the Adjustment there, in less than three weeks. And I had this horrible dream about Neville. I think it was a taffa dream. A warning."

"We'll be home before the Adjustment," she said. I recognized her tone of voice; it was her bracing, everything-will-be-okay tone. We were falling into a familiar pattern, of sharing worries and comfort. "And I'm not sure taffa dreams mean anything, Ash. You've probably heard about them a lot since you've been here, because they're the particular obsession of someone in this city, only—"

"You know the Lion?"

"Of course! Wait, you do?"

"He got us into the house. Jules traded some rare beans for his help."

"*Beans?* He should've helped for free if he thought I was in trouble!"

"I don't think he does anything for free—and I'm not sure he was convinced you were in trouble. How do you know him, anyway?"

"Ah. That's—I mean—Ash, he's my brother."

It was my turn to stop in the middle of the street, and Ember's to tug me along. *"Which one?"* I demanded.

"Five."

Five to nourish land and heart. Yes, I could see that being Leo. And he was high on the list of those who could be trusted, right after Dominic and Em. I sighed in relief.

Then I scowled. "Got anything *else* to tell me?" I wasn't sure if it was because everything was finally sinking in, but I was beginning to feel annoyed. "Any more relatives hanging around this place?"

"No. I'm sorry, Ash. I was going to send you a message telling you where every one of my family was, once I had a location on them all."

"You should have told me years ago."

"I know, and hush!"

I had spoken too loudly. But I was suddenly, overwhelmingly angry at her for hiding things from me, for not having any faith in me, for . . . *oh.*

"Em. Sorry. It's not me. Well, not entirely. It's Connor."

"What?"

"I'm picking up on what he's feeling. He's somewhere nearby. And he's *really* mad."

I oriented myself on the sense of approaching fury and headed toward it. "This way."

"Why is he so angry?"

"Probably because I shot him."

"You *shot* him?"

"With the stunner. I didn't want him coming to the house; I was worried he'd go after Terence."

"Ash . . ."

"I had to keep him safe." I sounded defensive, even to myself. "I mean I—it seemed like the right thing to do. At the time."

We made our way into another street—and there was Connor, racing toward us with two yellow-robed figures following behind.

"Are you all right?" he demanded, tearing up to me.

"I'm totally fine."

He pulled me into the light of a streetlamp and scanned my face. Whatever he saw must have satisfied him, because he nodded and took a step back. I knew he'd wait to yell at me later when we were alone. Or maybe he wouldn't yell at all, which was much worse. There was a coolness to his rage, a terrifying sense of distance.

Ember nodded at the people who'd been following him. "Who are they?" she whispered.

"Help. From the Lion. I'm not sure if you know—"

"I know him." She peered around. "Is Jules with you?"

"He was. He's . . ." Connor paused, and when he spoke again, his tone was very gentle. "Ember, there's something wrong with Jules. He became very ill, very fast. I left him with the Lion's Mender, but . . . I'm afraid it doesn't look good."

Ember swayed. I put my arm around her, hugging her to my side. "Em . . ."

She drew in a ragged, shaky breath, focusing on Connor. "Let's go to Leo."

THE ATTACK

Elle was waiting to meet us at the entrance to Leo's tent, which, like the market itself, was as busy as it had been during the day. She escorted us past the people talking about dreams, through the room where we'd met Leo earlier, and into the house that adjoined the tent. We followed her along a series of hallways to a large, bright room filled with two rows of neatly made beds. *An infirmary of some sort.*

She ushered us in and left. The only occupants of the room were Jules — lying in a bed at the far end — and Leo, standing beside him with his broad shoulders resting against the wall. The Lion straightened as we entered, focusing on Ember. "Hello, little sister."

Connor drew in a sharp breath.

"Em says he can be trusted," I whispered hastily. "He's the fifth."

He nodded in acknowledgment as we hurried over to Jules, who was asleep. I was shocked by how frail and worn he was, and the way there somehow seemed to be less of him than there had been before. *He looks like he's dying.* He looked like he was dying *soon.* How had he gotten so sick so fast?

"He was conscious a minute ago," Leo told us. "One of you can try speaking to him if you like."

Ember settled on the bed. Connor and I moved away, giving her space.

"Jules?" she said softly. "Can you hear me?"

There was no response. She tried again, speaking more loudly this time. "Jules? It's Ember."

His hazel eyes blinked open, widening in delighted recognition. "Red! You're okay."

"Yes. And you're going to be all right as well."

"Don't trouble yourself about me." He reached up with obvious effort and tugged on one of her curls. "Think I don't know when the game is done?"

She clutched at his shaking hand, holding it to her cheek. "It isn't. You're going to be *fine.*"

"It's okay, darling. No regrets. Glad to go out . . . doing something right." He smiled his crooked smile at her. "You were a good bet, Red. The best."

She bent to kiss him, a long kiss filled with heat and desperation. I understood what it was to kiss someone like that. I looked away, only to meet Connor's steady gaze. I knew he was remembering, as I was, the kiss we'd shared outside the center, when I'd been trying to pour life into his broken body. His heart had started to beat, and that kiss had become a single perfect moment where the two of us had been each other's world. Tangled up together, Jules had called us, and he'd been right.

Connor's expression grew distant, and his eyes flicked away from mine.

I felt as if someone had sucked all the warmth out of the room. It was my own fault, this breaking of trust between us, but knowing that didn't make it one bit easier to bear. *What have I done?*

Ember spoke. "Sleep." I glanced back to see she had her hand resting on Jules's chest. *She's talking to her nanomites.* Jules's eyes slid shut and his breathing deepened.

Em stared up at her brother out of a white, miserable face. "What's wrong with him?"

"That requires some explanation." Leo jerked his head at Connor and me. "What do these two know about us?"

"You can say whatever you like in front of them."

He raised an eyebrow. "You didn't used to share information so easily. That toxin Terence doses his servants with—"

"I got rid of the toxin!"

"Yes, I deduced that much. However, every system in Jules's body is shutting down, and the Mender cannot heal it. He seems to have been deprived of something that he is hopelessly dependent on—not the toxin, I think, but the antidote."

She went even paler. "I told him he didn't need the antidote anymore, not when I'd taken the toxin away!"

"There was no reason for you to think otherwise. Unfortunately, it appears that prolonged use of the antidote results in a dependency upon it. It's either an unexpected side effect, or . . ."

"Or Delta engineered it that way on purpose," Ember finished, a bitter note in her voice. "So that even if someone found a way to purge the toxin from their system, they wouldn't survive. It's the sort of thing Terence would have asked her to do."

"And the sort of thing she would have done, simply

to see if she could. I've tried giving him the antidote—
I've had some stockpiled for a while now, in case it
was ever useful—but it's made no difference. Once
the shutdown starts, it seems to be too late to use it."

She swallowed. "How long . . ."

"My Mender thinks he has a week."

Em let out a whimpering noise.

I hated to see her like this. "We can go back to the
house, find Delta, see if she can help—"

"She won't want to help, Ash," Em whispered.

"Nor would I be inclined to trust any solution she
presented you with," Leo put in. "It'd be just as likely
to kill him faster. Delta is exceedingly careless with
human life."

"There isn't anything you can do for him with
nanomites, Ember?" Connor asked.

She shook her head. "I could only help before
because I'd already figured out how to deal with the
toxin, years ago. I have no idea what to do about this!
I need time. Longer than a week."

"Well," Leo said, "if time is the problem, there's
always the stasis chamber."

I mouthed at Connor, "Stasis chamber?"

He answered in a low voice, "I'm not sure what it
is. But to keep something in stasis is to preserve it."

His tone was clipped and shorn of emotion. *Doesn't particularly want to talk to me. Got it.*

"It might not be completely functional, of course," Leo continued. "It's been sitting around for a hundred and twenty-three years now."

"I didn't think you still had it!" Ember said. "Where is it?"

"You remember the cave where Father used to work? I've been using the place as a storehouse. It's there."

Hope lit up her face. "It's worth a try. Only I'll need a vehicle to reach it. And a sample of the antidote would also be useful."

"I suppose I am to provide you with these things?" Leo sighed. "Are you quite sure it wouldn't be better to let this human go now? Before you become even more attached? He will die eventually, you know. And you won't."

What a horrible thing to say! I cast an indignant glare at Leo. But Ember didn't seem to mind. "I'll take whatever time I have, Leo. The same as you did, with Peter." She reached out to squeeze his hand briefly. "Are you really going to tell me it wasn't worth it?"

The Lion smiled his rare, sweet smile. "No, I am

not going to tell you that." He patted her shoulder and strode to the door. "I'll get the antidote."

I opened my mouth to ask Ember exactly where this storehouse was, and thought the better of it when she leaned over to brush Jules's hair gently back from his face. *Let her be, for now.* Connor still wasn't looking at me, and I could sense both his anger and his absolute unwillingness to discuss it at this moment. No point in speaking to him, then. I wandered over to a bed and stretched out, sitting up with my back against a pillow. After everything that had happened, it would be nice to sit for a while and absorb the events of the evening.

I have decided how you can repay your debt.

On the other hand, perhaps what I *really* needed was a conversation with an ancient spirit.

Starbeauty came padding in and leaped up onto the bed to loll at my feet. **You must keep the chaos from returning.**

Do you mean . . . the great chaos? The Reckoning?

Those were bad times. Difficult to survive. Even for cats.

There were suddenly a thousand cats in my head, yowling in pain and terror. Their voices merged and changed, turning into a mournful roar that lingered in my ears, and I knew I was hearing one of the lost lions.

The sound vanished as quickly as it had come, leaving an empty silence behind.

Shaken, I said, *Starbeauty, I had this bad dream about a hill, and bodies, and the death of the world. Is that what you're afraid of? Was it about the future?*

If life is a ball of string, then what is before, and what is after, depends on where in the ball you begin.

I thought about those words for a second, in case they would make more sense if I did. Nope. *The man in the dream . . .*

He is a bad man.

You know about him?

I know about taffa dreams.

Of course she did. It couldn't be a coincidence that those dreams only happened in a city where an old earth spirit resided. Maybe they really *could* show you lives beyond this one. Or the future . . . *What does the dream mean? I don't understand how Neville could cause the end of the world.*

We each of us cause the end of the world, or its beginning. And you will ensure that there is no death of cats.

I don't know how to do that.

You must learn to understand your power.

What was this, some ancient-spirit conspiracy to deliver me the same mysterious message? *LISTEN*—

She sat up, ears twitching. **Quiet.**

I went obediently silent; I wasn't sure if I was imagining it, but she seemed suddenly anxious. After a second she said, **There is trouble.**

What? Where?

The tent. Come!

She jumped down, bounding out of the room. I scrambled off the bed and ran after her, calling over my shoulder, "There's something wrong in the tent!"

Connor followed. Ember didn't; she must have decided to stay with Jules. *Or she thinks I've gone crazy, chasing after a cat.* I'd found the chance to tell Connor what Starbeauty was right after we'd left the Lion earlier in the day, but Ember didn't know.

Connor reached into his pocket to toss me something as we pelted along behind Starbeauty. *The stunner.* I gripped its reassuring weight as we tore through the house. I could hear screeching and shouts, faint at first, and growing steadily louder and more discordant as we neared our destination. The three of us ran into Leo's dream journal room and burst past the curtain to the tent beyond.

We'd arrived in the middle of a huge fight. Cats were pouring in through the front entrance, deadly, wailing storms of teeth and claw.

Starbeauty plunged into the fray to attack the other felines. Everywhere, people were fighting off cats with fists and feet and . . . abilities? Small bursts of fire were popping. Water was splashing down out of nowhere, and those taffa vines that I'd thought were mere decoration were winding out of the pots to grab hold of furry bodies. *Waterbabies, Firestarters, Leafers* . . . How many Illegals did Leo have guarding this place?

A few cats surged toward us, and Connor threw out his hands, flinging them away with air. I raised the stunner.

You cannot kill a cat in my city!

I couldn't even distinguish Starbeauty from the other cats anymore, but she was obviously keeping an eye on me. Would the stunner kill an animal? I didn't know. I stood there, not knowing what to do, and abruptly noticed that *no one* was really hurting the cats. The water wasn't drowning them, the fire was only singeing them, and the vines were just holding them in place. Even Leo, fighting in the center of the room, was tossing them away without too much force. Cats were the perfect weapon in Spinifex City, and that couldn't be an accident. Someone was using them to strike at us.

There had to be a Yowler somewhere in this tent.

I scanned the turmoil and finally spotted him. It was the mousy-haired boy who'd been guarding Terence's house, the one Marta had drugged hours ago. He threw back his head to let out a wail, and the cats became more frenzied. I pointed the stunner but couldn't get a clear shot. *Starbeauty!* I shouted out in my mind. *It's the boy near the entrance who's doing this. He's using an ability!*

An awful high-pitched screeching split the air. I clapped my hands over my ears, and so did everyone else. On it went, rising in pitch and intensity until it drowned out every other noise. When it ended, there was total silence in the tent. The cats had lost all interest in attacking; they were milling placidly around, and the Yowler was on his knees.

Starbeauty stalked forward, stopped in front of the Yowler, and purred.

Suddenly *all* the cats started purring, even the ones being held up in the air, filling the tent with the low rumbling of felines. Starbeauty lifted up her front paw and pressed it against the Yowler's leg. He whimpered. Then he began to tremble, wrapping his arms around himself as shivers racked his body.

She let her paw drop. **I have saved you all.**

I cast a dubious glance at the boy, who was still shaking. *What did you do to him?*

He speaks the language of cats. Therefore, he belongs to me. All that is of cat belongs to me. I have reminded everyone of it.

Leo strode over to Starbeauty. He was bleeding from a dozen vicious scratches but seemed to be moving all right. He stared incredulously down at her, and she stared back as if to say, *What do you expect? I'm a very clever cat.*

He shook himself, clearly deciding that whatever mystery surrounded his pet could be dealt with later, and glared at the boy. "Why did you attack us?"

"You attacked Terence," the boy replied through chattering teeth. "You all turned on him." Tears began to stream down his face. "I was trying to do what he would want. To earn redemption . . . redemption through service. But I'm not . . . I don't belong . . . I don't know anymore!"

He dissolved into helpless sobs. Leo sighed. Then he drew back his fist and struck.

I jumped as the Yowler collapsed to the ground, unconscious.

It is best that he sleeps. When he wakes, I will make sure he knows that he is mine forever.

That sounded a little scary, but better to belong to Starbeauty than to Terence. *Listen, he'll probably have a toxin in his system. He'll need to take this . . . um, actually, don't worry about it.* Leo had the antidote, and the Yowler was a source of information about Terence; the Lion wasn't going to let him die.

Leo began to issue orders. Secure the tent . . . treat all wounded. . . . People started to organize themselves. Taffa vines unwound to deposit cats gently onto the floor, and Connor allowed the ones he was levitating to drift to the ground. A few Menders were already moving through the space, laying hands on people to heal them, but I was pleased to see that no one seemed to be gravely hurt. Certainly no cats.

The Lion stalked past us and through the curtain into the journal room. He motioned for Connor and me to follow. When we were alone, he snapped, "Has Terence gone mad, launching an attack on me? And with an Illegal? Neither of us wants the governments of the rest of the world looking into the people who work for us!"

"I'm not sure that Terence did send him," Connor

replied. "The Yowler said he was trying to do what Terence would want. Anticipating orders, rather than following them."

"Delta and Terence were fighting when Em and I left," I put in. "Really fighting, I mean, like a knock-down battle. I think maybe the minions — um, Terence's Illegals — believe the other aingls are acting against Terence."

Leo blinked in surprise. "Delta and Terence were in a physical fight? What about?"

Well, he basically desecrated your brother's remains. I couldn't say those words; I wouldn't want someone I barely knew giving me news like that about my little sister. "I think maybe you better ask Ember about it."

His eyes narrowed. "Do you, now? Then you'd better follow me."

The three of us made our way back to the infir-mary, where Ember was standing in front of Jules. She was watching the door with a fierce glare, clearly deter-mined to beat off any potential attackers.

"Is everything all right?" she demanded as we came in. "What happened?"

"It's fine. Now." I rushed through an explanation, leaving out the part about Starbeauty being an ancient spirit—that was the cat's secret to tell Leo, if she wanted—and finishing with, "Um, Leo was wondering why Terence and Delta were fighting."

She sighed. "It's about Dominic."

He frowned, and she drew him aside, speaking softly. Connor threw a questioning look in my direction, and I gave him a brief summation of the origins of the black box, without telling him that Dominic was also Nicky. That was too long a story for now. He must have been as startled by it all as I had been, only he didn't show it. He had a tight grip on his emotions at the moment; if I hadn't been able to sense his anger I'd never have known he was mad by looking at his flawless, impassive face. That wasn't good, of course. It was the mask he wore when he felt things the most deeply.

There was a sudden roar from Leo. "Terence did *what?*"

I looked over at him. The Lion's big body was shaking, and he was clenching and unclenching his fists. Ember said something to him, and he snarled, "He will answer to me for this!"

Leo took a single step toward the door.

Ember darted in front of him. "Vehicle, Leo!

You need to give me a vehicle. And a sample of the antidote, remember? Then you can do what you like to Terence."

It was obvious Leo wanted to go charging after his brother right this moment. But he bowed his shaggy head in a reluctant nod. "Very well, little sister."

THE RESOLUTION

Fifteen minutes later, Ember, Connor, Jules, Leo, and I were moving through the house. We formed a strange procession. Leo strode ahead, with Jules floating behind him, levitated by Connor. He walked at Jules's side, and Ember and I followed. I was wearing my pack, and Connor his; Ember had Jules's, which was where she'd put the antidote sample Leo had given her.

I expected that we'd have to go outside to get to the vehicle. Instead we seemed to be heading deeper into the house. The Lion led us to a staircase that went downward, and we trailed after him into a well-lit basement. There was a weird black car in the middle of the space. It had huge tires and a boxy shape; I'd never seen a vehicle like it. In fact, I wasn't sure there *were* any other vehicles like it. But there seemed to be one very serious problem.

"Um. How do we leave?"

Leo put his hand against a small panel by the stairs. I jumped as the wall ahead of the car slid upward, revealing a long tunnel with tiny lights running up either side.

"That will take you out of the city." He glanced at Em and sighed. "Please don't crash my car. I know how you drive."

She walked over to hug him. "Good-bye, Leo. Try to remember there's more to life than taffa. And thank you."

He wrapped his big arms around her. "Farewell, Ember."

We got into the car — Connor and Jules in the back, Ember and me in the front. There was a bewildering array of screens and lights in front of Em. I watched as she adjusted a few dials and entered a set of numbers — coordinates? — into a keypad beneath a small display. Then she pulled on a lever and the car rocketed forward.

I clutched the door, bracing myself as we barreled

along. In what seemed like no time at all, the end of the tunnel loomed ahead.

We were hurtling toward a flat, blank wall.

Connor shouted, "Ember!"

"It'll open."

We got closer and closer. The wall was still there. "Are you *sure*?" I demanded.

But even as I spoke, it began to slide upward, revealing sand and hills and a starry sky. We shot into the desert, barely making it out under the still-rising wall. Ember was navigating by a screen that showed her the contours of the surrounding countryside, and she didn't slow down one bit, even though we were now bouncing over rocks. We lurched one way and then another as she wrestled the wheel left and right. My teeth rattled and my chest hurt from being thrown against the seat belt; all I could do was hang on and hope that it would end. Soon. Really soon.

It didn't. We bounced and swerved for hours, and almost overturned twice when Ember took a turn too sharply. When she finally screeched to a halt, the orange rays of what was sure to be a spectacular sunrise were shooting across the sky.

She'd parked us in front of a huge cave. Em flung open her door and ran to it, calling over her shoulder,

"Bring Jules." I staggered out, feeling battered, and took in a few calming breaths. When my legs felt steady enough, I made my way into the cave, following Connor and the floating, still-unconscious Jules.

I arrived in time to see what appeared to be a solid rock wall sliding back. At this point, I wasn't a bit surprised to find another hidden space. *There are layers and layers to this world.* . . . The room beyond the wall was filled with—well, stuff, but that was about all I could tell because everything was covered with dust sheets.

Ember dragged one of the sheets off some kind of giant elongated metal container and stood at the panel set into one side of the thing. She pressed a button and a lid rose, revealing a cushioned interior.

"Connor? Put him in there."

Jules floated in and Ember shut the lid.

"Are you sure he can breathe?" I asked.

"He's fine." She pressed a few more buttons. "He's in stasis."

"I don't know what that is, Em."

"This chamber will preserve him exactly as he is. He won't get any better, but he won't get any worse, either. At least, not for a while." She smiled at Connor. "Thanks for the help."

He nodded at her and didn't look at me. "I'll be outside if you need me again."

I cast a glum glance at his retreating back. "I should go talk to him."

I didn't actually move. I was hoping Ember would argue with me, or give me a task to do, because I didn't want to talk to Connor, not yet. I was terrified he was going to say that I'd gone too far and it was over between us.

Ember was unhelpfully silent. Then she whispered, "Ash . . ." She sounded stricken.

I dashed to her side. "What is it?"

She waved her hand at a small display. "This is . . . it's all information about what's wrong with Jules."

The display was filled with numbers and symbols that were completely mysterious to me. "And?"

"And he's been affected worse than I thought. Much worse."

"But you've got lots of time to fix him now."

"Not that long. This chamber is an experimental model. Anyway, it isn't that. He's in such a bad state, I only know one way to save him."

"Um. Surely you only need one way?"

"It's not that simple, Ash! What I'd have to do — I'm not sure if it's what he'd want."

"So wake him up and ask."

"I can't. By the time he recovers from stasis well enough to hold a conversation, it'd be too late to act. If I'm going to do this, I have to start the moment I take him out of the chamber." Her gaze fixed on mine. "I need your advice. About death."

"*Death?* Em, I'm not sure that's something I'm good at giving advice about."

"You have to be." She looked a little panicked. "You see, my family, we have trouble dealing with — endings. It's part of the reason Terence hates Illegals. Before Dominic . . . we didn't know that we could die."

I could see how it would have upended Terence's world to discover he might not be immortal after all. "It isn't only what happened to Dominic that makes him hate us, is it? He's afraid of the *idea* of death. Of having to end."

She nodded. "Then there's Leo. The love of his life died over a hundred and twenty years ago, and he still hasn't recovered."

"Is that who he's searching for in the taffa dreams?"

"Yes. You would've liked Peter, Ash. He was a Mender." She reached out to put her hand on the chamber. "We built this for him. Leo wanted to stop him from deteriorating while he found a way to extend his life."

"What happened to Peter? Did the government hurt him?"

She laughed. "No. He was dying of old age. He and Leo were together for nearly sixty years, except he wouldn't let Leo help him in the end. He said everyone has their time to move on to the next existence."

"Jules isn't old, Em."

"I know," she answered impatiently. "What I'm saying is, Peter didn't *want* his life extended by artificial means. And to help Jules . . ." She bit her lip and said in a rush, "I'm going to have to flood his system with nanomites. To have them take over the functions his body would normally perform on its own."

That really didn't sound so terrible. "And there's a reason why that's bad?"

"First off, I'm not sure how it'll affect him, or even if it will work. Second, if it does work, he won't be completely organic anymore. He'll be something else, and I don't know what that'll mean for him. He might feel he's less . . . human."

Now I got it.

"I need you to tell me what to do, Ash," Ember whispered, "Because I'd do anything to save him. But I'm not sure he'd do anything to live."

I didn't answer her right away. This was a serious

337

question, and it deserved serious consideration, although she'd chosen the most unsuitable person in the world to ask. I'd actually walked in the greater Balance once, when I'd been dying, and I *knew*—as Grandpa had once told me—that death was a great transformation, not an end. Despite that, I'd *still* done something stupid to hang on to Connor, making a choice for him that I'd known he'd never make for himself.

Everything became clear in my head.

"Em, this isn't about what I think, or what you think. It's about what *Jules* would think. What choice he'd make."

I weighed everything I knew about Jules. How he lived life as it came, making what deals he could today and letting tomorrow take care of itself. How he hated Terence—but not Ember. He was capable of understanding that composition didn't determine character. *Or greatness of soul.* "For what it's worth, if Jules was offered the choice, I think he'd choose to live. I think he'd take the bet."

Ember stared down at the shell, her gaze drilling into it as though she could see through the metal. As though she could see him. "I hope he doesn't hate me for saving him."

The way Connor hates me right about now. I rubbed at my chest. "I have to go talk to Connor. Are you okay on your own?"

She blinked, as if she'd temporarily forgotten I was there. Then she enveloped me in a hug. "Thanks, Ash. For coming after me. For believing in me."

I hugged her in return. "You're my Tribe. My family. My sister. You know that." I let her go and added fiercely, "But from now on, you tell me the truth. Always."

"I will. I'm really sorry."

I nodded and stepped back. "Go save Jules, Em."

She pushed me toward the opening in the wall. "Go make up with Connor, Ash."

I made my way out into the cold morning air. Connor was leaning against the car with his back to me, looking toward the far-off trees of the Firstwood. They were a long way away, over rocks and red sand and pale spinifex grass, a faint blur of green beneath an endless orange-streaked sky. I suddenly, desperately wanted to go home. No, I wanted to go *back*. Back to the Firstwood, and *back* to how things had been between Connor and me, before Spinifex City.

I stopped a few paces away. He didn't turn around. But he spoke.

339

"I know about Talbot."

Anger roared through his voice. He was radiating so much fury that standing near him was like standing beside a bonfire. But I'd take heat over cold. I'd take anything over the deathly chill of distance.

"Jules told you?"

"He had to. He was too sick to come after you, and he wanted me to know what I was walking into." He spun to face me, blue eyes ablaze. "You should *not* have shot me."

"I was trying to protect you—"

"Because you didn't trust me! You thought I would abandon you to chase after Talbot."

"If I had the chance to get the people who killed Cassie . . ."

"I have a little more self-control than that, Ashala," he spat.

"Well, I don't. And I watched you die once already." I tried to make him understand. "Connor, when you're in danger, I see that moment when you fell from the sky. It's as if I'm back there, experiencing it all again, and no matter how hard I try, I can't escape it."

"Then try harder!"

"Don't you think I have been?"

"I think you're acting as if it's your job to stand

between me and danger," he shouted. "I am *not* every other member of the Tribe, Ashala."

"No," I yelled back. "You're not. Because you matter more!"

"What?"

"You matter more. And you shouldn't, because I'm the leader and I'm supposed to care about everyone the same. But I don't." It was hard to say something out loud that I'd only ever admitted inside my own head. "Everyone else . . . they all rely on me for something. They all look to me as if I'll always be able to make everything right. And I . . . I rely on you." I stared toward the Firstwood, seeking comfort from the distant trees. "Ember told me once about these binary systems, two stars orbiting each other. When you fell from the sky—it was as if I was falling, too. Endlessly and forever. You're the person I can't lose, Connor."

He was quiet. After a while, I dared to switch my gaze from the trees to him. He didn't seem quite so angry. Instead he seemed—thoughtful?

"Do you know how Georgie and Ember knew you were alive when we were in Detention Center Three?" he asked.

I frowned. "They couldn't have known. I always thought they must have been really worried."

"They weren't—at least, not that you were dead. Because they knew that if you'd died, I would have gone through the place like a tornado. If the center was still standing, it meant you were alive." He sighed. "Do you really think I don't understand, Ashala? You're the person I can't lose, either."

I took a hopeful step, only to freeze when he added softly, "The difference is, I was willing to let you risk your life when you asked me to."

I hunched my shoulders. "I guess that makes you braver than me."

He bit back a laugh. "No one is braver than you. Only I knew that if I didn't respect who you are, I would lose you. And Ashala, if you cannot respect who I am, you will lose me." He shook his head in frustration. "Do you even know who I am anymore? Who we are together?"

"Of course I know—"

"Then tell me what you said to me when you asked me to let you walk into the center!"

"I don't remember."

"Yes, you do."

And I did, of course. "I said . . . I said that the Tribe and the Firstwood were the essence of who I am. My soul." I shoved my hands in my pockets and muttered the last bit, "That they were the part of me that went on, which was more important than my life."

Connor nodded. "I am of the forest now, as you are, and this is not a safe world. There will always be times when we both need to stand between the Tribe and the trees, and danger. Ashala, you and I — we are warriors. We are partners. Or we are *nothing*."

I stared at the ground. He was right, I knew he was right. But I couldn't shake off the way I'd felt when he died, or the terror of it happening again. Which was why I'd shot him. *Now I'm in danger of losing him because I'm scared of losing him. . . . I'm creating what I fear.* More than that, I was betraying him. Betraying us. I'd always been a better person with him than I was on my own. Except I hadn't been that person for him.

And that I could not bear.

I lifted my head. "I shouldn't have shot you."

"No. You shouldn't."

There was a wariness, in his eyes and in his voice. It wasn't enough to apologize; he needed to know that I really understood I'd been wrong. "I think . . . I've been trying to move past that moment when you died in one big leap. Only that's not how it works. It has to be done in lots of little steps. Lots of choices, every single day. I made a bad choice." I drew in a shaky

343

breath. "Sorry isn't even a big enough word. But I *am* sorry. And I know the choice was bad, and I won't make it again, and—and I love you."

He took three quick steps toward me. I flung my arms around his neck, burying my head in his shoulder and holding on very tight. He was laughing now. "I'm not going anywhere, Ashala."

I haven't lost him. I clung on tighter all the same. Then I let go, just a little. Enough so I could see the laughter lighting up his eyes, the perfect curve of his lips.

Enough so I could kiss him.

Heat engulfed us, a firestorm of shared emotions that burned away all thought and left only a multitude of glorious sensations. It was a perfect moment, and I could have lived in it forever. I would have, too, except I gradually became aware that I could hear Leo's voice, calling out Ember's name. We broke apart, and I leaned against Connor's chest, dizzy and pleasantly disoriented.

Leo spoke again. Somehow, his voice was coming from the car. "Ember. *Ember.* Are you there? Answer the radio, little sister. There's going to be trouble in your part of the world."

THE WARNING

We darted around the side of the car.

Connor flung open the door and threw himself into the front seat. He grabbed hold of a small black device connected by a cord to the dashboard and spoke into it. "Leo, it's Connor. Ember's with Jules. Is someone coming our way?"

It seemed an eternity before Leo responded. "Not to where you are now. But there's going to be some kind of attack on that detention center near your forest."

I grabbed Connor's wrist, pulling the radio between us so we could both talk. *"When?"* I demanded.

"During the Adjustment for the former Chief Administrator."

The Adjustment. *Neville, and the hill of death . . .* I shivered, calculating how long it would take us to get to the center. We were going to have to leave in the next couple of days to make it in time.

"Do you have any details about the attack?" Connor asked.

"I fear my information is sketchy. I'm getting this from the Yowler boy—he's woken up and is being surprisingly cooperative, except he doesn't know much. He seems sincere, although I suppose it's possible he's lying."

Connor raised an eyebrow at me.

"He's telling the truth," I said. I trusted Starbeauty to make sure of it. "What about Terence, Leo?"

"Escaped." Even through the radio, I could hear the snarl in the Lion's voice. "And Delta appears to have been rendered unconscious by some kind of weapon. All I can tell you right now is that Terence has sent three of his Illegals to the Adjustment. The ones Jules calls 'minions,' although I have no specifics on exactly which ones. Oh—and you *do* know the Adjustment has been moved up?"

My heart jumped. "Moved up to when?"

"It begins on the sixteenth."

Three days away. *Too soon* . . . I should've paid more attention to what was happening back home, only no one in Spinifex City had been talking about the Adjustment. It wasn't big news here the way it would have been in Gull City.

"I thought it better to warn you immediately, but I'm afraid I have nothing else at present," Leo said. "My people are searching Terence's house. If I discover anything more, I'll contact you again. Tell Ember I want my car back."

The radio crackled out.

I shook my head. "We're too far away!"

"Not with your ability, we're not," Connor pointed out. "You can Sleepwalk us home."

Of course I could. I'd gotten so used to my ability not working that I'd almost stopped counting it among our resources. How hard would it be for me to get us home? Not that hard. I couldn't make myself perform complicated missions when I Sleepwalked, because a set of three simple instructions was the maximum I could follow in a dream, but three should be enough. Only problems were, first, it would be a bit of a test, because I hadn't used my ability on purpose since it started functioning normally again. *Guess*

347

I've got to try it sometime. Second, it was a big distance to cover, which meant I'd be using up a lot of energy. And when I got too tired, I woke up. If I did that at the wrong time . . .

"You realize I could accidentally land us in the middle of saber territory?"

"If you do, I'll fly us out." He didn't seem a bit concerned about the prospect of finding ourselves surrounded by ferocious people-eating cats. "We can do this, Ashala."

We could, too. *Because we are warriors, we are partners . . .* I beamed at him. He leaned across to kiss me, a quick, fierce kiss that left me breathless and fizzing with happiness.

"You get the packs," I told him. "I'll go tell Ember what's going on."

I found Ember sitting on the floor next to the stasis chamber, cross-legged and still. Her eyes were closed. I shook her shoulder. "Em?"

She blinked up at me. "Ash?"

"Leo called, on the radio, I mean, and —" I stopped. She didn't seem to be focusing on me.

I kneeled down in front of her. "Are you okay?"

"I'm programming nanomites. It's difficult. What did Leo want?"

"There's going to be an attack on the Adjustment. Also, Terence got away, and Delta has been shot, probably with the same weapon Jules used on you. Plus Leo wants his car back."

"What kind of attack?"

"He doesn't know. Just that three of the minions are going there."

"*Minions?* This is bad, Ash."

"I know—"

"No, listen to me. I always knew Terence had some bigger plan, and this could be it! Or at least part of it. He might be trying to derail the reform movement by having the minions disrupt the Adjustment, or, or assassinate the Prime, or Neville . . ."

"*Neville?* Why would he do that, when they were working together before?"

"My brother doesn't have friends. He doesn't even really have allies, not ones he won't eventually betray. And we don't know how much Neville knows or has guessed about Terence. He could be a loose end, someone Terence wants to silence."

True enough. "Well, I can't say I'll be sorry to see Neville dead."

"Yes, you will!" she snapped. "Don't you see what this could mean?"

I rolled my eyes at her. "Obviously not, or you wouldn't be yelling at me."

"Sorry. It's just—one of the reasons the reform movement has so much support is because a lot of people don't see abilities as a threat. But if Prime Willis, or Neville, or anyone else gets assassinated by someone using an ability . . ."

"Every Illegal becomes a potential killer." And I *did* see what that could mean. I could gaze into the future as if I were Georgie. It wasn't only a matter of the Citizenship Accords not being revoked. It was about having them made much worse. More detentions, fewer Exemptions, or no Exemptions at all. Enforcers everywhere. And the governments of the seven cities throwing everything they had into destroying the Tribe and all the other groups of Illegals hiding out in the countryside. Not only that, but if Illegals killed someone so close to the Firstwood, the Tribe would be immediate suspects. We'd be the first ones the enforcers came after.

It would be the world Terence Talbot wanted, and Neville, too, if he was alive to see it. Was this what the taffa dream was about? Could all that death come from Neville himself dying? I didn't know.

What I did know was that it was only going to take

one calculated act of violence, orchestrated by Ember's lunatic brother, and Illegals everywhere would be paying the price for decades to come.

I drew in a shuddering breath. "I get it."

"And you're the only one who can stop this. Those enforcers at the Adjustment don't stand a chance; they'll only have swords now that the government's discontinued the use of streakers. It won't be enough."

"They've got rhondarite swords," I protested. "They'll stop an ability—"

"Only once they're in contact with someone's body, and the enforcers will have trouble getting close enough."

She was right about that. Enforcers were used to dealing with Illegals who were ashamed of what they were and had little control over what they could do. They'd never have encountered anything like the minions. "I'll stop it, Em."

She gave me that same look she always did, the one filled with so much faith that I never felt I could live up to it. *"Go."*

I raced back out to where Connor was waiting. He was wearing his pack and holding mine; he handed me a flask. "I've mixed in the herb with the water already."

I resisted asking if he'd made sure it was the right herb; I knew he would have. We both carried a small selection of useful Firstwood herbs with us whenever we left the forest, including the one that helped me to sleep. *And* the one that stopped me from dreaming, but that obviously wasn't what I wanted right now. I drank a few mouthfuls of the mixture, then handed the flask back to Connor and lay down on the ground.

Closing my eyes, I began counting backward, letting the world recede until I'd reached a state somewhere between sleeping and not-sleeping. This was the point at which I could give myself instructions, so I imagined a blank piece of paper in my hand and thought about what I needed to do. *Take Connor. Get home fast. Don't let anyone see you.* There probably *wasn't* anyone to see us out here, but we might still be close enough to Spinifex City for someone to spot me doing whatever impossible thing I decided was a good idea. I repeated those three commands over and over until they appeared on the paper, crisp and black and clear.

As soon as the instructions were there I let the note go, allowing myself to sink into sleep.

I was floating among stars. *Moving* stars. They clustered together and exploded into blinding light. When the light finally faded, there was a girl where the stars had been. A brown-skinned, curly haired, bright-eyed child. Joy shot through me. *Cassie.*

It was wonderful to see her. Except I was dreaming. I had to be, because my little sister was dead. The moment I realized that, Cassie smiled and vanished. In her place was a note. It floated gently downward, hovering in the air above me. Words shone out from it, and I knew what I had to do.

Everything changed. I was standing atop a strange red ocean that rose and fell oddly, bursting up into surges of water that seemed frozen in place. Beside me was a tall winged being. A friend. But the two of us shouldn't be here. *We have to be somewhere else.* . . . There! That island in the far distance, the one overgrown with trees. We needed to reach the middle of it. Only we had to be sneaky, to avoid spying eyes.

I took hold of my friend's hand and focused on our surroundings, changing the landscape and all the spies within it into mist. Everything gradually faded into an insubstantial shadow of itself, until only the two of us were real and solid. The spies were lost in fog. They could not find us now. I propelled us forward taking my friend with me through the mist-world. But I wasn't going fast enough. I concentrated. *This is my dream, and I can do anything I want!*

We got faster, moving at super speed through faded surges of red water and then hazy trees. On and on we went, rocketing to the middle of the island. *No one can see us! Nothing can stop us!* But I was starting to have trouble. The world was fighting back, wanting to be solid again, and I struggled to maintain it in a shadow-state. And some unseen force seemed to be dragging at my body, making it harder and harder to move. I flung it off impatiently.

My friend crashed into me from the side, knocking me over.

What was he doing? Had he fallen? Was he sick? I twisted to see—

—and found myself sprawled in the dirt, one hand pressed to Connor's chest. He was lying across me, pinning my shoulders to the ground and shouting my name. "Ashala!"

"It's okay. I'm back. I'm back!"

He let go and rolled away. I sat up, body shaking and stomach heaving, feeling about as bad as I usually did after a big Sleepwalking effort. But I'd done it. There were tuarts rising up around me, and the scent of eucalyptus in the air. *We're home!*

I leaned into the nearest tree, waiting to feel better and wondering how long it had taken to get here. I couldn't tell; I had no sense of the passage of time in a dream.

"Connor? How long?"

"An hour or so. No more."

His voice sounded strange. I looked over at him. He was sitting with his back to a tuart like I was, but his skin was as pale as I'd ever seen it, and tremors were racking his body.

I straightened in alarm. "Connor! I didn't—I couldn't have hurt you!"

"No. But we went *through* things, Ashala."

"Through things?"

"Hills. Trees."

I thought about the dream. "I changed the world into mist. Only you and I were solid."

"The world didn't look like mist to me!" He ran a trembling hand through his hair. "And then you started shaking, and I knew you must be getting tired. I tried to stop you with air and couldn't—I thought you were going to wake up inside a tree!"

I imagined hurtling toward solid things and passing right through. Then I imagined snapping out of Sleepwalking with a tree through my arm, or leg, or chest. Or through his.

That must have been . . . absolutely terrifying.

"Well," I told him brightly, "you can't say being with me isn't an adventure."

He began to laugh. I joined in, and crawled over to him. "Sorry, sorry . . ."

"Don't be silly. I'm just happy you woke up." He shifted to pull me against him, and I snuggled into his chest.

"Exactly where do you think we are?" I asked.

"We passed by the rock pool not long ago. Must be about a day and a half away from the caves. Walking distance, that is."

Faster to fly, but better not to. We'd need his ability to get across the grasslands and to fight the minions; there was no point in depleting it unnecessarily. *Wish I could've gotten closer.* Still, not bad for an hour's work.

We sat there until we had enough strength to move. Then I picked up my pack, which Connor had dropped on the ground nearby, and we began to trudge through the forest in the direction of the caves.

As we went, I talked, catching Connor up on everything he didn't know. What had happened in the house when I'd gone in to rescue Ember. The taffa dream. Nicky. And Ember's thoughts on what Terence might be up to with the attack on the Adjustment. It was comforting, to walk together among the trees in the cool autumn air. I skimmed my hand across tuarts along the way, relishing the feel of the rough bark beneath my fingers and the warm, familiar sense of belonging it brought me.

We'd been walking for about an hour when there was a whooshing sound, and Daniel materialized in front of us.

I took a startled step back. "Daniel? Is something wrong? Georgie? Nicky? The Tribe? Is everyone okay?"

"Everyone's fine, Ash," he answered soothingly. "All the people and all the dogs. Georgie sent me here. She said that when you came back from Spinifex City, this is where I meet you."

That was a Georgie reason for doing something if ever I'd heard one.

Daniel glanced from Connor to me. "Where's Jules? And . . . did you find Ember?"

I nodded. "We did, and she's good. She's with Jules. He's — not well. We came back ahead of them. There's going to be trouble at the Adjustment."

"It's been moved up —"

"We know," Connor interrupted. "We think Terence's minions are going to launch some kind of attack."

"They might be trying to kill the Prime," I added. "Or Neville. Or simply cause chaos." I shivered a little at that last word and plunged onward. "Has anything happened there yet? Any kind of disturbance?"

Daniel shook his head. His hair was bit scraggly and uneven, I noticed; he must have let Georgie cut it again. "It's been quiet, and between us and the Saur Tribe we've kept a close watch. If anything was wrong, we'd know it."

"Has Neville been brought in yet?"

"Yes. Grey, too. And the Prime arrived late yesterday. You don't know when the attack will be?"

"Unfortunately not," Connor responded. "But if the purpose of it is to derail the reform movement, which Ember thinks it might be, then the minions will want to make a spectacle, in front of as many people as they possibly can. Do you have any idea what kind of events . . ."

"There's going to be a big opening ceremony on Tuesday morning," Daniel replied promptly. "A dinner the night after that. And tomorrow there's a memorial service, right before lunch. For the detainees who 'died' escaping the center."

They really *had* been keeping watch. But that was a lot of events to cover, and the attack might or might not take place during any of them. They all sounded like good targets. Except . . . maybe one more than the others.

"The memorial service," I breathed.

Connor nodded. "Illegals causing mayhem during a ceremony meant to mourn other Illegals? It's before the Adjustment officially begins, but it would be hard for the minions to pass up that kind of opportunity."

"It's tomorrow!" I spluttered. "That's so close. Even flying—or Running—it'll take us the best part of a day just to get across the grasslands." Or rather the best part of a night, in order to avoid being seen.

"Also," Daniel said, "if the service *isn't* the target, what do we do? We can't exactly lurk around the center waiting for something to happen, at least not without getting arrested."

"No," Connor agreed thoughtfully, "but we don't have to. If we could reach Prime Willis, or Jeremy Duoro or Rae Wentworth, they'd listen to a warning from us. We could try to get them to evacuate the Prime, or shut down the Adjustment, or . . ." His voice trailed off and he sighed. "I don't know. Something. At least if we've warned them, they'll be better prepared."

"Plus they'll know the Tribe isn't responsible for the attack," I said. "That we tried to help. That could be important if someone tries to blame us later, or if . . . things go bad, for Illegals."

There was a moment of grim silence as the three of us contemplated exactly how bad things could get. Then Daniel spoke. "I don't know about Willis or Wentworth, but I think we can get to Duoro."

"How?" I demanded.

"He has this routine. In the morning, first thing, he comes out of the center, walks to the edge of the grasslands, and just stands there, staring at the grass. Then he goes back inside. He's done it every day since he arrived."

I knew what that was about. "He's looking out at where the children died. I mean, where he thinks they died." Jeremy Duoro had done his absolute best to save the detainees from being eaten by saurs. In fact, he'd almost ruined our rescue with his bravery. It was sad that he was still mourning their deaths so deeply. But helpful.

"If we're going to reach Duoro tomorrow," Connor said crisply, "we'll have to cross the grasslands tonight. The three of us need to get to the caves, get supplies, and work out exactly what we're going to do."

Daniel nodded. "I'll see you both there."

He vanished, leaving only a stirring in the air behind him.

I turned to face Connor and held out my hand, ready to fly. He twined his fingers in mine. I had a sudden panicked thought that this might be the last time we were alone before we went into the center. "Connor? In this or any other life . . ."

He understood, of course. He raised my hand to his lips, pressed a kiss to my knuckles, and finished the sentence. "We will find each other."

And we flew, soaring toward the caves so we could plan out the details of how we would stand between the Tribe and the trees, and danger.

THE CENTER

The next morning, I was skulking outside Detention Center 3 with Daniel at my side.

Yesterday had gone past in a frantic blur as we formulated a plan and decided who should put it into action. In the end it hadn't been hard to determine who came on this particular mission. First, Connor, both because of his superlative control of his ability and because he was the one who'd befriended Belle Willis and Jeremy Duoro six months ago. Second, Daniel, because he could control his ability almost as well as Connor, and he was pretty much the only other Tribe member — except for Em, who wasn't here —

who could be trusted to keep their head. The absolute last thing we needed was someone panicking under fire. Third, Jaz, to hide on the grasslands and relay messages by mindspeaking. And finally me, because . . . well, I hadn't been about to let them leave me behind. But also because I was the one who knew Rae Wentworth, and that might be important. She'd never interacted with Connor, except as an enforcer; she'd only trust me.

Now we just had to activate our plan.

Jaz and Connor were at the front of the center — Jaz crouched in the grasslands, and Connor hiding in the forests that ran along the road leading to the main gates. Daniel and I were lurking at the back, concealed by a pile of tumbled rocks. Fortunately, there was no shortage of convenient rocks to conceal ourselves behind in the Steeps, the hilly granite country that bordered Detention Center 3 on two sides.

I whispered to Daniel, "Are you sure you know where you're Running to?"

He gave me a look. It was a tolerant look, because Daniel had endless amounts of patience, but I got the message. I'd drawn him a map of the locations of the major structures within the center, and of the storage building where we were headed now. He'd said he'd memorized it, and there was no need whatsoever for me to keep checking. "Sorry. You know what you're doing."

"I really do, Ash."

I shifted my attention to what was in front of us. Most of the center was surrounded by a high boundary wall with a walkway along the top that was continually patrolled by enforcers. But at the back, half the wall had collapsed in the fire Connor had started to cover our escape the last time we'd been here. There were still guards strung along the crumbled section, standing about twenty paces apart, as well as patrols that came by at regular intervals. It was the patrols we were concerned about; we didn't want to pass close enough to one for an alert guard to notice something strange about the movement of the air.

I watched as two enforcers appeared, pacing slowly past the standing guards. It seemed to take forever before they'd covered the length of the gap and disappeared behind the wall again. Daniel checked his watch. "Fifteen minutes since the last time they came through."

That was more than enough time for us to get in, especially with the help of a strong breeze to cover Daniel's Running. He picked me up and held me tight against his chest. I called out to Jaz. *Tell Connor. Now.*

The wind grew abruptly stronger, scattering stones across the ground as it gusted through the center. Daniel drew in a deep breath and Ran.

The whole world seemed to disappear into a big smear of paint, all the colors merging into one another. There was nothing concrete to focus on, and no sound except the roar of air rushing past me. Then everything solidified, only I wasn't where I'd been before. Daniel and I were inside a building, one that was filled with crates and had a staircase leading up to an open floor above.

He put me down. It was the first time I'd ever Run anywhere with him, and it had been — pretty amazing, actually. "How do you find your way when everything is a blur like that?"

"Georgie asked me that once. I don't see a blur. For me, it's as if I'm moving normally and everything else has slowed to a crawl." He glanced around curiously. "So this is the place? Where you showed Jeremy Duoro and Belle Willis the cache of streakers?"

"It's where Connor showed them the cache," I replied. "Plus the rhondarite from the secret mine Neville had in the Steeps." I jerked my head toward the upper floor. "I was hiding up there."

The storage building wasn't very different from how I remembered, except for the roped-off areas and little signs everywhere. It was an exhibit, now that the center had been made into a museum.

Ash? Are you there yet?

Yep. Has Duoro come out?

Nope. I'll let you know when he does.

"There's nothing happening at the front so far," I told Daniel.

He nodded and began to stroll around. Like me and Connor, he was dressed entirely in Gull City blue; we wanted to be able to blend in with the Citizen delegates to the Adjustment if we had to. I leaned against a crate, fingering the stunner in my pocket. It was the only weapon we had, other than our abilities. *And the collars, I guess.* Daniel had three of the rhondarite collars that we'd taken from the rescued detainees bundled into a small backpack. He thought that, with his speed, he might be able to get close enough to clip a collar on a minion. That was why he was also wearing thick gloves, to prevent contact between the rhondarite and his skin. Connor had tried to move a collar with air, in case he could find a way to use one as well, but it turned out it was unwise to rely on an ability to shift anything made of rhondarite.

One stunner, three collars, our abilities, and our wits. I wished we had more. I wished we had an army.

I hoped we had enough.

"Listen to this," Daniel said. He was bending over a sign positioned next to an empty crate. "It's a quote from Jeremy Duoro. 'I couldn't believe my eyes when I saw what this box contained. Weapons. Row upon row of shiny, deadly streakers. What terrible plan was lurking in the devious mind of Chief Administrator Neville Rose?'" He shook his head. "Does he really talk like that?"

"He's a dramatic kind of guy." I smiled. "But a good one. He'll help us if he can."

Ash? He's coming out.

I straightened. "Duoro's outside the center!"

He's strolling. . . . He's strolling. . . . He's heading across the gravel to the grasslands. Now he's standing at the edge of the grass, all sad, boohoo. What a terrible tragedy, sixteen children eaten by saurs. Okay, Connor's sending the rock.

I imagined our rock being propelled through the grasses to stop at Duoro's feet. We'd tied a short note onto it, saying that the Prime and the Adjustment were in danger and asking Duoro to meet Connor in this building.

It's hit his foot. He's glancing back at the gate guards. . . . Wait, he's doing the old "just bending down to tie my shoelace" trick. . . . Nice. Very nice. He's got the rock. . . . He's reading the note! He's reading the note! Now he's walking to the center—a bit quickly—whistling loudly—don't overdo it, friend.

A long pause, then, **He's back in.**

Thanks, Jaz.

Good luck, Ash. And Connor says he's headed your way.

I grinned at Daniel. "It went well. They're coming."

He nodded, and we waited. The moments seemed to crawl by until the door finally opened and Connor slipped inside.

I sighed with relief to see that he'd made it in all right. "Any sign of trouble out there?"

"Not that I saw. Not yet." He walked over to stand at my side. "Duoro shouldn't be far behind me."

He was right—it wasn't long before the door opened for a second time and Jeremy Duoro bounded in. He charged up to Connor, seizing his hand and shaking it enthusiastically. "You're alive! Belle and I thought Neville might have killed you for telling us his plans."

Connor shook his head. "I got away. But I must

tell you I'm not quite what you thought I was. I am an Illegal."

Duoro's gaze dropped to the Citizenship tattoo on Connor's wrist. "Got the better of an Assessor, did you? Good for you!" He let go of him, beaming at Daniel and me. "Are you Illegals as well?"

I nodded; there seemed little point in lying. "I'm Ashala, and this is Daniel."

"Ashala?" he breathed. "Not . . . *the* Ashala? Ashala Wolf? Leader of the Tribe?"

"Um, yeah."

"It's such an honor to meet you." He turned shining eyes toward Daniel. "And you, too, of course. I never thought I'd meet anyone from the Tribe!"

"Thank you," Daniel replied, and I could hear the suppressed laughter in his voice. "I only wish we weren't here on such serious business."

Daniel, the diplomat of the Tribe; it was a polite way to remind Duoro that we had more urgent things to discuss than his love of all things Illegal.

"The attack, of course!" Duoro exclaimed. He turned to Connor. "I've already warned the Prime. She's increased security. Don't worry, though; I didn't tell anyone else where the information came from, or that you are here." He stepped closer and said in a lowered voice, "Is Talbot behind this?"

I bit back a gasp.

"You mean, former *Prime* Talbot?" Connor asked carefully.

Duoro nodded. "Stories are being passed around his old supporters that he faked his own death to thwart an Illegal plot to assassinate him, and that he's about to make a triumphant return. Have you heard anything?"

There was a small silence. Daniel and Connor were leaving answering that question to me. *If there're rumors, I bet Terence is the one spreading them.* In fact, maybe this whole attack was part of a plan for his "triumphant return" to save the world from vicious Illegals.

I made a decision. "It is Talbot. He's alive. And he has Illegals helping him."

"I *knew* he wasn't dead!" Duoro exclaimed. Then bewilderment crept over his face. "But why would Illegals help him, or attack the Prime? She's trying to get rid of the Citizenship Accords!"

I sighed. "It's complicated. The Illegals who are helping him, he's made them hate themselves, the same way he hates anyone with an ability. They're young and twisted up."

He frowned. "How young?"

I thought about the minions Ember had encountered on the road out of Fern City, and the Yowler who'd attacked Leo. "About my age," I replied. "Or a bit younger. Why?"

"There's a delegation of students from all the cities here to witness the Adjustment. But they're teenagers — surely they couldn't be assassins?"

I exchanged a horrified glance with Connor and Daniel. It had never occurred to us that the minions might actually be part of the crowd *invited* to the Adjustment. My thoughts raced. *We might have even warned the minions we're onto them with the increased security. . . . This is a disaster.* But there was no time for regrets. "Believe me, they're not ordinary teenagers, and you don't want to see what they can do close up. Where's that delegation right now?"

"Probably in the old dining hall, at breakfast with everyone else."

"Including the Prime?" Connor asked.

Duoro nodded, eyes wide. "Yes. I never thought — I didn't think the danger could come from inside!"

We hadn't, either. "We've got to get to the hall."

"Wait," Duoro said. "I don't know if this means anything, but one of the teenagers was ill this morning. Or said he was. He went to see Dr. Wentworth."

"Where's she?"

"She's set up an infirmary in the old hospital."

Oh, no. "That's right near the cells!"

"Ah, yes. Why does that matter—"

"Because Neville's in the cells!"

He looked puzzled, and I realized I'd done a terrible job of conveying the dual threat. *And I can hardly say, Rose might be in danger because he knows too much about a paranoid, three-hundred-plus-year-old aingl. . . .*

Daniel intervened to deliver a short, masterful explanation. "We think Talbot was allied with Neville Rose in some way, including being involved in some of Rose's unlawful activities. Talbot might now be trying to cover his tracks by getting rid of him. Rose could be a target, along with Prime Willis."

"Then we have to protect them both!" Duoro said. "Not that I think Rose deserves any help, but an assassination by an Illegal would be a disaster for the reform process."

He was a little erratic but not at all stupid; I should have remembered that.

"We'll need to split up. I—" I stopped, interrupted by a hissing sound from outside. *What's that?*

The four of us ran out to find a massive fireball hovering in the sky above the center. We started toward it, but the fireball simply hung there for a moment, popping with small bursts of flame, before vanishing completely.

"Is that the attack?" Duoro asked.

Connor gave a grim shake of his head. "It's a signal. For the attack to begin."

We'd run out of time. "Daniel and I will take the hospital and the cells. Connor, you go to the Prime. And be careful."

Be well, be safe, come back to me. . . .

He met my gaze. "You, too." And I knew he was saying that in answer to both the words I'd spoken and the ones I hadn't.

I nodded.

Connor leaned over to grasp hold of Duoro's arm. "We're going to have to fly. Don't worry, I won't let you fall."

An expression of sheer delight flitted across Jeremy Duoro's face, and the two of them soared upward.

I reached out to Daniel. He lifted me up again, and we Ran.

THE SACRIFICE

When the world resolved into itself, we were at the old hospital building. Daniel set me down and zoomed inside, tearing through one room after another. I could only follow his progress by seeing doors fly open down the central hall; I couldn't actually see *him*.

He materialized in an open doorway, looking shaken. "Ash? There's a woman in here . . . and if this is Wentworth, she's dead."

I sprinted forward, my heart slamming against my ribs, and stopped at Daniel's side to take in the terrible scene. *Dr. Wentworth.* The brown-skinned Mender was sprawled on the floor, red robes pooling around her.

Half the back of her head had been caved in with a blood-soaked rock that was still sticking out of her skull.

"The minion who was here has probably gone after Neville," Daniel said.

I nodded. I knew I should say something, or do something, only I couldn't seem to move or speak. *My friend is dead. I wasn't in time to save her. My friend is dead.*

Daniel shook my arm. "Ash? We've got to stop them from assassinating Neville, or this is all for nothing. And she's *gone*. No one could survive that."

He was right. No, I realized with dawning hope, he was half right. One of us had to stop the minion, and *almost* no one could survive. I shoved the stunner into his hand and started toward Wentworth. "You go. I'll catch up."

"I can't take the weapon, it'll leave you defenseless."

"There's no reason for anyone to come back here. It's Neville they'll be after." I kneeled on the floor and called over my shoulder, "Stop the minion, Daniel, and that's an order!"

He vanished in a whoosh of air. I felt frantically at Wentworth's neck. Was that a pulse? It was so faint I couldn't be sure. But, just as Firestarters didn't burn and Waterbabies couldn't drown, Menders were difficult to kill. Their bodies clung to life, and the more powerful the Mender, the harder it was to kill them. Wentworth was the best Mender I'd ever seen. Only she didn't seem to be Mending, not from this. Had I imagined the pulse?

I hovered over her, biting back a whimper. Then I noticed the rock. It was a funny shape, all pointed and sharp, almost as if it were—crystal? *It's not a rock*. It was unprocessed rhondarite. The minions must have swiped it from one of the displays in the center. And it was partially embedded in Wentworth's head.

Which meant it was blocking her ability.

I grabbed hold of the rhondarite, trying to be gentle as I pried the awful thing out.

"It's gone, Rae," I whispered when I had it free. "Get better. Please get better." I threw the rhondarite away and wiped my bloody hands on my pants. Then I brushed her dark hair back from her face so I could see her eyes, hoping they'd flutter open. They didn't, but . . . was her skull repairing itself? It was hard to tell, so I felt her neck again. There was a definite pulse this time, growing stronger by the moment. She was Mending. I heaved a sigh of relief and leaned back.

That was when I saw it.

There were letters scrawled across the wall to my

right. Letters written in blood. *We are everywhere.* I fought a sudden urge to throw up. Whoever had been here had taken the time to use Wentworth's blood as she lay dying, so they could—what? Inspire fear? *No, inspire terror.* To make people believe there were Illegals everywhere ready to attack them the way Wentworth had been attacked. It was cruel and twisted and . . . effective.

The doctor stirred. She stared up at me out of dazed dark eyes. "Ashala? What are you doing here?"

I got control of my rage and replied in something approaching a normal tone of voice. "Long story, and you've been badly hurt, Doc. You need to lie still."

"There was a boy. He said he was sick. Did he hit me with something?"

"Yeah. With rhondarite, but you're getting better now. Listen, he's an Illegal, and he's here to hurt people. If you're okay, I have to go."

"People are hurt?"

She struggled up, rising to her feet. I stood with her, trying to keep her steady. "You need to lie down!"

"If someone's hurt," she said stubbornly, "I need to help."

"No, you don't, and anyway no one's hurt yet, I hope. . . ."

"Ashala." She shook free of me. "Explain to me what is happening. Why would someone attack me?"

I didn't think I'd ever admired Rae Wentworth more than I did in that moment—covered in blood, barely recovered from a wound that should have killed her, and *still* determined to help.

"This isn't going to make much sense," I told her, "but you'll have to trust me. There are bad Illegals here who work for former Prime Talbot. Um, he's not dead, I don't know if you've heard the rumors. Talbot is trying to derail the reform movement, stir people up against Illegals, and we think the Illegals who work for him are going to assassinate Prime Willis, or Neville. The one who hurt you has probably gone after Neville, and a member of my Tribe is out there, too, and I have to go help."

She nodded. "Then go, and I'll follow as soon as I can."

I ran, out of the hospital and into the center. As I neared the cells, I could hear sounds of a struggle. I peered around a corner to see that the door to the cell block was wide open. An enforcer was lying on the ground with his skull caved in, by a rock this time instead of rhondarite. *Didn't even have time to draw his sword.* I could make out a white-haired figure and a dark-haired figure huddled in the shadow of the next building, both dressed in the plain brown clothes of prisoners. *Neville and Grey.* And in the open space between the structures, Daniel was fighting with a sandy-haired boy.

The two of them were struggling for the stunner, and one of them must have had his hand on the trigger, because every now and then a blast would shoot out. I gaped in surprise. *Daniel's so fast, how did the minion manage to get anywhere near him?*

In a moment, I had my answer. The boy disappeared, just vanished completely, and reappeared behind Daniel.

I shouted a warning as the minion aimed two sharp, vicious blows at Daniel's side. He staggered, and the boy grabbed the stunner. I sprinted over. Before I could tackle the minion, someone slammed into me from the side, throwing me to the ground. I hit the dirt, twisted, and struck at — Miriam Grey?

I'm trying to keep you from being killed, you idiot! Or at least keep Neville from being killed, although I doubted Terence would care if Grey was collateral damage. But there was no point in telling her that; she had always been crazy, and confinement clearly hadn't agreed with Miriam Grey. Her green eyes were even more devoid of sanity than they'd been the last time

I'd met her. She hissed and spat, clawing and scratching at my face. I flung up an arm to protect myself and punched her in the stomach — once, then twice. She gasped, and I threw her off me, aiming a last kick at her middle as I stood to make sure she stayed down. Grey howled, curling up into a ball.

A bolt from the stunner flashed past, forcing me to duck, then roll as another one sizzled by. Except the minion — the Blinker, I decided to call him — wasn't actually aiming at me. In fact, he seemed to be shooting in all directions, following something around the space. *It's Daniel. He's Running.* And I was only going to get in the way. I scrambled for the shelter where Neville and Grey had been hiding. Neville wasn't there anymore, which was worrying. I tried to spot him amid the stunner blasts. *He's probably trying to escape in the confusion.*

Daniel appeared out of nowhere, ramming into the boy and pushing him backward so fast he dropped the weapon. I ran for the stunner as Daniel slammed him against a wall, holding a rhondarite collar to his throat. The boy struggled, trying to get away from the collar. Daniel was holding it in place, keeping it in contact with the boy's skin. *If I can stun the minion, I can end this!*

I'd nearly reached the weapon when Neville darted

in. He was carrying a sword; he must have taken it from the dead enforcer. *What is he doing, trying to help us?* I shouted at him to run. He ignored me, raised the sword—and plunged it into Daniel.

I gasped in shock as Daniel collapsed, the collar clattering to the ground. My hand closed on the stunner and I swung it up to fire at Neville. Only before the blast hit its mark, the Blinker appeared, grabbing hold of Neville's arm. They both disappeared.

The shot dissipated into the air just as someone crashed into my legs, knocking me over. I had barely enough time to register that it was Grey before my head slammed against the corner of a wall, and for a second everything went black. I blinked woozily as the world returned, and scrambled to my feet.

Grey was gone. So was Neville, and the Blinker. A red-robed figure staggered out from among the buildings, and I almost shot her before I realized it was Wentworth. She stumbled to Daniel's side, dropping to her knees and putting her hands on his chest. I backed up toward them, swinging the weapon back and forth, ready to fire the moment I saw danger.

There was no one to shoot. The dreadful truth sank in. Terence hadn't sent the minion here to kill Neville.

He'd wanted to *rescue* him.

Everything seemed to be going a little blurry at the edges, and there was a ringing sound in my ears. I kept looking for a target, determined not to let Daniel be hurt again, as I struggled to comprehend what had happened. Neville wasn't disposable to Terence after all. *They're still allies.* Maybe Neville had something Terence wanted, or . . . I didn't know, but I shuddered to think what a master manipulator like Neville Rose could accomplish with Terence's support. And — *wait, there they were!*

Neville and Grey and the Blinker were standing on a rooftop, three buildings away.

I fired. The energy died out before it got anywhere close. I was too far away, and I couldn't risk leaving Daniel and Wentworth unprotected to get any nearer. So I settled for glaring instead, especially at Neville, who was still carrying the sword wet with Daniel's blood.

I aimed the stunner at him. He raised the sword, and for a second I thought he was going to throw it at me, which was about as useless as me pointing a weapon at him.

Then he twisted and stabbed it into Miriam Grey.

She didn't even have time to scream before he shoved her off the roof, sending her tumbling downward with the sword still sticking out of her. I shuddered at the sound her body made as it slammed into the ground. *Why?* Except I knew why, because it made a dreadful kind of sense. He didn't need her anymore. And she'd known too many secrets about him, secrets that someone as insane as she was couldn't be trusted to keep.

Neville smiled. I couldn't make out the details of his smile, but I didn't have to. I knew it was the one that belonged to his true self, to the face kept hidden behind the pleasant mask he showed the world. The knowing smirk of a monster who understood exactly how monstrous he was, and took joy in it.

Neville pointed to his eyes, then to me, and spoke. I couldn't make out his words, either. I still knew what he was saying.

I'll be seeing you, Ashala Wolf.

He and the Blinker vanished.

I waited a few moments in case it was a trick, in case they came back to get us. They didn't. I'd been too slow and too stupid and too late, and Neville had escaped.

I turned back to Wentworth. Daniel was lying on the ground with his eyes closed. He didn't seem to be bleeding anymore. "Will he be okay?"

"He should be." Wentworth's skin was sallow and she was sweating. "He's not entirely out of danger yet, but I have to rest my ability a little before I can use it again."

I kneeled down, handing her the stunner. "Take this. I think there're other Illegals trying to get to the Prime; I've got to go try to stop them."

She pushed it back at me. "No. You need it." She stood up. "Help me drag him inside. We'll hide until this is all over."

Good suggestion. Wentworth was thinking more clearly than I was. I leaned down, and between the two of us we pulled Daniel into one of the nearby buildings.

"Stay here," I told her. "Lock the door and don't come out."

She frowned, peering into my eyes. "Ashala, have you hurt your head?"

"Knocked it a bit. I'll be okay."

"I can try to help —"

"No. Save your strength for Daniel." I gripped her arm. "I'm counting on you to keep him alive. I know you won't let me down, Rae."

She raised her chin and nodded.

I ran for the dining hall, stunner in hand. My balance

seemed to be a little off, but I was confident I'd be okay. At least, I was until I tried to call Jaz so he could let Connor know I was coming. The message bounced back and forth inside my skull, seeming to scramble my brain. I leaned against a wall, waiting for the pain to pass. *No mindspeaking with a head injury. Good to know.* Maybe I should've let Wentworth help me. Only she'd looked bad, and Daniel had looked worse. And I was not leaving one of my own to die in this place.

The pain faded, and I righted myself, continuing my slightly shaky journey toward the dining hall. As I got closer I smelled the dreadful scent of burned flesh. *Firestarter.* I slowed, and huddled between two buildings to spy out what was ahead.

Small fires were burning everywhere, and there were charred bodies strewn across the ground. It seemed as if a lot of enforcers had converged on this place and died horribly for their trouble. The big doors to the dining hall were closed, but I could see odd flashes of light through the high windows. Connor was in there, I could sense it. And burned across the wall were words, the same ones that had been written in blood in the hospital. *We are everywhere.*

Despair crashed over me. People would see those words and come after Illegals, after the Tribe . . . *No.*

I hadn't failed yet. Wentworth would speak for us, and as long as we could keep the Prime alive, there was hope. I had to find the Firestarter. Maybe in the dining hall?

I was contemplating a dash across open space to the door when a fireball came flying toward my head.

I hit the ground. It sailed over me and set my hiding place alight. *Can't stay here!* I ran out, shooting the stunner in the direction the fireball had come from. I caught a glimpse of the Firestarter—a tall, skinny boy—two buildings away. He was laughing as he lobbed more fireballs. I dodged and kept firing as I weaved my way closer, trying to get a clear shot. But my head was spinning, and all my movements were a little off. Fire caught the edge of my arm and hand, burning me and the weapon. I dropped it, rolling back and forth across the ground as I tried to put out the flames. I expected to be incinerated at any moment.

The fire went out, and I staggered up, in terrible pain from my burned arm but miraculously alive. Then I saw why. The Firestarter was down, flat on his back with a sword in his side. Jeremy Duoro was sprinting away. "Run!" he yelled. "Take cover!"

I didn't need to be told twice. The Firestarter was badly hurt, and when one of them died, their body released an inferno that reduced everything in the immediate area to ash. I had no idea if having rhondarite in him would prevent a death inferno or not, and I wasn't prepared to put it to the test. I stumbled away, collapsing into the shelter of a wall, and looked back.

Just in time to see the Firestarter yank the sword out of his body and send flames blazing at Duoro.

I screamed a warning. Duoro flung himself to the ground. *Not fast enough!* The fire caught him across his shoulder and left side. The Firestarter collapsed again, and I lurched out, throwing myself on top of Duoro to smother the flames. Then I grabbed hold of what remained of his shirt and dragged him into a corridor between buildings, ignoring his screams of pain. I had to get him away from the Firestarter and out of the vicinity of another attack or a death inferno, whichever came first.

I crouched at his side, trying to assess how seriously he was hurt. *It's bad.* A significant amount of Duoro's body was burned. Too much of it. He needed more help than I could give him.

He blinked, staring at me out of unfocused eyes.

"Jeremy, it's Ashala. I'm going to get Dr. Wentworth."

Even as I spoke I knew it was useless. I doubted Wentworth had the power to save another life, and I'd never get her back here in time even if she did.

Duoro seemed to understand that he didn't have long. "Please . . ." he whispered. "Don't leave. Stay with me."

I slumped, reaching out to take his uninjured right hand.

"Got him, didn't I?" he rasped. "Saved you."

"Yes." I wanted to cry; I held the tears inside and kept them out of my voice. "You saved me."

"Always wanted . . . to do something that mattered. Couldn't save . . . the others."

He was dying and there was nothing I could do about that. But there was something I could say. Leaning over, I hissed fiercely, *"The children are alive.* Do you hear me? The detainees weren't eaten by saurs. It was a trick, a way for us to save them without anyone knowing the Tribe was involved. They're alive and they're *free."*

His face changed, shifting into an expression of incredulous joy. I'd never seen anyone look so— hopeful.

Then the light vanished from his eyes, and his stare became blank.

Jeremy Duoro was dead.

Only moments ago I'd thought that I wouldn't leave

one of my own to die in this place. I felt as if one of my own just had. I wanted to sob and to shout and to scream at the injustice of it. I wanted to rip Terence Talbot and Neville Rose and everyone like them to pieces. Instead I hauled myself to my feet and peered out into the center. The Firestarter wasn't there anymore. There was only the sword, lying where he had been.

I could easily track where he'd gone by the blood trail he'd left behind — not toward the dining hall but away from it, around a corner and out of sight. It didn't matter; he wasn't going to last long. I went for the sword, picking it up. It wasn't much of a replacement for the stunner, but it'd do. Then I started toward the dining hall, and Connor.

That was when my battered, half-scrambled brain kicked into gear. *The blood trail.* There was only one thing the Firestarter could be heading for in that direction. The main gates, and then . . . *the grasslands.*

From what I'd seen of the minions, it would be about right for one of them to want his death to cause as much damage as possible. He couldn't pick a better target for fire than grass, and he had a strong ability. *The fireball in the sky . . . all those burned bodies outside the hall . . .* His death inferno would be nearly impossible to put out, even for the saurs with their armored scales.

If he reached the grasslands, everything would burn.

Jaz? I yelled. The mental shout seemed to bounce off the walls of my skull, sending pain shooting through my head. I couldn't reach him that way. *The saurs will stop the Firestarter before he gets to the grass.* Only—would they? All they'd see was one injured boy limping toward them, and it took exceptional circumstances for the saurs to step off the grasslands. They might not recognize the nature of the threat until it was too late, and while Jaz and the saurs might be immune to fire, the rest of the kids in his Tribe were not. How many of those wild children were hidden in the grasses today? A lot, they'd been out in force to keep watch on the Adjustment. Not to mention all the animals, the pretty speckled snakes and spiky hedgehogs and furry hopping dunnarts and the hundreds of others that made their home in the grass.

I wanted to run to Connor. Whatever he was dealing with must be bad, or he would have defeated it by now, besides which I could feel a faint sense of exhaustion tugging at my senses. He needed me. But I had to make the right choice, the choice he would want me to make. We stood between our Tribe and Jaz's Tribe, and the trees and the grasses, and danger.

He is of the forest. I am of the forest. . . . I had to take care of this first.

I snarled and sent Connor the only help I could. I sent him my faith, my absolute confidence that there was nothing he couldn't do, casting that belief out into the air and hoping he received it. *You are Connor, and you can do the impossible.*

Then I went after the Firestarter.

THE BATTLE

When I rounded the corner I could see two charred bodies ahead of me. The gate guards must have still been at their posts when they were attacked. Now they were dead. They were away from the gates, too — they'd clearly run toward the Firestarter, either because they'd seen him as a threat or because he'd fooled them into thinking he needed help. He was only a skinny kid, after all. Jeremy Duoro's voice echoed in my head: "But they're teenagers — surely they couldn't be assassins." *Oh, Jeremy. I warned you.* This teenager was able to kill without a moment's thought, as if it were nothing. As if life were nothing.

And he was headed for my friends.

I hurried to the gates, which had been pushed open just enough for someone to get through. The Firestarter was about three quarters of the way over the long stretch of gravel that separated the front of the center from the grasslands, where saurs were stalking around in the distance. Some of them were watching him, but none of them seemed overly concerned. As I'd feared, they didn't understand the danger.

I'd never get to the Firestarter in time. But I didn't have to. All I had to do was warn the saurs, and their hearing was exceptional.

I clung to the gate and screamed at the top of my lungs, "Firestarter! Firestarter! *Firestarter!*"

Reptilian heads swiveled toward the boy, and scaly bodies began to move in his direction. He reacted, flinging three fireballs ahead of him in quick succession. Flames tore across the grasslands, licking at the sky. The boy began to run to the grass. Even in his injured state, he was fast.

The smallest of the saurs was faster. Hatches-with-Stars came hurtling through the fire with Jaz clinging to her back. She raced across the gravel, skittering toward the Firestarter. He tried to dodge. He wasn't quick enough; her clawed feet trampled right over the top of his body. It was enough to kill him.

I knew it by the sudden, massive storm of fire.

The heat was so intense I could feel it from where I stood. I huddled behind the gate, hoping desperately to see Hatches and Jaz emerging from the blaze. Only they didn't. *Come on, come on* . . . Firestarters didn't burn, and saur scales were so tough they were immune to pretty much anything. But a death inferno incinerated the body of a dead Firestarter. Would it destroy them, too?

My heart thumped against my ribs, every beat more painful than the last as anxiety constricted my chest. Out on the grasslands, the saurs rolled, trying to put out the fires started by the fireballs. And, gradually, the inferno began to die.

I was terrified of what the dying flames would reveal. Terrified of seeing a small burned body and a larger reptilian one. I peered into the fading inferno — and gaped at the sight of Jaz, arms outflung, fire streaming into his body.

The firestorm wasn't dying. It was being *absorbed.*

Jaz's skin seemed to glow from the inside as he took the flames into himself. *I've never heard of a Firestarter being able to do this!* But I'd never heard of a Firestarter being caught in another Firestarter's death inferno, either. I watched, awestruck, as the flames vanished and Jaz shone. For a second he sat there, a beacon of blazing light, and I worried that he'd burn from the inside out. Then he lifted his arms to the sky and sent flames shooting upward, disappearing harmlessly into the air.

I sagged in relief. Hatches wheeled toward the grasslands, and Jaz looked back, worried about me. I didn't think I could manage another yell, so I gave him a thumbs-up signal and pointed to the grasslands. *I'm okay. Go put out that fire.*

The two of them sped away, Hatches screeching her triumph, and the other saurs trumpeting back. I went in the other direction, heading for the dining hall with the sword clutched in my hand.

My head spun, and my burned arm hurt. It seemed to take forever to get there. When I finally reached it, I crept up to the big doors and eased one open. The scene inside was so chaotic that it took a few moments to make sense of what was happening.

A slim black girl was standing a few meters ahead. She had her back to me and her hands raised, sending blue bolts of energy crackling into the hazy air in front of her. She was firing her bolts into whirling dust and little stones, a dirt storm that occasionally thinned enough for me to catch a glimpse of people huddled behind upturned tables. I couldn't find Connor, but he had to be responsible for the mini tornado of earth. *He's making it hard for the—Electrifier?—to see.* Hard for her to aim.

That wasn't all he was doing, either. Every time a shot of electricity sparked out, something flew in its way—a chair, a tray, a table. Objects were flying toward the Electrifier, too, except she just blasted them away. *It's a stalemate.* Only it couldn't last forever, and Connor was going to lose this fight. He was trying to protect all the people in the room. She didn't care who she hurt.

I slunk into the hall, sneaking up behind her. I was weak, but I wouldn't have to wound her that badly. All I had to do was hurt her enough to distract her, and allow Connor to get in a good shot. One step. Two. Three . . . I lunged.

I was quick and I was quiet. But she was alert and faster than me. She spun, sending a bolt arcing in my direction. A chair flew in front of my body. It wasn't enough to shield me. Some of the electricity came sizzling through, striking my right side. The blast seemed to set my wounded arm on fire all over again, and it was agony. I screamed and staggered, the sword falling from my hand as I collapsed onto the ground.

Everything went dark. Then the world blinked back into being.

Impossibly, I was on the grasslands. *No, I'm not.* I was inside my own head. I had to be, because I'd been in the hall a second ago. *Unless I'm dead?* No, surely Grandpa would have been here to meet me if I were. Besides, I knew I'd go to the Firstwood when I died, not the grasslands. So what was happening?

"Woof!"

I spun to find a familiar black Labrador behind me. "*Nicky?* Are you responsible for this?"

He wagged his tail, seeming very pleased with himself. "Nicky, I don't know what you think you're doing, but I can't be here right now. Send me back!"

Nicky bent to nose at something in the grass, rolling it onto my foot. I picked it up. A flask? He pranced, his black body quivering with excitement as if he'd given me the best present ever. I took a cautious sniff of the contents and recognized the faint citrus scent. This was the herb I used when I wanted to fall asleep and Sleepwalk.

I sighed in exasperation. "I don't know what you think you're up to, but this isn't helpful right—"

I stopped as a crazy, wonderful idea burst upon me. Nicky could link directly into my mind. He'd proved that many times over. And — at least according to Em — the connections that made abilities work were all in the brain.

"Nicky," I breathed, "can you help me Sleepwalk? Is that what you're trying to tell me? Because I'm in terrible trouble!"

"Woof!"

Call me crazy, but that sounds like yes. I eyed the flask. Did it represent Sleepwalking, in this world of my mind? *One way to find out.* I tipped back my head and drained the contents.

There was a blinding flash.

And when I could see again, I was in a different place.

I was sprawled on the floor of a cave, one filled with dozens of different forest creatures — birds, tree cats, lizards, frogs. A hissing electric storm hovered above them. There was something wrong with that storm, a twisting at its heart that made it vicious and mean. It wanted to eat the animals, to rip their little bodies to shreds, but a mighty winged being was standing in its way. *My friend.* And everywhere, numbers were falling through the air.

15, 14, 13 . . .

I was dreaming. I knew it with utter certainty. And

the numbers mattered. They were . . . *a countdown.*

They were telling me how long I had to act.

Lightning crackled toward me, and a tree branch flew in the way, taking the hit. The storm sent out more spiteful blasts, this time at the helpless animals. My friend raised his hands and other branches whirled, blocking the bolts.

12, 11, 10 . . .

I lurched to my feet. *I have to stop the storm!* I called up vines, magic vines that hurtled upward from the ground and into the storm. They seized its heart, drawing its energy downward into the earth.

The storm fought back, sending a thousand bolts sizzling in my direction. Branches flew to shield me. A single bolt got through, striking my leg, and I stumbled to one knee. *This isn't right!* I should be invincible in my own dream. Only I wasn't. Something was wrong with me. I'd been wounded, weakened. And the countdown was continuing.

9, 8, 7 . . .

The vines were slipping from the storm. *No!* I tried desperately to make them stronger, only I had no strength in me. Then, out of nowhere, an enormous possum scurried to my side. She gathered my battered body into the shelter of her furry arms, and healing energy flowed into me. I called up more vines, and more, entangling the storm in shining green strands.

6, 5, 4 . . .

The storm shrieked its rage, and I shrieked right back, pouring all my will into keeping it contained. It was trapped, but it was taking everything I had simply to hold it. I could not defeat it, not alone.

Only I wasn't alone.

My winged friend grabbed something from the floor of the cave, a strange warped spear. He threw the spear into the storm, and it collapsed in on itself, the hissing energy sputtering out.

3, 2, 1.

Everything changed again.

I was in a room. A big room, filled with gradually settling dust, and no animals at all. Just people hiding behind bits of furniture. Connor was standing to my left, and there was a girl on the ground in front of us. She had a sword through her leg, and a couple of enforcers were holding her down as she tried to pull it out. "I have to serve!" She sobbed. "I *need* to serve!"

Dizziness swept over me, and I staggered. Someone caught my shoulders from behind, helping me to keep my balance. The possum. *No, not a possum.* Wentworth. Except the doctor was staggering herself, and shaking even worse than I was. I shoved her in the direction of a nearby chair, stumbling a little as I went.

Connor sprinted to my side, grabbing hold of another chair and setting it next to Wentworth's. He pushed me into it. "Ashala. Breathe."

I did, leaning over to rest my arms on my knees. "Doc," I whispered. "Daniel?"

"He's fine. He'll live."

She cast a quick, curious glance at Connor, and I realized she'd recognized him from when she worked here. I shook my head at her and she nodded; she understood not to let on to anyone that he'd once been an enforcer in this place.

I focused on breathing. Surprisingly, other than the usual Sleepwalking-induced nausea, I didn't feel so bad. My head wasn't hurting and neither was my arm. I glanced down to find it covered in a network of scars, as if I'd been burned long ago.

"Sorry," Wentworth whispered. "Didn't have enough power left to heal it completely."

I opened my mouth to tell her I didn't mind one bit, only before I could speak, a shout cut through the air. "Arrest those Illegals!"

A black-bearded administrator was striding out of the dust, pointing in my direction. Wentworth made an indignant protest, and Connor put himself between me and the rest of the room. I struggled to my feet, ready for a fight as enforcers began to advance toward us.

Someone called out, "Stop!"

Everyone froze, heads turning in the direction of that distinctive, powerful voice. Prime Belle Willis was rising to her feet from where she'd been crouching behind a table, throwing off the staff who'd been trying to keep her sheltered and safe. She was exactly as I remembered — stout, with blond hair and an ordinary sort of face. It was her voice and her sheer presence that held people's attention.

Willis gestured to the Electrifier, who was still being held down by enforcers. The girl had gone quiet now and was gazing into space with empty, defeated eyes. "Someone find a collar for that girl," Willis ordered. "But," she added, with a stern glance at the bearded man, "leave the Illegals who saved our lives alone."

Prime Willis to the rescue. I watched as she motioned people over, issuing crisp instructions. In no time at all, there were enforcers guarding the room and Menders circulating among the wounded. Willis looked at Connor. "Should we expect another attack? What happened to the other one, the Firestarter?"

"He's dead," I answered. "And there won't be any more attacks. There was only one more of them, and . . . well, I'm afraid he got away. Along with Neville Rose. The Illegal, um, rescued him."

There were gasps and murmurs from the crowd.

"What about Grey?" Willis demanded.

"She's dead, too. Rose killed her."

The bearded man snorted disbelievingly. "Why would he do that?"

"I saw it with my own eyes, Lewis," Wentworth put in. "I suspect Grey had become more of a liability to Rose than an asset. And I'll tell you something else. Illegals might have been the weapon of this attack, but they weren't the masterminds. This was organized by former Prime Talbot as part of a plot to derail the reform movement. I overheard one of them say so."

With an effort, I kept my expression neutral. Wentworth had overheard no such thing. I'd been the one who told her the Illegals were from Talbot, and what he was trying to do. *She's a good friend to have.*

And an excellent liar.

An administrator piped up, "That's impossible. Talbot died of a stroke."

"People say he's coming back," someone else called out. "That he faked his death."

403

And a third, bewildered voice, "But Talbot hates Illegals!"

There was a sudden hubbub of chatter. Willis held up her hand, and everyone fell quiet. "I've heard the rumors about his return," she said. "And I doubt he's above using Illegals to further his own aims. Rose was once planning something similar. In fact, it explains why they came for Rose—he was one of Talbot's biggest supporters. Jeremy was investigating the rumors. . . ." Her voice trailed off, and she glanced around the room. "Where is Jeremy?"

Of course. She doesn't know yet. "Prime Willis?" I knew only too well that there was no way to make news like this any better. I tried to deliver the blow as fast as I could. "He was killed saving me from the Firestarter."

There was a hushed silence. Willis stood very still, her expression rigid. Lewis scowled at me. "I'd like to know how you got into this place. And who are you? One of the Tribe?"

I considered lying, and decided against it. People would assume the Tribe was involved in today's events anyway, given how close we were to the Firstwood. And I wanted to make sure they associated the Tribe with the Illegals who'd helped them rather than the ones who'd attacked. "I am Ashala Wolf."

Everyone seemed to breathe in at once.

"You're the leader!" Lewis sputtered. "How do we know that your Tribe isn't part of this?"

"We saved you," Connor snapped.

"Lewis." It was Willis who spoke. Whatever she was feeling about Duoro, she'd put it aside; she looked and sounded capable and in control. "The reason they are here is because Jeremy asked them to come."

I ducked my head, letting my hair fall over my face to hide my surprise.

"He heard whispers of a possible attack," Willis continued. "Nothing concrete, but enough to make him concerned. He thought the Tribe might be needed to defend us against other people with abilities. Obviously, he was right."

I'd forgotten how quick she was on her feet. It was a good story. No, it was a *great* story. And she'd just cemented our position as saviors. Allies of the government, not its destroyers. *Thank you, Belle Willis.*

I looked up at her, only to find that *everyone* was looking at me, and in a disturbingly expectant kind of way. As if they were waiting for me to say something, like I was supposed to make some sort of speech. I wasn't any good at speeches; that was something politicians did.

Politicians, and leaders of the reform movement, like Jeremy Duoro.

Suddenly there were words in my head. Because even though Duoro hadn't really asked for our help, I knew what he would have said if he had.

I cleared my throat and said, "I came here today because Jeremy Duoro . . . he told me the world was changing." I glanced around, trying to address the whole room, the way I thought he would have done. "He said that there was going to be a fight, and it was the only fight that was going to matter anymore, except it wasn't between Citizens and Illegals. It was a fight between the people who want to stop the hating, and the ones who don't." I glanced at Willis, checking to make sure she was happy with what I was saying. She gave me a tiny nod, and, reassured, I went on. "Jeremy said whatever side you were on in this fight was more important than whether or not you had an ability. Neville Rose, and Terence Talbot, and the Illegals who attacked everyone today—they're on the side of hate. But that wasn't Jeremy's side. And it's not mine, either."

That was the end of the words I had, the words I imagined he would have spoken. I added some of my own, only for Willis and straight from my heart,

"I'm so sorry he's gone! I would have saved him if I could."

"I think," she said gently, "that you and your Tribe have saved more than enough lives here today, Ashala Wolf. Including my own."

She walked over to me and extended her hand. I clasped it in mine, and did what Jeremy Duoro would have done. I played to the audience.

"It was an honor, Prime Willis."

Someone began to clap. Then another person, and another, until the entire hall echoed with the sound of applause. I wasn't sure what it was for, and I don't think they knew, either. It probably didn't matter. Under the cover of the noise, I whispered to her, "He took a bad injury, but he died peacefully, and he wasn't alone. And he looked so happy and hopeful at the end."

Her lip quivered. "He always did have enough hope for the whole world." For a second, her composure slipped, and I glimpsed the raw, howling grief that she was keeping locked inside. "We will not let his death be in vain, Ashala."

I met her gaze squarely, letting her see that my resolve was as fierce as her own, and made a promise to the Gull City Prime. "No. We won't."

THE PARTY

Ten days after the events at the center, we were having a party.

Georgie was organizing it, and she'd banned me from helping; she wanted to manage everything herself. It was nice to see her happy about something, because she'd been hovering anxiously over Daniel ever since we returned to the Firstwood. His near death was a future she hadn't glimpsed, and it had shaken her.

I'd left her to her preparations and gone out to sit by the lake in the fading light of the day. I could hear the eerie wailing of saur songs in the distance; the lizards were having a celebration of their own, and had been for almost a week, rejoicing in their victory over the "burner-of-grass."

Grandpa didn't seem to be around, but I still found it soothing to sit and stare at the water with Nicky at my side. Nicky had been my shadow ever since I returned to the Firstwood, the faithful companion who trotted at my heels and understood the worries of my heart. It was a strange thing—he'd been Ember's little brother in his last life. He was my dog in this one. And he seemed to know that I needed him nearby right now.

I was afraid of so many things, but most of all of the future.

No one had any idea where Neville Rose was, or Terence Talbot, for that matter. The Electrifier wasn't talking. We'd arranged for Leo to warn Belle Willis about the toxin in the girl's system, and to supply her with the antidote. He'd told Willis that he'd acquired it in the course of watching a shady character in Spinifex City who he'd only just realized was the former Prime Talbot. Willis appeared to believe him. She seemed quite charmed by Leo. But I had no hope that the Electrifier would betray Terence. My only comfort was that both Leo and Delta were hunting him, so wherever he was, Terence was on the run. Except I couldn't shake the dream of Neville standing on the hill of death. I was haunted by his escape, and by what might come from it.

There was a noise behind me, and I twisted to see Ember coming through the forest. She'd returned five days ago, along with Jules. He was alive, but his body was struggling to accept the nanomites; he had good days and bad days. On the good days he was almost normal; on the bad he could barely move. Ember didn't know how to fix it yet, or even if she could. Strangely, the situation seemed to bother Jules a lot less than it bothered Ember. He didn't mind at all that she'd put nanomites in his body to save him, and he'd been dealing with his poor health with endless optimism and good humor. I'd never liked him so much before. I had to concede that maybe Ember had been right all along to see more in him than I had.

She sat down on the other side of Nicky. "Hey."

"Hey."

"Ash, I wanted to . . ." Her voice trailed off. "What's wrong?"

"Nothing."

"*Something's* wrong."

I sighed. "I can't stop thinking about the taffa dream. I know you don't believe in those dreams, but I think Starbeauty has something to do with them,

410

Em. I think they're real." I'd filled her in on Star-beauty and everything else she'd missed out on after she came back. "It was a warning. But how am I sup-posed to stop the death of the *world*? And about the only advice Grandpa and Starbeauty gave me was that I need to understand my power, and I don't know what that means!"

She opened her mouth to speak.

"Before you say it," I told her, "they're not talking about Sleepwalking."

"I know."

I blinked at her. "You do?"

She nodded. "Think about it this way, Ash. You changed something that could have derailed the reform process into a rallying point for revoking the accords. You've changed the world. Again."

"I didn't do it alone—"

"That's my point! You were able to save Prime Willis, in the end, because Jeremy Duoro saved you, and Rae Wentworth Mended you. And because of Nicky, who helped you to Sleepwalk. And Connor, of course, who was little more than an assassin before he met you. And then Belle Willis convinced everyone the Tribe were saviors, and she wouldn't even have *been* Prime if she hadn't been caught up in what happened at the center the last time you were there. Don't you understand what that all means?"

I frowned at her, puzzled. And then I saw it, stretching out like one of Georgie's webs — the many linkages I'd made on which events had turned.

My jaw dropped. "My power. It's . . . to connect. To — to love."

Everything connects, Grandpa had said. *But not everyone sees those connections.* I finally understood the danger he and Starbeauty were worried about for the future. People were good to the earth now, but they weren't good to one another, and it wasn't enough to value only one kind of connection. *All life matters, or none does.* And if preventing that terrible future of Neville and the hill of death depended on me making connections . . . I grinned, immensely cheered. That was something I knew how to do; it was as natural to me as breathing.

Ember cleared her throat. "I thought we should talk. About what I did before. The accords and everything."

We hadn't discussed this since she returned. We didn't need to, except she obviously didn't realize that. "I already forgave you, Em. And the only reason you're having trouble accepting it is that you don't believe you deserve to be forgiven."

She bowed her head. "I don't."

Yeah, I'd figured that was how she felt. "You know, there's so much hate in this world." I nodded down at Nicky. "Those people in Vale City hated him for being different. Terence hates people with abilities. I hated Citizens after Cassie died."

"This isn't about that—"

"Yes, it is!" *I'm not on the side of hate. And you shouldn't be, either.* "Ember, what I'm trying to say is, I have hated, and you have hated. But sooner or later someone has to stop the hating or it goes on forever. And I think the only way we're ever going to be able to truly let go of it is if we start with the hate we have for ourselves."

"Oh, Ash. I don't even know how to begin to do that."

"It's easy. You just have to remember something that Georgie once told us. Love is the only thing more powerful than hate."

Ember stared at me for a moment, then smiled. I smiled back. I knew she hadn't fully understood what I'd said, but I didn't try to explain it further. She'd get it eventually, and my own journey to forgiveness had shown me that it took more than words to show the way.

Some truths cannot be told. Only discovered.

We sat there in comfortable silence, watching the light fade from the sky. After a while, music drifted through the forest.

"You know," I said, "I think it's possible Georgie forgot she was supposed to tell us when the party was starting."

Ember giggled. "I think so, too. Let's go, Ash."

The two of us wandered through the Firstwood, heading to the clearing we used for summer camp, with Nicky at our heels. As we neared it I stopped, taking in the scene before me.

There was a bonfire burning in the center of the clearing, and solar lamps hanging in the trees above. The glow of the flames and the lamps turned the gray bark of the sheltering tuarts to a soft, magic silver, and the entire Tribe seemed to be enclosed within that light. Mai and Jin were hovering over the fire, roasting vegetable skewers. Micah and Keiko and Andreas stood at the edge of the clearing, playing their flutes, while Trix sang in a high, clear soprano. Some people were dancing, while the rest gathered in small clusters, eating and laughing and talking. That included Georgie and Daniel, who were sitting side by side, sharing a plate of food. And Connor lounging on a fallen log at the edge of the tree line. *My Tribe.*

Jules came running up to Ember as we approached, lifting her up and twirling her in the air. He was having a good day. He set her down, and she twined her arms around his neck to pull him into a deep, passionate kiss.

I looked away, smiling, and walked on. Nicky padded ahead to stake out the food with the other Tribe dogs, and Georgie bounced over to me.

"You were supposed to tell us when the party was starting," I reminded her.

"You and Em were talking!" She waved her hand at the clearing. "Do you like it, Ash?"

"It's beautiful."

"You have to remember it," she told me, sounding almost stern. "What this looks like. How it feels, to have all of us here together."

Was she worried I was going to run off to the wolves again? I was long past that, but maybe she didn't realize it.

"I will—"

"I mean it, Ash!"

I patted her arm. "I won't forget, I promise you I won't. Don't worry, Georgie. I know how much I need the Tribe."

She reached out to take my hand, clasping my fingers

lightly before letting me go. "We need you more, Ash."

Then she trotted back to Daniel, and I made my way over to Connor.

I'd been avoiding having a particular conversation with him since we returned from the center, but I couldn't put it off any longer. I dropped to sit on the log beside him, wondering how to begin.

He did it for me. "You want to ask if I'm going after Talbot, now that we're not in immediate danger. And you're afraid of my answer."

That was pretty much a perfect summary of what I felt. "I understand if you have to go. But I can't come with you. Not with Terence and Neville out there somewhere. I've got to stay with the Tribe."

"I dedicated most of my life to finding a way to kill him," he said, "before I met you."

"I know."

He drew me to him. I leaned into his body, but only lightly in case I had to let him go, and he added, "Except that was my father's choice. That revenge."

My pulse quickened in hope. "Does that mean . . ."

"I'm staying, Ashala."

"Are you sure? I don't want you to stay for me."

"I'm not. If anything, it's for my mother." He sighed, resting his cheek against the top of my head. "You shared my memories of my father. But you never knew my mother. She was everything he wasn't. Strong, without being cruel. Quick to laugh, and slow to anger. In love with the beauty of the world and with being alive in it."

I snuggled closer. "I think I would have liked her."

"She would have liked you. And when you made me part of the Tribe, you showed me that I didn't have to follow my father's path. That I could make a different choice." He reached out to tip up my chin. In the soft light, his face was a marvel of sculpted perfection, an unearthly beauty made real by the smile at the corner of his mouth and the warmth in his eyes. "And I choose to be my mother's son."

He leaned in to kiss me, a slow, sweet kiss that sent molten heat flowing through my veins. When it ended I whispered against his lips, "Connor. Let's dance."

We ran out to spin among the rest of the dancers and became part of the night, the two of us moving in rhythm with each other and the Tribe and the turning stars above. For a second, the silver glow of the tuarts seemed to twist and elongate into shining lines that flowed between us all, and extended outward to the animals and the trees and the earth. *I see the connections, Grandpa. I do.*

The wind grew stronger, swirling sparks of fire and the scent of eucalyptus through the clearing. I gave myself up to the music and the laughter and the dancing; to these people, and this moment.

We are the Tribe, and we are here.

Author's Note

What is it to be human?

The denial of humanity in the world of the Tribe is what underlies the Citizenship Accords. This is what Ember is speaking of when she says: "What I never told you is that *ideas* can be violent. That they can shape violence, and justify it and perpetuate it." One truth known to all writers and to any peoples who have ever suffered oppression is that ideas are powerful things. It is one of the reasons that the way in which we speak of other peoples and other cultures matters so much. Words shape the world we live in and the way in which people are treated. And in general, sustaining inequality of any kind—at least if it is to be done over time and is not a one-off occurrence—requires an idea: a way in which discrimination can be explained and justified; a means by which it can be made acceptable. Thus, the unraveling of discrimination in Ashala's world begins with attacking the idea that supported it, by asking variants of the question "Are people with abilities part of the Balance?"

When I was writing *The Disappearance of Ember Crow,* I also had to consider humanity from a different angle—in particular, whether composition (organic or synthetic) made a difference. And I knew where I needed to go for my answer. Because the Tribe series is a work of Indigenous futurism, a form of storytelling in which Indigenous authors use our cultures, knowledge, and experiences to confront colonial stereotypes and imagine Indigenous futures. So to understand the nature of humanity in the world of the Tribe, I needed to look at it from an Indigenous perspective.

The first thing that occurred to me was that Indigenous peoples of the earth know what it is to be denigrated as less than human. In the colonial era, the denial of our humanity was often the basis for discriminatory laws and policies that caused great suffering. For nearly a century in Australia, Indigenous children were forcibly taken from their families. Those children are now known as the Stolen Generations. Two generations of my own family were taken, and much of the history of the Stolen Generations has been woven into the Tribe series. For example, in *The Interrogation of Ashala Wolf,* the government keeps files on runaways. In the Stolen Generations era, the government kept files on Aboriginal people. The feel of what it is like to be a child or teenager in a cold government institution, with your entire existence governed by a vast bureaucracy, is drawn from this era too. And Australia was not the only nation in which Indigenous children had something like this happen to them. The experiences of the Stolen Generations have parallels with the experiences of Indigenous children in Canada and the United States in Indian residential or boarding schools.

Because of this history, it seemed to me that I should be cautious in ever concluding that any other form of life was less than human. Indigenous peoples know what it is to bear the cost of such thinking.

The second thing I had to consider is what the ancient stories of my people tell me about the nature of reality. I come from the Palyku people, and our oldest narratives speak of a world in which everything is alive. Animals, plants, trees, wind, rock—they all have language, culture, and law. Human beings cannot know all of this language, culture, and law, because we can't see the world from the perspective of every other form of life. Only rock truly knows what it is to be rock. But just because we can't experience it doesn't mean it doesn't exist. This is why one of the assumptions made by Indigenous systems is that it is not possible to know all of the world. There is therefore no reason that new forms of life could not emerge in a synthetic form.

So in the end, I came to the point that is captured by Alexander Hoffman: "Whether we are organic or synthetic, whether we walk on two legs or four, whether we are creatures of claw or hoof or wing or feet—it matters not. Composition does not determine character. Or greatness of soul."

I have always loved speculative fiction, and perhaps this is because my ancestors taught me to always look to the future in hope. They held on to that hope through the hardest of times and in the cruelest of circumstances. I wish they hadn't had to, and I wish I didn't have to look forward now to find a better world. I want the times I live in to be the ones in which human beings end discrimination for good. Only we haven't, yet. But I believe that we can, because I think the human species is smarter and more compassionate than our collective past might suggest.

Anyway, I believe in the young. It's why I chose to write about a teenager. Ashala is going to save her world, and I found it hard to imagine an adult doing that. We grown-ups are often too inclined to speak of injustice as an inevitable feature of the landscape rather than as something that humans create or at least contribute to, even if only by failing to challenge it. Teenagers ask more questions, and are far less satisfied with answers suggesting that anything they view as an injustice cannot be changed.

What is it to be human? If our species has a single, all-powerful ability, it is to imagine. It is in us all to dream of a better world.

And as we imagine, so do we create.